Christmas 2021

Dear Pat,
I hope you enjoy this
book as much as we
did. Love, Doug and Judy

CRACKS
in the
FLOOR
of
HEAVEN

Michele Renée DeRouin

D1248066

SHINE-A-LIGHT
PRESS

Visit Shine-A-Light Press on our website:
www.ShineALightPress.com
on Twitter: @SALPress
on Instagram: @Shine_A_Light_Corp

Visit Michele Reneé DeRouin on her website:
www.cracksinthefloorofheaven.com

Edited by Chris and Andrea Elston. Book layout and design by Chris Elston. Cover design by Liana Moisescu

ISBN: 978-1-953158-10-9

Library of Congress Control Number: 2021940989

Printed in the U.S.A.
U.S.A. $16.99

DEDICATION

For my children, Alyssa and Dane. I love you to the moon and back.

CONTENTS

CONTENTS (cont'd)

ABOUT THIS BOOK

I am by nature a very curious person. I analyze, contemplate, and question how things work, sometimes to a fault. The day God spoke to me about writing *Cracks in the Floor of Heaven*, a question came to the forefront of my mind. What if our souls exist in Heaven prior to our conception, and in agreement with God, we are born for His special purpose and at His appointed time?

> *Before I formed you in the womb I knew you, and before you were born I consecrated you; I appointed you a prophet to the nations.*
> Jeremiah 1:5

> *Your eyes saw my unformed substance, in your book were written, every one of them, the days that were formed for me, when as yet there were none of them.*
> Psalm 139:16

> *...even as He chooses us in Him before the foundation of the world, that we should be holy and without blemish before Him...*
> Ephesians 1:4

> *And we know that for those who love God all things work together for good, for those who are called according to his purpose.*
> Romans 8:28

> *For everything there is a season, and a time for every matter under heaven: a time to be born, and a time to die...*
> Ecclesiastes 3:1-2

Cracks in the Floor of Heaven is a work of fiction. I tried my best to be as biblically accurate as possible while still using my God-given creativity and imagination. I believe we have one life to live. I want to use mine to help facilitate healing in people's lives and bring as many souls to Christ as possible. I truly hope this story impacts you in a positive way. God Bless.

CRACKS

in the

FLOOR

of

HEAVEN

CHAPTER 1
ANTE-TERRA

I strolled down the winding path; Buddy kept pace with me, his whiskers tickling the side of my arm as we walked. I reached up to rest my hand on his gigantic head and could feel the vibration of his content purring. I grabbed ahold of his thick mane and climbed onto his back as we made our turn and entered into the dense canopy of the Garden.

Buddy stopped beneath our tree; the same one we have visited for a thousand years. From this specific tree hung fifteen different types of fruit. I picked a ripe lilikoi and dug my thumbs into the outer layer, pried it open, and scooped out the contents with my fingers.

I picked a pear next and tossed it in the air. Buddy caught it with his enormous jaws, then licked his lips and let out a low growl, indicating he wanted another tasty snack.

"Yummy, huh, Buddy?" He wagged his tail and moved to position himself underneath the lowest hanging branch. He glanced back at me as if to say, "Are you climbing that tree *again?*" *Of course, I am*, I thought. *It's about time I show this tree who's boss.* I stood up, carefully balanced myself, then reached up and grabbed the lowest limb to hoist myself up. I picked another ripe, round, tasty piece of fruit and dropped it down to Buddy.

I slowly made my way to the highest branch possible and looked toward the City of God. It was one of my favorite things to do. I could see the pearly gates surrounding it, and the structures beyond glistened in the light that poured from within. I scanned the horizon from east to west. Beautiful, wildflower-covered plains in the east extended for thousands of miles until they reached massive canyons to the west. Hundreds of blue topaz-colored lakes shimmered in the light and herds of animals both earthly and heavenly dotted the landscape. It was an area of natural wonders, so expansive; not one soul had explored it entirely.

I closed my eyes and listened to the beautiful songs of praise and the prayers of intercession offered by the saints for their brothers and sisters who, for then, remained on Earth. I softly sang along. Oh, how I admired the saints. These mighty warriors and martyrs had been born on Earth and fought valiantly against the Evil One. Maybe one day, I, too, will be blessed with that same opportunity.

I opened my eyes and saw Michael walking down the path toward the tree where I was perched. I watched him in awe. He was the most magnificent angel in Heaven. When he took flight, it was spectacular. His wingspan was so massive it measured well over thirty-five feet. I instinctively knew he was looking for me and couldn't help but wonder why. Curiosity got the best of me, and I started my descent a little too quickly.

Halfway down, the branch below my right foot shifted out from under me. I held on tightly and moved my right foot to another limb to balance myself. Then, *that* branch, along with the one under my left foot, shifted. I lost my grip and began the hundred-foot drop to the Garden floor. Buddy tried to break my fall but missed the mark and I landed on the soft ground, which decided to join in on the fun and retracted like a piece of elastic, then snapped me up into the air. Like a feather, I slowly floated back down. Buddy walked over and licked the fruit juice off my face while I laid there laughing. The tree had bested me once again.

"I know you did that on purpose!" I called up to it. The tree's leaves rustled as if there were a sudden breeze; however, I knew the truth. It was laughing at me. That tree had knocked me out of it more times than I could count. You would have thought by now I would have learned my lesson and climbed up a different tree, but this one was the tallest and had the best views. *Besides, no tree was going to push me around.*

Michael walked up and stood over me. I stared in wonderment at his radiant splendor. "Ante-Terra, did you fall out of that tree again?"

"I don't fall out of trees, Michael. That tree purposefully knocks me out of it." Michael looked up the tree, then back at me.

"Then maybe you should climb a different tree, Anima," he suggested.

"What fun would that be?" I responded.

Although I am sure he understood what I meant, angels don't have feelings or experiences associated with fun. They were created to worship and obey God. Many times, I would try to get Michael to laugh. The only response I ever got was, "You are very interesting, Anima." I finally gave up trying.

I was called by many names; however, none were like the ones the saints had. Their names were the most beautiful and given to them by their earthly mothers. Angels called me Ante-Terra, which in Latin means "before Earth," or Anima, meaning "Soul." I often daydreamed about being called Karen or Cynthia. One day, I hoped to have a real name, but I would have to be born, and that time had not yet come.

"*He* is waiting for you," Michael said. "There is something important that requires discussion today."

"Thank you, Michael. I am headed there now," I replied, jumping to my feet. Michael turned and leaped into the air. It was a breathtaking sight. *Angels, always straight to the point, no time for small talk.*

I got up and brushed myself off. "Let's go, Buddy." I couldn't help but wonder what was so pressing that *He* would send Michael for me. Usually, we met up at the same time, but that day, *He* was early. I turned toward the center of the Garden and began the walk to our favorite spot.

The Garden was the most magnificent place in the entire Kingdom. Light filtered down through the canopy and brightened blades of grass and leaves of bushes and ferns that covered the Garden floor. Coconut palm trees swayed gently from side to side in the breeze, as if dancing to a soft melody. Every flower made its home here, from the plumerias and gardenias to the jasmine and giant lilies. On my way to see *Him,* I often stopped and took the time to inhale as many scents as possible. But not that day. *He* was waiting for me.

Buddy sensed my urgency and did not dawdle either. Usually, he would chase butterflies, and I would take my time handing out my favorite earthly names to the thousands of animals that made the Garden their home.

As much as I enjoyed spending time there, my favorite part of the day was that spent with *Him*. I quickened my pace. The closer I got, the more excited I became. My soul longed for *Him*. I knew *He* could see me coming before I arrived. The light of my soul shone exceptionally bright as I closed the distance between us.

Every soul emits its own unique, bright light that can be seen from miles away. The color of my soul is yellow, like a dandelion, and some have told me it's exceptionally bright, hence *His* nickname for me, "Little Light." Little, because of my small stature. I knew every soul in the Kingdom and their corresponding color. It made it impossible to play the game hide and seek, even though many have tried.

Our meeting place was the most gorgeous part of the Garden. There was a large, granite boulder, perfectly positioned under a tall, sturdy oak tree. The tree's expansive branches extended for hundreds of feet, and a multitude of birds and animals made their homes in it. A bubbling spring poured out from underneath the boulder and formed a beautiful pond. The water made its way downstream and turned into a creek which joined other streams less than a mile away. These connected to one of the many rivers that eventually emptied into the crystal-clear lake on the south side of the winding trail I followed to the Garden.

We always enjoyed sitting on top of that rock, dipping our toes into the small pool of cool water. Each day, fish journeyed from the distant lakes and swam up the rivers, streams and creeks in order to greet us.

We would giggle together as they kissed the bottoms of our feet.

I closed my eyes and listened to the sounds around me. Birds communicated with each other through whistles, chirps, and clucks. Some sang musical tunes, while others mimicked sounds emanating from the Garden floor. Hummingbirds and bumble bees buzzed from flower to flower, and lemurs called out to one another from high up in the trees. I could hear water bubbling over and around rocks from dozens of streams nearby and the loud crash of water from distant falls.

Then I sensed *Him*. I opened my eyes and saw *Him* standing in an open meadow. I couldn't help myself; I started running.

I nearly knocked Him over as I leaped into His waiting arms. He held me close for several moments and planted kisses on my forehead and cheeks. There was nothing more I desired than to be with Him, learn from Him, and be loved by Him. The overwhelming feeling and total satisfaction of His presence filled my heart and soul to its capacity.

"Jesus!" I repeated over and over, returning His affection by kissing the scars on his wrists. He had many names such as Immanuel, Jehovah, Yeshua, El Shaddai, Father, and God. But Jesus was my favorite. It means *Deliverer*.

"Good afternoon, My Little Light," He said with the utmost affection. Hearing His endearing nickname for me filled me with undiluted joy and love.

Jesus stood six feet tall. He was medium-built with bronze-colored skin. His hair was dark brown, and He had a matching mustache and beard. His eyes were the colors of a rainbow, if a rainbow had a thousand colors.

Unlike the angels, Jesus loved having fun. So many times, I had tried counting the colors in His eyes. Every time I made significant progress, He somehow switched them around, and I would lose track. He always thought this was hilarious. He liked to tease me and say, "You almost got it that time. Let's try again."

He wore a white robe that glistened and embroidered on it were the words "Faithful" and "True." A purple sash that read "King of Kings" and "Lord of Lords" ran across His chest. He wore a gold crown on His head, full of the most precious stones ever made. It had a name engraved in the base that only He knew. His perfect holiness and transcendent glory flowed from Him, and a rainbow encircled His entire body.

Sometimes we ran around and climbed trees. Other times, we sat for hours talking about anything and everything concerning Heaven, the saints, the angels, or any topic I found interesting. He loved to teach me the names of plants and animals in the Garden, pointing out the marvelous mysteries of His creation. He was the best teacher, always patient and kind. He had a funny sense of humor, and there was absolutely nothing I enjoyed more than His companionship. He was the most beautiful being in all of Heaven and Earth. From Him poured all things good. When I was with Him, everything faded away, and my focus sharpened as I concentrated on His every word, movement, and expression.

"Jesus, you sent an angel for me today."

"Yes," He replied.

"You knew I would be here, as usual."

"Yes," He said again. "There are important things to discuss today, but, for now, let us spend time together. We will get to those matters soon enough. What questions do you have for Me today?"

Jesus loved my questions. Every day, when walking through the Garden, I made a mental list of what I wanted to ask Him. However, I was in such a hurry that day; I had only one: *What does He want to discuss that's so important?*

"You always have such good questions, My Beloved Soul. You must have a list for today."

I looked at Buddy, who was resting his head on the Lord's knee, purring loudly. I knew Jesus could see I was struggling, but thankfully His patience was endless. Suddenly, I thought of one.

"Do people have lions as their best friends on Earth?" Buddy looked up at Jesus, tilting his giant head, awaiting His answer. Jesus reached down and ruffled Buddy's mane, causing him to purr loudly with satisfaction.

"Lions do not normally befriend humans on Earth. They are wild and not easily tamed." Buddy abruptly stopped nuzzling the hands of Jesus.

This answer shocked me, as well. *Lions and humans were not friends on Earth?* That was the weirdest thing I had ever heard. I couldn't imagine not having Buddy by my side. He was my trustworthy companion. *Who else would help me climb trees and explore the Garden's endless supply of fruits, nuts and vegetables?* I started thinking about that mischievous tree that kept kicking me off its branches.

"Did that tree knock you out of it again today?" Jesus asked with a twinkle in his eye. He already knew the answer.

I nodded, yes. "Michael told me to climb a different tree next time."

"What fun would that be?" He asked. "I think you need to hold on a little bit tighter next time." We both started giggling. Suddenly, I thought of another question.

"What kinds of animals *do* people befriend?" I asked.

"Dogs, small cats, birds, and turtles, to name a few."

"Turtles!" I exclaimed. I tried to think of a single fun thing I have ever seen a turtle do. Nothing came to mind.

"Any other questions, My Cherished One?" He asked. I loved His nicknames for me.

"Why can't angels have fun?" I blurted out. Jesus tossed His head back and laughed again. His laugh was contagious, and I joined in.

"Do you think I should teach them how to have fun?"

"Yes!" I said and ran my fingers through Buddy's soft, thick mane. Jesus grabbed me up in his arms again and held me tight.

"Alright, My Little Light, let's now talk about why I sent for you." A serious expression replaced his smile as He sat me back down next to Him. "This is an important matter, Daughter."

"Yes, Father," I responded and looked deep into His eyes. Nothing was more important to me than pleasing Jesus.

"You know of the saints, Daughter." It was more of a statement than a question. Jesus and I had spent hundreds of years discussing the saints, and He knew of my admiration for them.

"Yes, Jesus. The saints are souls like me, born on Earth and sent to battle Satan."

"You are so smart and have an excellent memory." He tousled my hair lovingly. "There is still much work to be done on Earth, and I have an important mission, specifically designed for you. Are you ready to be born, Little Light?"

I could not believe my ears. I knew the Lord was serious by the look on His face. I had been waiting for Him to ask me that question for a very long time.

"YES, YES, I will go! I am ready! I am willing!" I exclaimed excitedly. Jesus paused for a moment and looked deep into my eyes.

"Daughter, I must tell you, although Earth has an abundance of joy and love, there is also pain and suffering." I looked down at the scars on His wrists and feet. I had never felt pain or suffering. I had heard the stories of the martyrs and the saints, and even though I understood the meaning of those words, I had never *experienced* them. A hundred thoughts swirled around in my head.

"May I ask you a few things, Jesus?"

His smile returned. "Of course, you can. You are brilliant and ask great questions."

"Will I experience pain and suffering?"

"Yes, Child," Jesus replied.

"Will you be with me, Jehovah?"

Jesus smiled and answered, "Yes, I will be with you. I will never, ever leave you."

My third question came out more slowly and a little softer. "Will I get to return to you?"

This time, Jesus waited a moment before answering, choosing His words carefully. "I *want* you to return," He replied. "But that decision will be yours. Only you will be able to make that choice."

That was such a strange answer. *Of course, I want to return!* I looked around the Garden and down at Buddy, then back up at Jesus. I stared at Him and worked hard to memorize every detail of His face. I traced the lines on His forehead and the shape of His eyes and mouth. He stared right back at me. It was as if He was doing the very same thing.

I was ready to ask my fourth question. "Will I have weapons to fight against the Evil One?"

"Yes, you will have many weapons at your disposal," He assured me, then continued, "And I will no longer refer to you as 'Little Light' for you shall be 'a Mighty Light,' and together we will work to drive out the darkness."

Excitement and joy caused my soul to shine even brighter as I asked my final question.

"Will I get to have a *real* name?" I contemplated the saints and their beautiful names.

The Lord laughed and scooped me up into His loving arms again. "Yes, you will have a name!" Finally, I will have something spectacular for the angels to call me. No longer will I be referred to as Ante-Terra or Anima.

Well, then, that settled it. If Jesus wanted me to go to Earth, I would go. I would do anything for Him. Exhilaration and anticipation started bubbling up inside me. I wanted nothing more than to please the Lord. I collapsed in His arms, feeling a sense of relief from the heaviness of the conversation. I laid my head on his shoulder. He stroked my hair softly and sang a song about His love for me. My eyelids became very heavy. I tried to resist the urge to close them but did not win that battle, and for the first time in my entire existence, I fell into a deep, deep sleep.

CHAPTER 2
A BIRTHDAY WISH

"Wake-up, Alina! Time to rise and shine, birthday girl!"

I opened one eye and scowled at my mother, who stood in the bedroom doorway. "Mom, it's the first day of summer, and you're waking me up?" I moaned, rolled over, and covered my head with the pillow.

"It's your twelfth birthday, and I have a surprise for you." She grabbed the pillow off my head, sang "Happy Birthday" in a French accent, and placed a giant kiss on my forehead. My little brother, Gavin, joined in the morning harassment by jumping up and down on my bed while singing "Happy Birthday," trying to copy Mom's French rendition. I grabbed his hand and pulled him down next to me to cuddle, gripping him firmly. "Good morning, Little Bear," I said to him as he attempted to wiggle free. I held him tighter. Gavin was two years younger than me and still thought Mom was hilarious. I was at the stage where everything Mom did was just plain embarrassing.

"We're not *French*, Mom," I said, protesting her accent. Gavin finally broke my grip and jumped off the bed.

"Your grandmother was French," she retorted, ignoring my morning grumpiness. "You were born in 1977, on a hot summer day. I almost didn't make it to the hospital in time." I rolled my eyes. I had to suffer through this story every single birthday.

"I held you in my arms all night long. You didn't even cry; you stared up at me with those beautiful, green eyes of yours. In those days, babies got mixed up at the hospital all the time, so I refused to let them take you to the nursery." Then she whispered just loudly enough so Gavin could hear, "I'm not sure your brother is even mine."

Mom thought she was funny and laughed at her own jokes all the time. My brother stuck his tongue out as she left to finish breakfast, singing "Happy Birthday" again on her way out.

"You always say that!" he yelled at Mom as she headed down the hallway. Gavin looked at me, "Are you having a birthday party this year, Nia?"

Gavin couldn't pronounce Alina when he was little, so he shortened it to Nia. I didn't mind so much. I despised my real name. Why couldn't Mom have picked a regular name like Kim or Sarah? I had the weirdest one in my school: Alina Gabrielle Sheridan. Several years ago, I asked Mom why she gave me such an unusual name.

"An angel appeared to me in a dream one night when I was about six months pregnant. He told me that I was to name you, Alina Gabrielle." I had a hard time believing her. *Why couldn't that angel have told her to name me Kate or Jessica?*

Gavin distracted my train of thought by asking about the party again. "No, Gavin, I don't want a birthday party." This statement was a bald-faced lie. There was nothing I wanted more than to have a birthday party. The problem with parties is you must have kids that want to come to them. I didn't have anyone to invite. The one friend

I used to have moved to Arkansas in the middle of sixth grade the year before, and I had spent the last four months of school eating lunch all by myself. Summer was probably going to be dull, but it was better than being bullied at school.

"Well, maybe you can invite Amy to the party," he said casually.

"Who is Amy?" I asked as I got up and started making my bed.

"The girl who just moved in next door. I think she's in your grade. She has a brother my age named Christopher. We already met."

Of course, they had. Gavin did not have problems making friends. He was smart, outgoing, funny, and athletic; everything I was not.

The smell of breakfast was heavy in the air. My stomach growled.

"I'm going to eat all the bacon!" Gavin teased and ran out of the room.

"Don't you dare!" I yelled after him.

All morning long, I wondered about our new neighbors. Amy and Christopher, yet another example of perfectly common names. *Why couldn't Mom have picked out a name from a baby book like everyone else?*

Mom was anything *but* ordinary. For example, every room in our house had a different theme. I could have appreciated a room with a floral motif. It would've been nice to see multi-colored vases perfectly set on wooden furniture. Or how about a beach theme? I would have loved to have seen decorative baskets with shells of different types and sizes centered nicely on the end tables and a painting of the ocean hanging on the wall. But, no, Mom wanted nothing to do with anything normal, or traditional.

For example, our living room had the biggest Santa Claus collection on the planet. I hated having people over. I imagined them asking themselves, "*Why don't these people ever put away their Christmas decorations?*" It was as if Mom was going for the Guinness World Record or something. I can't tell you how many times she'd hauled us around to garage sales looking for Santa Clauses, trying to convince us we had room for *one more.* Even though mom was eccentric, she could be a lot of fun.

I don't think she had any idea how drop-dead gorgeous she was. Her long, thick, blonde hair went down to her waist. She was tall and slender with a perfect figure, even though she never exercised. Her eye color changed from blue to bluish green, depending on her mood. She had a perfect smile and a fair complexion with a few well-placed freckles.

On the other hand, I, looked nothing like my mom. I was short, with green eyes and crooked teeth. I had thin, straight, light brown hair, and wore thick-lensed glasses that were a little too big for my small face. I was skinny as a rail, even though I ate like a horse. My nickname at school was 'Toothpick,' and I hated it. I had bronze-colored skin that deepened in the late summer months. I was shy, clumsy, a little awkward, and I struggled with making even the smallest of chit-chat. I was anything but witty. There wasn't an athletic bone in my body, so team sports terrified me. I had concluded I must look like my father, whom I had never seen.

It had been just the three of us for as long as I could remember. Our mom liked to call us The Three Musketeers. Gavin and I didn't know who our father was. Mom never talked about him, and there were no photographs. The only remark she ever made was that he had refused to marry her after Gavin was born, so she left him. That was it. Gavin and I pressed for answers, but she would always change the subject. The last time I brought it up, she became sullen and depressed for days afterward. I hated seeing her like that, so my brother and I agreed to never ask about him again.

My mom had a younger brother, too. Of course, we knew nothing about him either. Our grandparents died in a car accident before we were born. Mom never voluntarily spoke about any of them. It was another reason I felt like an outcast. Everyone at school had aunts, uncles, cousins, and grandparents. Sometimes I would fantasize that we had a big, extended family who loved us very much. I imagined Christmas and Easter with a house filled with relatives, talking and laughing, but then reality always slapped me in the face and reminded me, *"You are different."*

I headed toward the kitchen and accidentally activated one of the Santa decorations that spilled out of the living room and into the hallway. "Ho, Ho, Ho . . . Merry Christmas," it announced in an automated tone.

"Mom, can't we keep the Santa Claus collection isolated in the living room?" I asked with frustration. She ignored my bad attitude and set breakfast on the table.

The dining room had not escaped from Mom's peculiar decorating style either. It was covered wall-to-wall in angels. Now to be fair, I loved angels. However, I pictured them as beautiful, majestic, human-like creatures with giant, white wings, not chubby babies, floating on clouds, holding harps. And for Mom to decorate an entire room in them was bizarre.

While eating breakfast, Mom asked, "So, Alina, what do you want to do for your birthday?"

What does it matter? I thought. I was feeling especially melancholy that day. What I wanted more than anything, but would never admit, was a birthday party with lots of friends in attendance. Mom kept pressing, so, shrugging my shoulders, I said, "How about we go shopping for a new shirt?"

Gavin frowned at me and with a mouth full of bacon and sarcastically and emphatically said, "Boring!"

It was then I noticed a strange scratching and whining noise coming from the garage.

"You're right, Gavin, that is boring," Mom said, smiling. She stood up and walked over to the garage door. Mom opened it and started singing "Happy Birthday" again. The most adorable puppy I'd ever seen came bounding into the house. He was golden brown with bright, blue eyes, and no bigger than a football. With tears in my eyes, I bent over and picked him up. He licked my face, and his entire body wiggled wildly. Gavin screamed and ran over to share in the birthday surprise.

"You bought me a puppy for my birthday?" I asked. My brother and I had begged Mom to get us a dog for years, but she always refused. She said we weren't old enough yet and that they were a lot of work.

Gavin jumped up and down with excitement. "What are you going to name him, Nia? Can I help? Will you share him with me? Can I hold him?" I was still in shock and disbelief.

"Gavin, settle down and give your sister some time with him."
Gavin pouted a little.

"I'll share with you, Little Bear," I said and handed him the puppy.
I stood up and gave my mom a big hug. "Thank you. He's perfect."

Mom beamed at me. "You are welcome, Honey."

A dog of my very own, I couldn't believe it.

Gavin was already throwing out ideas for names, "How about naming him, Charlie or Rex? My friend Brian named his dog Aslan, like in the book *The Lion the Witch and the Wardrobe.*"

There was no way on Earth my beautiful puppy would have a weird name; however, I didn't want to hurt my brother's feelings, so instead, I said, "Let's pick something else, Gavin." I thought for a moment and then came up with a perfect one. It was simple and accurately represented what he was, a new friend. "Let's call him Buddy," I said with a finality that even my brother couldn't challenge.

"Buddy! Come here, Buddy!" I called. Gavin looked slightly disappointed but didn't argue.

"I love it! That's a wonderful name!" Mom said with a big smile on her face. She went about cleaning up after breakfast, leaving us to enjoy our new dog. Gavin and I ran around the house with Buddy, taking turns playing with him.

While washing the dishes, Mom lectured me about feeding Buddy and keeping the yard clean. "He's your responsibility, Alina."

I barely paid attention but heard enough to answer, "Yes, Mom."
Gavin offered to help too.

We laid on the floor with Buddy, calling his name and wrestling with him. Buddy took turns, licking, and nipping us.

The doorbell rang, and Gavin jumped up. "That's Christopher. I can't wait to show him, Buddy." He ran to the door and threw it open. I looked up to see his new friend standing in the doorway, and he was not alone. A girl, my age stood behind him. Christopher's sister was my height, with dark hair and brown eyes. She was very, very pretty. My heart sank a little. Pretty girls never liked ugly ones like me.

"Hi Christopher, check out the new puppy my mom got for my sister's birthday," my brother said excitedly, then added, "Alina said she would share him with me."

"Hey, your sister came, too!" Gavin exclaimed as he opened the door wide enough for them both to enter. I was suddenly so self-conscious that my mouth went completely dry.

"Come in! Welcome!" my mom said in her French accent. *Please don't embarrass me,* I thought and shot her a look that said exactly that. I was suddenly and acutely aware of the Santa Claus and cherub collections. *Why does my mom have to be so weird?*

Christopher immediately noticed and said, "Hey, you still got your Christmas stuff up! That's so cool!" I could feel my face turn beet red. His sister walked straight up to me without hesitation, said with a smile, "Hi, I'm Amy. Nice to meet you."

"I'm Alina. Nice to meet you too," I replied politely. Buddy ran circles around our legs.

"I love your name. It's so unique." She bent down. "Look at him. He is so cute! Can I hold him?" she asked, her voice full of excitement. I was shocked at how nice she was being. It was probably because my mom was in the room.

"Yeah, of course," I said, barely audible, my shyness in full bloom.

Mom picked up on it and said, "Alina speak up; a mouse couldn't even hear you." I shot her another dirty look, which she ignored.

I picked up Buddy and handed him to Amy. She stroked Buddy's coat and smiled at me. "You are so lucky!" She gently gave Buddy back to me. "Puppies always have such sweet breath," she said. I listened as she talked about her dog and cat. One was named Foxy and the other, Jasper.

Amy's brother looked at Gavin and said, "Then they turn into adult dogs, and their breath smells like poop." At the word "poop," both Christopher and Gavin laughed hysterically. Amy and I rolled our eyes.

"Brothers are gross," she whispered, dramatically.

Who is this girl? She *seemed* to like me. Usually, girls my age would notice my appearance and awkwardness and look down their nose at me. They would scrutinize my non-designer clothes and whisper secrets about me. They would say things like, *"Alina? What kind of name is that?"*

I was sure Amy had never experienced bullying in her whole life. She was way too pretty. Her teeth were straight, and she had the latest haircut. Her clothes and jewelry matched perfectly and were the most recent style. She had a bubbly, contagious giggle that made you want to laugh along with her.

"Happy Birthday, Alina! Or do you like being called Nia?" she asked.

"Either one is fine," I replied politely.

"I love them both! They are nothing like my boring, old name." She giggled again. The melody of her laugh pulled me in, causing me to giggle too. I found it ironic how neither of us liked our name.

"I'll trade you," I said, trying some humor on for size.

"It's a deal! What are you doing for your birthday?" she asked.

"She is going shopping for a new shirt," Gavin yelled from the other room. Gavin and my mom seemed to be having a contest to see who could embarrass me the most. They were both winning. *Amy will figure out how dull I am, for sure.*

"Sounds fun! Do you mind if I come along?" she asked. I could feel my jaw drop. *Did she just ask to hang out with me?* How I wished I could be as outgoing as Gavin.

"Of course, you can!" my mom and I answered at the same time. *Don't sound too desperate,* I thought.

"Great, I'll go ask my mom. I'm sure she will say yes. She is still unpacking. My dad is the new pastor at the church down the street. Oh, that reminds me, youth summer camp is in two weeks. You *must* go! It's a blast! I'll be right back and tell you all about it, okay?" And with that, Amy ran out the doorway. I was relieved she missed the shocked look on my face. I stood there, staring where she had just been, bewildered by what had taken place. *A funny, cool, pretty girl wants to go shopping with me for my birthday and invited me to summer camp!*

"Mom, can I go over to Christopher's house while you guys go shopping?" Gavin begged.

"Yes, but, be on your best behavior and don't get in the way of his mother unpacking. Moving is very stressful," Mom lectured. She planted a kiss on his cheek.

"Gross!" he stated and wiped his face as they ran out the front door.

After a few minutes, I started doubting Amy would return and made a mental list of all the excuses she would use. The doorbell rang, and I held my breath, waiting for the letdown as I opened it.

"I'm ready to go! Mom said she would love for you and Gavin to go to camp with us!" Simultaneously we both turned to face my mom.

"Can I?" I was desperate, and I would do anything to get to go. I'd clean the house every day and wash her car once a week. I didn't say this out loud, but I was hoping Mom would pick up what I was putting out there. My mom looked at me, then over at Amy, then back at me again. It felt like twenty minutes had gone by before she answered.

"I guess I can take care of Buddy while you're both gone," she finally said, a little disappointed.

"Thank you, Mom!" I exclaimed, trying hard not to sound too overjoyed.

"Now go get ready for the day," she ordered. I hadn't noticed until now, but I was still in my pajamas.

"Yippee!" Amy cheered and hugged me tightly. "You are going to love it! There are games and crafts. You can hike and swim in the lake or even paddle around in a kayak. We have bonfires every night and make S' mores."

As I brushed my teeth, Amy continued talking about all the fun activities that take place at summer camp. However, what Amy didn't know, and what she couldn't have known, was that as exciting as camp sounded, what I cared about the most was having a friend. It was the best birthday present I could have asked for. I felt like the luckiest girl on the planet, and no camp or bonfire could ever compare to that.

CHAPTER 3
CAMP PINE ROCK

"Mom!! Where is my bathing suit?" I yelled from the bedroom, frantically trying to pack for camp. The church provided a list of needed items that included: sunblock, a hat, a notepad, a pen, five pairs of shorts, five shirts, and so on. When I got down the list to the Bible, I panicked.

"Mom, I need a Bible!" I had never been to church before, let alone owned a Bible.

Mom popped her head into my room and said, "Calm down, Alina! Ask Amy. Her father probably has a thousand Bibles."

How embarrassing. I didn't want to ask to borrow a Bible, but it was on the list and probably very important. I shoved the remaining items into a duffle bag and headed for the door. Amy must have read my mind because she met me half-way between our houses with something in her hand.

"I thought you might need this," she said with a smile and handed me a beautiful pearl-colored book. It had gold engraving on the cover that read, *Holy Bible*. When I had shared with her that my mom had never taken us to church before, unlike most girls our age, there was no judgment, just pure excitement to share this new experience with me.

"You can keep it," said Amy. I got a new Bible for Christmas, and this is my old one."

"Are you sure?" I asked.

"Of course, I am!" she exclaimed. "I even wrote your name on the inside." I opened it and found her inscription. In beautiful penmanship, Amy had not just written my name but, "To my friend, Alina Sheridan. May God bless you in all that you do."

The pages were thin and delicate. I was afraid to handle them. I read the first line: "In the beginning, God created the heavens and the earth." It was lovely, and the most precious gift anyone had ever given me. I hugged her tightly and whispered, "Thank you."

"Did I spell your name, right?"

I nodded, holding back tears. Amy's thoughtfulness and kindness were overwhelming. We were scheduled to leave in a few minutes, so I wanted to spend that time saying goodbye to Buddy and Mom. I ran back to the house, carefully holding Amy's thoughtful gift.

"Now listen here." Buddy tilted his head as I spoke. "I will be back before you know it. Mom is going to take good care of you while I'm gone." He glanced over at Mom, then back at me, and tilted his head as if to say, "Don't leave me with this crazy woman." He licked my face, and I hugged him tightly. Gavin had already said his goodbyes and was headed next door.

I gave Mom a quick hug and thanked her again for letting us go.

"Be good. I love you," Mom said and kissed my forehead. She took Buddy from my arms and held him protectively. I was a little concerned, leaving them both for a week. She must have read my mind.

"Don't worry; we will be fine." I had never been away from home for more than one night. Mom looked a little sad saying goodbye but tried her best to put on a brave face. Gavin had packed the night before and was already in the car with Christopher waiting to leave. I picked up my duffle bag and walked out the door.

Amy's parents drove us to church, where we met up with the rest of the kids from her youth group. A big, yellow bus was waiting in the parking lot, and kids were piling in. Excitement filled the air, and even though I was thrilled, I was also very nervous. Gavin didn't seem anxious at all. He was already talking and laughing with a bunch of boys his age.

Amy stayed right by my side, guiding and supporting me. We found a spot near the back of the bus, and she introduced me to several other girls seated nearby.

The bus ride was crazy. After leaving the city limits, we started the three-hour trip to camp. Flat desert scenery slowly turned into rolling hills as cacti gave way to shrubs and small trees. We wound our way through curvy mountain roads, and I witnessed the emergence of the legendary Ponderosa Pine tree. Some of these trees grow as tall as one hundred and eighty feet and grow in abundance at this elevation, or so I've been told.

The atmosphere on the bus was electric. As we got closer to our destination, everyone was talking about past experiences at camp like, "Remember that time we rode the zipline over the water?" and "Remember when Brian fell out of the kayak and into the lake?" I watched their expressions and listened to their stories as Amy added her personal experiences.

We pulled into the parking lot, along with at least fifteen other yellow buses. Adults tried to keep some sense of order. The first thing I noticed when I walked off was the incredible smell of pine. Birds were singing, and I caught my first glimpse of a squirrel. It was chirping angrily and chasing another squirrel up a tree.

We grabbed our belongings while the counselors handed out instructions, the schedule for the week's activities, and our assigned cabins. Amy never left my side. She was attentive and an excellent tour guide.

"This is the snack bar and store where you can buy candy or toiletries you may have forgotten," she said as she pointed to the various out-buildings. "Here is the pathway to the chapel where we gather twice a day. The boys' cabins are that way; we aren't allowed over there. The cafeteria is on the other side of the chapel, and here is the lake." It was so incredibly beautiful. The turquois water shimmered, and I spotted half a dozen multi-colored ducks hanging out in the middle. Kayaks lined the shore, and, sure enough, a zip line ran across to the other side.

"Hey, Amy!" a tall, blonde called out and ran over to us. She hugged Amy close. "I missed you so much!"

On the bus, Amy had explained to me that she had been to Camp Pine Rock many times when her father pastored another church in Tucson before they moved to Phoenix, so I expected she would know other people. What I didn't expect was how jealous and nervous it made me feel. *What if she ditched me for some of her old friends? What if she realized how boring and insecure I am and left me all alone?*

"Hi, Laura!" Amy embraced her friend. "This is Alina. She is my best friend and lives next door to me." *Did Amy just refer to me as her best friend?* I tried to hide my shock and jubilation. I waited for Laura to give me a dirty look or stare at me in disbelief, but she surprised me.

"Oh my gosh! You have a beautiful name!" She gave me a quick hug. "So nice to meet you. I live in Tucson. I've been coming to Camp Pine Rock for years. We are going to have so much fun together!" she exclaimed. I wasn't too sure about this new threesome. I confessed to myself, as lovely as Laura was, I didn't want to share Amy's affection or attention.

It was as if Amy knew what I was thinking because she leaned over right when Laura started waving at someone else and whispered in my ear, "Don't worry, Alina. Laura is obsessed with boys. She won't be with us very much." I let my breath out in a rush. I didn't realize I had been holding it in.

Trying to sound cool as a cucumber, I said, "No big deal, she seems nice."

Laura saw another friend she recognized and said, "I'll catch up with you guys later." I was relieved as we set off to find our cabin and put our stuff away. A big announcement came from overhead that chapel was starting in thirty minutes. Amy told me to grab my Bible, notebook, and a pen.

As we walked down the path, Amy continued to introduce me to different kids. Friends linked arms and sang catchy tunes as we all made our way to the chapel. Thousands of ladybugs completely covered a fallen log on the right side of the trail. Amy and I, along with several other kids, stopped to look at it. I was mesmerized. Not enjoying the attention, all the ladybugs took flight at once. A couple of girls screamed as the they started getting caught in our hair and landing on our shirts, arms, and faces. I couldn't help but laugh. Camp Pine Rock was more beautiful than I had ever imagined. It was like a dream world. No wonder Amy went back year after year.

The chapel was a large log cabin with tall windows that wrapped around the entire building, and a giant wooden cross that hung above the stage. The windows were made of stained glass and pictured a man and a dozen or more sheep grazing on green rolling hills. I did not recognize the man, but he had dark hair, a mustache, and a beard. It looked as though he was standing guard over the sheep. The colors of the artwork were bright and beautiful. The light shining through them made fascinating patterns on the inside of the building. I was so drawn to its beauty that I almost tripped. Amy caught my arm just in time.

I saw Gavin and Christopher sitting in the front row. Amy and I picked a middle one and sat down. Music started playing as the last few kids filed in and found their seats. I didn't know what to expect, so when everyone stood up started singing and clapping, I tried to look like I knew what I was doing. I had difficulty following the songs. Amy closed her eyes while singing; she knew every word. I attempted to concentrate on learning the words and melody, but I couldn't stop staring at the stained-glass windows. I didn't understand why it seemed so familiar and comforting.

As I scanned the chapel, I saw kids smiling and singing, clapping, and swaying. A few even had their hands raised in the air as if wanting to ask a question. I suddenly got goosebumps for no reason, and a feeling I was not familiar with overcame me. I peeked at Amy. Her eyes were closed, and her hands were in the air.

After several songs, the music died down and a man they called Pastor Steve made several announcements relating to the schedule for the week. He then told us to open our Bibles, turn to 1st John 1:9 and read with him aloud. Amy helped me find the page and pointed to the chapter and paragraph.

"If we confess our sins, He is faithful and just to forgive us our sins and to cleanse us from all unrighteousness."

I listened as Pastor Steve talked about a man named Jesus, whose Father had sent him to die for our sins. I wondered what kind of father would do that. I'd never met my father; however, I didn't imagine he would have ever done that to Gavin or me.

Then, the pastor went on to discuss how full of sin we all are, that not *one* human is perfect, and we all need to ask for forgiveness. He talked about the love that God has for us and how that love continually draws us near to Him. The pastor said that our sin separates us from God. That is why Jesus had to come to Earth, be born, and then die on a wooden cross. I stared in wonderment at the one that hung above the stage.

Next, the pastor asked us to turn to John 3:16 and, again, we read aloud with him. *"For God so loved the world, that He gave His only begotten Son, that whosoever believes in Him, shall not perish but have everlasting life."*

All this new information had my head spinning. At the end of the service, Pastor Steve asked if anyone wanted to accept Jesus into their hearts and have Him wash them clean from their sins. Hands throughout the chapel went up. Pastor Steve called for them to join him at the altar for prayer.

I did not raise my hand. First, I did not completely understand what was going on. Second, I was too scared to go forward and have every person in the chapel stare at me. I kept my butt glued to the seat, one eye open, and one eye closed. As everyone prayed, I noticed Gavin standing up front. Other adults had joined Pastor Steve. They had their hands laid upon the kids' shoulders, eyes closed, and they were talking out loud. I assumed they were praying.

When the service ended, I felt out of sorts. So many things happened in the chapel that I didn't understand. *Who was the man with the sheep? Why are we so full of sin?* My mind was swirling with questions, but Amy interrupted them.

"Let's go kayaking on the lake," she suggested.

"Just us?" I asked shyly.

"Yes, just us!" she exclaimed and grabbed my hand. Amy had a way of making me feel like the most important person on the Earth.

We headed to the lake and climbed aboard a bright yellow kayak. Amy threw a life jacket at me and grabbed the oars. We took turns paddling around, splashing other campers who paddled by us, and laughing and screaming as others returned the harassment. After a while, we found a sheltered little cove and paddled over to it.

We were by ourselves for the first time since arriving at camp. Something I heard in the chapel service had been bothering me, so I took this opportunity to ask Amy a few questions. Since her dad was a pastor, I figured she could give me some clear answers.

"I have a question about what Pastor Steve said at chapel today," I said, looking around once again to make sure we were by ourselves.

"I figured you would. Ask me anything," Amy said confidently. "I'll do my best to answer."

"Why would God let His only son die? My mom would never willingly let Gavin or me die. I don't understand that part. That sounds so cruel. Didn't He *love* His son?"

Amy answered, "Yes, He loved His son very much, and He didn't *let* Him die, Jesus *wanted* to die. He knew it was the only way to save us. The story doesn't end with His death though, Alina. Three days after Jesus died on the cross, He came back alive. And, because God knows everything, He knew His son's death was not going to permanently end His life."

"So, He died but didn't stay dead?" This concept puzzled me.

"Exactly!" she confirmed.

"What was He saving us from?" I asked.

"From sin and, ultimately, from missing out on spending eternity in Heaven with Him."

"What is sin?"

Amy looked deep into my eyes and said with conviction, "Sin is everything that separates us from God."

"Like what? I need specific examples," I pressed.

"Well, being mean, cruel, and hateful. Telling lies, cheating, unforgiveness, and stealing, to only name a few. God is like this perfect being, and He can't live in us until He washes us clean from sin. We are a dirty towel and Jesus is the soap. He comes in and cleans us. Then God can dwell in us because we are pure and spotless."

"Why did He have to die though? Sounds pretty extreme to me," I said, trying my best to understand.

"Sin is a huge deal to God," she explained. "He is perfect. If we want to be with Him and go to Heaven when we die, then we got to get cleaned up."

"Well, what is in Heaven, and how do you get there?"

"Heaven is the perfect place. It's kind of like summer camp but *way* better." I looked around at the lake. Giant mountains surrounded the camp. I could hear the buzz of insects and the chirping of birds. Camp Pine Rock was the most fantastic place I had ever been.

Amy continued, "Heaven is where you live forever, and you never feel pain or suffer." She paused for a moment. Something flashed across her face. She looked like she was going to cry for a minute. I wanted to ask her if something was wrong, but she composed herself and continued.

"Jesus is there. We will get to meet Him face-to-face and hang out with Him all the time. But only if you ask Him into your heart." Amy had the perfect way of explaining things, but with each answer came more questions.

"And if you don't get cleaned by Jesus, where do you go when you die?" This question caused a frown to pull at the corners of Amy's mouth. I was afraid I had upset her.

"If you don't believe in Jesus and ask Him to forgive your sins, you go to a place called Hell." She whispered the last part as if the mere mention of the word "Hell" was taboo, and anyone hearing it would be shocked and frightened.

"Well, what is Hell like?" I whispered. I had heard that word before but only as a curse word. Mom would get annoyed when trying to fix something and occasionally would yell, "Ah, hell!"

"Hell is a bad place. Dad says it's the opposite of Heaven in every way. It's a place of pain, suffering, hopelessness, and darkness. In Hell, we are completely separated from God and all Godly qualities such as love, friendship, hope, happiness, and peace. The Bible says it's a place of punishment that you can never escape."

Hell sounded terrible. Once when I was six years old, I burnt my hand on the fireplace. It was a third-degree burn, so they had to perform a skin graft. It hurt for a long time and I had to wear a bandage for months. That was the worst pain I had ever experienced. I couldn't imagine it lasting for all of eternity.

Just then, an announcement was broadcast saying it was time to get ready for dinner. It had been a long day, and I was exhausted. My brain was overloaded from all the new information. I could have easily skipped dinner and gone straight to bed; however, I wasn't about to let Amy out of my sight. She might come to her senses and decide I wasn't worth the time and effort.

"We better get back," Amy said. "We can talk more about this later."

"I'm sorry I have so many questions," I said, feeling very vulnerable and worn-out.

"You have great questions, Alina," she exclaimed. "I'm happy to help answer them!" I felt relieved but still drained. Amy had a way with words. She was more mature than most kids our age. We paddled back, jumped out, and rushed to the cafeteria.

I could barely get through the meal. My eyelids were heavy as bricks. I remembered seeing this funny movie once where a small child fell asleep, face-down in his food. I could relate, and that night, I swear, it almost happened to me twice.

I think Amy could tell I was struggling, so after dinner, we went straight to our cabin. We were going to miss the bonfire, but instead of acting disappointed, Amy yawned and expressed how tired she felt. I knew she was saying it just to be nice. Amy helped me unroll my sleeping bag and tucked me in. I didn't even brush my teeth. I literally crawled into bed, closed my eyes, and immediately drifted off to sleep. That night I had the most vivid dream of my life.

I found myself in a magnificent garden. I had to blink several times to adjust my eyes to the scene before me. Nature had invaded this place with a determination that would rival any rainforest, garden, or jungle.

The ground was soft against my bare feet. It had a bouncy feeling to it, like a mattress. I bent my knees and prepared to test it out with a jump. Before I got the chance, as if it were alive, the ground suddenly retracted then with rapid momentum shot up and sent me flying high into the air. I was too shocked to scream and flapped my arms wildly, trying to stay upright. For a second, I thought the landing was going to hurt, but instead, the Earth sank in and cradled me. It felt like the ground was giving me a warm and welcoming hug. I sat up and giggled, I would have to try that again.

Flowers with colors I never knew existed blanketed the ground around me and the grass was a thousand shades of green. There was not one single dead or brown blade of grass or leaf. Everything was alive and thriving. Hesitating to get to my feet, I stared straight up at the canopy of a giant tree. A dozen koala bears stared down at me, babies clinging tightly to their momma's chest. Pink and purple-colored butterflies flew around me in countless numbers.

The sky was multiple colors of blue, and dozens of rainbows stretched across it in different directions. I noticed the crispness of the air and drew in a giant breath then let it out. An infinite number of fragrances invaded my sense of smell all at once.

I noticed a gecko climbing up the stem of a fern, trying its best to blend in. It had one eye pointed towards me and the other eye pointed behind him. I followed its line of sight and caught a glimpse of something circling in the shadows. Even though I could barely see it, I knew it was a massive animal of some sort.

Then I noticed I felt different. I no longer felt things like shame, sadness, or loneliness. Instead, excitement, happiness, and love coursed through my veins. There were new emotions too. Ones I did not have words for.

I stood to my feet and watched again as something moved in the shadows. I had a sense I was supposed to meet someone, but I didn't know who. Whoever it was, I *needed* to see them. I *loved* them in a way I had never loved anyone in my life.

I was just about to start exploring when I heard loud, rolling thunder. There was not a single cloud in the sky. *That's weird.* Suddenly the ground shook with such great force; I fell to my knees and watched as the Earth cracked open around me. And within a split second, I felt myself falling right through one of the openings.

I woke up with a gasp and sat straight up. It was morning, and everyone was already getting ready for the day. Besides having a dull headache, I was beyond thrilled. I laid there and recalled every detail of the dream and admitted to myself I was a little disappointed to be awake. The Garden was the most stunning place I'd ever seen. But, even with all its beauty, what I remembered the most was how I felt. I never wanted to forget that dream.

Even though my head hurt a little, overall, I felt much better. I was rested and ready for the day's activities. I jumped up, grabbed my toiletries, and headed off to the shower. Amy had just finished getting ready and was excited to see I was up. I considered telling her about my dream but hesitated for some reason.

Amy and I ate our breakfast, and I listened as the other campers recalled the previous day's adventures. I was looking forward to our time in chapel because I wanted to hear more about this man named Jesus. I didn't know anything about Heaven, but I hoped it was something like my dream from last night.

The chapel service started at 9 a.m. sharp. I was beginning to learn the words and melody of the worship songs and was feeling a little more comfortable in my surroundings. Pastor Steve told us to turn to Jeremiah 29:11 and read with him aloud. That morning, Amy had shown me how to find the books on the index page. It took me longer than everyone else, but I finally found the chapter and verse:

"For I know the plans I have for you, declares the Lord, plans for welfare and not for evil, to give you a future and a hope."

Pastor Steve continued to talk about God's good plan for our lives. He told us how, when we follow Jesus, He protects us and gives us hope for our future. Not just our future here on Earth but in Heaven as well. I thought about the message from the night before. Everyone sins. God wanted to wash me clean from my sin. Now Pastor Steve was telling me that God had a good plan for my future. He had us then turn to Proverbs 3:5-6:

"Trust in the Lord with all your heart, and do not lean on your own understanding. In all your ways acknowledge Him, and He will make straight your paths."

I wanted to learn how to trust God. Something tugged at my heart. It got stronger each time I came into this special, wooden building. When Pastor Steve asked if anyone wanted to accept Jesus as their Savior and spend eternity in Heaven with Him, I knew I wanted it. I still didn't fully understand what it all meant, but when the invitation was presented to come up front, I knew I wanted to go. I felt afraid and self-conscious but, I couldn't remember anyone snickering at the kids who went forward the day before.

As if Amy could sense my struggle, she whispered, "I'll go up there with you if you want." I nodded, yes. Amy took hold of my hand, and together, along with several other kids, we walked up front.

I squeezed my eyes shut and felt Pastor Steve lay his hands on my shoulders. He asked us to say a prayer with him. I didn't know how to pray, so I just repeated after him and said, "Dear Heavenly Father, thank you for your love. Thank you for your son, Jesus, who died on the cross so that I can be saved from sin. I believe in You, Lord Jesus. I believe that You died on the cross, then three days later rose from the grave. Forgive me for my sins and wash me clean and come into my heart." I could feel my own heart beating a million miles a minute. "Help me to become the person you want me to be. Fill me with the Holy Spirit and show me how to love others as you love me. In Jesus' name, we pray, Amen."

When we finished, I opened my eyes. I wasn't sure what to expect. I didn't feel any different. *What if it didn't work?* I turned to Amy, who had tears in her eyes. *Why was she crying?*

I whispered, "I don't think it worked. I feel like the same person." I had to admit I expected to feel different, and I was a little disappointed.

"But you *are* different!" she exclaimed. "On the inside, you are clean!"

I realized there was still so much I needed to learn. For now, I would trust Amy and Pastor Steve.

"I'm so happy for you, Alina. You are very brave," Amy said as she threw her arms around me. Just then, I felt someone else hugging me from behind. I turned around to see Gavin.

"Nia, I think we're Christians now! How cool is that?" We hugged each other. I couldn't explain it, but the emotions I suddenly felt were like the ones I had experienced in my dream. Tears welled up in my eyes.

"We have to help Mom next, Nia," Gavin said in a somber tone. I thought about Mom and instantly missed her. I couldn't wait to tell her about Jesus. It had been the best day of my life. I had a feeling everything was going to change for the better. *How could it not?*

CHAPTER 4
SECRETS AND LIES

It was challenging saying goodbye to Camp Pine Rock, Pastor Steve, and all the friends I made during the five days we spent there. On the ride home, we sang worship songs, recounted funny stories, and discussed all the things we would miss about camp. Spirits were high as ever, with only three more weeks until school was to begin.

I couldn't believe I was going to be in junior high. At least Amy would be going to the same school. I thought of all the future adventures and smiled as I imagined us riding our bikes to school, eating lunch, and completing homework on my bedroom floor together. The days of doing these things alone were over.

When we got to the church parking lot, I expected my mom and Buddy to be there, but Amy's dad said he was giving us a ride home. I couldn't wait to see them. We pulled up to Amy and Christopher's house and gathered all our belongings, thanked their parents, hugged our friends, and walked the short distance between our homes. Mom must have heard the car pull up and opened the front door to greet us.

"Oh, my babies are home!" she exclaimed. Buddy barked, ran out the doorway, and jumped on my leg, almost knocking me to the ground. I picked him up and couldn't help but notice how much heavier he was.

"Oh my gosh, Buddy, you grew a ton while I was gone," I said, happy to be reunited with my puppy. He licked my face and chewed on my fingers and hands. I set him down, so I could carry my stuff into the house. That was when I noticed Gavin still standing next to me with a look of shock on his face. I followed his gaze and saw a man standing next to my mom in the doorway. He had one arm wrapped around her waist, his hand protectively resting on her hip. In the other hand, he held what looked like a beer can. Mom smiled widely, but I could tell she was a little nervous.

"Kids, I want you to meet Frank. Frank is my, um, friend. He is going to be staying with us for a while." Gavin and I quickly exchanged glances, both of us trying to adjust to the bombshell. We had never seen our mom with a man before. She said he was just her friend, but we both knew better. *How long has she known this guy?* A knot started to develop in my stomach. I didn't have a good feeling.

"Now, don't be rude!" she lectured, sounding a little miffed at our reaction. "Say hello."

"Hello," Gavin and I said simultaneously.

"Hi, kids! Welcome home. I heard you went to Jesus camp!" He said with a laugh and a snort. His tone made it sound like he was making fun of us.

Our mother jabbed him in the ribs with her elbow and said, "Now I told you, Frank, it is called Camp Pine Rock." She turned back to us with a smile. "Did you guys have fun?" she inquired. Both of us nodded. I had been excited to tell Mom everything, but now, all I wanted to do was go to my room.

Frank only briefly looked at Gavin, but when his eyes landed on me, I got goosebumps, and the knot in my stomach doubled in size. His gaze was penetrating and off-putting. I did not like this guy or the way he looked at me. Pastor Steve told us we were supposed to love everyone just like Jesus did. Maybe he wasn't talking about Frank.

I tried to shake off the uneasy feeling and followed everyone into the house. *Mom has a boyfriend!* I screamed in my head. *And he's living with us!*

I went straight to my room and started to unpack, attempting to gather my thoughts and calm down. Mom made a big "welcome home" dinner. It was the most awkward meal of my life. I could tell she was getting frustrated because my brother and I barely said a word while we ate. Frank was on his sixth beer and was starting to slur his words. The more alcohol he drank, the flirtier he became with my mother. She would giggle and tell him to stop in a tone that made it sound like she was enjoying it. When she got up to clean the kitchen, Frank started staring at me in a way that made me feel very uncomfortable. I got up and offered to help Mom with the dishes.

After dinner, I took a nice, long, hot shower. It felt wonderful. While washing my hair, I sang a song I learned from camp, and it made me feel a little better. Everyone there had been so friendly. Not one time did I feel left out or bullied. No one told me I wasn't invited or asked me what I was doing sitting at their table. For the first time, no one teased me because of my looks. It gave me hope that there were kids in the world who would accept you for who you were. It helped to have Amy by my side. She was outgoing, kind, witty, and confident.

I could see why everyone liked her so much. It made me feel proud to have her as my best friend.

"Thank you for Amy," I said to God. "Best friends forever."

I wrapped a towel around me, quickly inspected the hall to make sure no one was looking and ran to my room to put on my pajamas. Buddy was waiting for me, curled up in a ball by my pillow. The drapes were wide open, as usual. The sun was setting, but you could still see the big oak tree in the backyard. I didn't think anything about the open drapes as I dropped my towel and started to get dressed. It wasn't until I had put my last piece of clothing on that I noticed Frank. He was staring at me through the window from the backyard. It took a moment for me to realize what was happening. He had been watching me dress.

I waited for him to turn away, embarrassed that I caught him staring, but instead, he smiled at me and took a drink from his beer can. My brain scrambled to process the events. He had been watching me change the whole time and wasn't apologetic or embarrassed.

Occasionally, you would hear a story about something like that happening, but I never, ever thought I would find myself in that type of situation. I was only twelve years old. *Why would my mom's boyfriend be staring at me through my bedroom window?*

I heard my mom yell Frank's name from somewhere inside the house. He took another sip of his beer and slowly walked away.

That night, I cried myself to sleep. I felt different on the inside, dirty for some reason. I tried to think about camp, but my mind kept replaying the events and the creepy look on Frank's face. God wanted us to love everyone, but I could never love my mom's new boyfriend. For the first time, hate tugged at the corners of my heart. Not only did I hate Frank, but I secretly hoped God hated him too. *How could God love someone like that?*

The next morning at breakfast, it was just Mom, Gavin, and me. Gavin was telling Mom about Camp Pine Rock. I didn't know where Frank was, but I wished he would never come back. I thought about alerting Mom, but doubt filled my mind. *What if she didn't believe me?*

I played out the conversation in my head. *What if she thought I encouraged it? Maybe I had imagined it?* I thought back through the events. I had not imagined it; I knew that for sure. Fear and anxiety plagued my mind. I decided to keep it a secret and hope that it would never happen again.

"You are quiet this morning," said Mom. "Everything alright?"

I nodded yes and got up to clear my plate as Gavin continued to fill Mom in on all his adventures. Buddy followed me to the sink, begging for scraps. I went into my room and pulled the drapes closed. They would never be open again.

I spent the rest of the day with Amy. I tried to pretend everything was okay, but I could tell she knew something was up.

"What's wrong, Alina?" she asked after lunch. We were lying on the floor in her bedroom, looking at magazines.

"Nothing really, I'm just tired," I lied. "I have a question, though." I tried to sound as casual as possible. "We learned at camp that God loves everyone." I paused for a moment. It felt like there was a giant frog stuck in my throat. "Does God love bad people too?"

"My dad told me once that God doesn't see people the way we see people. He said God sees who we can be and who He wants us to be." Amy always knew precisely how to explain things. "Dad also told me once that God never stops chasing after us."

"He even chases bad people? Do they know God is chasing them?" I asked.

"I think God uses us a lot of times to let people know He is chasing them," she answered. I wondered if I was supposed to tell Frank that God was chasing him. Maybe God would chase Frank right out the front door. I was about to tell Amy what happened when her brother burst into the room and told me my mom called and wanted me home.

"I told you to knock!" Amy yelled at her brother.

"Sorry," he replied insincerely.

We stood up, and Amy hugged me. "I'll see you tomorrow, Alina."

When I got to our property, I saw Gavin sitting by himself, tossing rocks across the yard. It looked like he had been crying. I noticed Frank's old, beat-up truck in the driveway. I walked over and kneeled in front of Gavin. He had a red mark on the left side of his cheek.

"Gavin, what's wrong? What happened?" I asked gently.

"He slapped me, Nia," he whispered, looking around to make sure there wasn't anyone listening. A tear slipped down his cheek. "I was arguing a little with Mom because I wanted to hang out with Christopher but Mom told me I had to do my chores first. All I did was ask if I could do them later. Mom said no, so when I went to finish them, Frank followed me to my room and grabbed me by the back of my hair and pulled it hard. When I cried out, he slapped me across the face and told me never to argue with Mom again." I could barely understand the last part because he had started sobbing uncontrollably.

I scooped him up into my arms and asked, "Did you tell Mom?"

"No! And please don't tell her, Nia! He warned me not to!" Gavin looked at me, confused. "Why would Mom bring someone like him around? Promise me you won't say anything!" I could see the panic on his face and reassured him I would not repeat what he had told me. He leaned on my chest, and I let him finish crying.

I felt like crying, too. Now we both had a secret. My heart hurt for my little brother and I was so angry with my mom. I didn't understand what she could possibly be thinking. Although I thought about telling Gavin what Frank had done to me, I decided he was too young and kept that secret to myself.

"Alina, where are you?" Mom yelled out the window.

"Don't tell her anything," Gavin begged again.

"Don't worry, Little Bear. I'll see what Mom wants and tell her you are riding your bike or something." I wasn't fond of lying, but I didn't think Jesus would be too mad if I told Mom a tiny, white lie. All I wanted to do was protect my brother.

When I walked into the house, Mom was in total panic mode. "Where are my favorite earrings? Frank and I are going out for dinner tonight, and I want to wear them. I need you to watch your brother. Where is he?"

"I don't have your earrings, Mom, and Gavin is riding his bike." That was two lies. *More questions for Amy,* I thought. Mom stomped off, determined to find her missing jewelry.

I went to bed that night feeling sad and hopeless. Buddy seemed to sense my mood and laid his head on my chest. I buried my face in his soft fur and tried to pray, but I didn't know what to say to God. All I had were questions and a broad sense of guilt from lying and keeping secrets from Mom.

It was one week before the first day of seventh grade when Amy suddenly fell very ill. At first, I thought she just had the flu. For five days, her mother would answer the phone and politely tell me she was too sick to take my calls. I started to panic the Sunday before school was to begin when I still had not heard from her. My worry was so great for my best friend that I decided to check on her myself. I snuck over the backyard fence and tiptoed to her bedroom window. What I saw shocked me to the core.

Not only was Amy in bed, she looked horrible. Worse than any sick person I had ever seen. Her skin was as white as a sheet, and even though her eyes were closed, I could tell she had dark circles beneath them. A bag of fluid hung from a pole, and a tube ran down from it. I could see where it was attached to her arm. A medical-looking machine with flashing lights was positioned next to her, as well. She opened her eyes, cried out in pain then, bent sideways, and puked into a bowl at the side of her bed. Her mom and dad ran in and immediately started tending to her. To avoid being discovered, I ducked down.

What the heck is going on in there? I wondered. *That looks nothing like the flu.* I recalled Gavin having it the previous year and he hadn't had to have machines or tubes hooked up to him. I had a sinking feeling in my stomach that something wasn't right. *More secrets,* I supposed as I quietly snuck back home.

I sat on my bed and cried. Buddy jumped up, laid his head my leg, and whined a little. Poor Amy, she looked so sick. Something deep down warned me that whatever was going on was super serious. A feeling of dread came over me. It was so intense that I bowed my head and said a prayer. It was the first time I had ever attempted to pray for someone else. I didn't know what I was doing, but I gave it my best effort.

"Dear Jesus, Amy looks very sick. Will you please help her get better? Amen." I didn't know what else to say, so I softly sang another song I had learned at camp.

Gavin came in utterly unaware of what was going on and said, "Nia, Mom wants us to pick our clothes out for school tomorrow and pack a lunch." I welcomed the distraction and tried to put a smile on my face to hide the pain.

Gavin had changed a little since the incident with Frank, and it made me angry. At first, I thought it was an isolated event. However, even though Gavin did not disclose any further altercations, I began to sense more had occurred. He continued to withdraw, and I often would see him attempting to hide another bruise.

There had been more incidents with me, as well. I did my best to avoid Frank as much as possible and block out the abuse that Gavin and I were experiencing. I wanted to tell someone, but I was afraid. Plus, I had promised my brother I wouldn't. I didn't trust that anyone could do anything about it, anyway. Both my brother and I learned to keep our heads down and our mouths shut. Telling lies and keeping secrets like that was depressing and filled me with shame.

As morning came, I still held out hope that Amy would be well enough to attend school. I imagined hearing a knock at the door and opening it to see her bright smile. I imagined riding bikes to school together, discussing our classes and what we packed for lunch.

When it was time to leave, Mom kissed us goodbye, wished us good luck on our first day, and sent us on our way. I glanced over at Amy's house, hoping she would come running out with apologies for being late, but it didn't happen.

In complete silence, Gavin and I started riding to our schools, which were only a block apart from each other. The last stretch was uphill, and Gavin was well ahead of me. I stopped for a moment to rest and drink some water.

As I turned the final corner, my front tire hit a gap in the pavement. My bike came to an unexpected stop, l flew over the handlebars, and landed in the middle of a giant puddle. It knocked the wind out of me, but I didn't hit my head. When I finally caught my breath, I looked down to see my new clothes covered in muddy water. My knees and elbows were scratched up, but luckily, I hadn't broken any bones.

I tried to hold back the tears, but they came uninvited anyway. Gavin was too far ahead of me to notice the wreck. Plus, he was almost to his school and past the turn to mine. I picked up my bike and walked up to the nearest house and knocked on the door to call Mom. She would bring me a change of clothes.

Great, I'm going to be late for the first day of school! I thought as an older woman answered the door. She had grey, short, curly hair and stared down at me through a pair of thick, gold-rimmed glasses. She looked like she could be anyone's sweet old grandmother.

"Honey, are you alright?" she asked with great concern.

From the look on her face and sound of her voice, I guessed I must have looked a total mess.

"Yes, Ma'am. I wrecked on my bike. May I use your phone?" I was sure she could tell I had been crying.

To my dismay, Frank answered the phone. "Is my mom there? I fell off my bike and need to talk to her."

"Nope. She went to the store," he replied flatly.

"Can you come to get me? I need to change my clothes and clean-up." The last thing I wanted to do was ask Frank to pick me up, but I had no choice.

He was silent for a minute, then asked, "Is anything broken?"

I surveyed my injuries again. "No, I don't think so."

He paused. "Well, then, you'll be fine." And with that, he hung up. I stood there in shock and listened to a dial tone for a while before hanging up the receiver. *What am I supposed to do now?* I wondered. *Go to school with mud all over my clothes?*

I could feel the woman studying me as I stared at the telephone in disbelief. I was sure she had overheard the conversation.

"Come in here, Honey. Let's get you cleaned up."

I numbly followed her to the bathroom as she pulled out a first aid kit and tended to my wounds. Neither of us said anything. I winced as she cleaned the scrapes and did everything in my power to keep from crying again.

The first bell was to ring in fewer than ten minutes. I would be late and dirty on my first day of junior high. I almost couldn't bear the thought of it. If Amy had been there, she would have known what to say to help me feel better. But she wasn't.

"Let's find you a clean shirt," the old woman said. She walked out and quickly came back with a blouse. It was a little too big for me and covered in obnoxiously large, bright flowers. I would never have worn a shirt like that before, but it was better than the dirty one I had on.

"Now, we can't do much about your shorts, Honey, but let me see if I can scrub some of that mud out."

The wrinkles on her face were deep, but there was a kindness about her that made me feel safe and secure for the first time in weeks. Despite my best efforts, I started crying again. She wrapped her arms around me until I stopped.

"There, there, Sweetheart, everything is going to be okay."

She offered to take me to school so I wouldn't be late. "You can leave your bike here. I'll clean it up for you and drop it off at the office once my husband comes home with the truck." Her warmth was so genuine that I almost started crying again.

"Thank you, Ma'am," I said softly.

"You can call me Doris. Now let's hurry. You don't want to be late for your first day of school."

I made it to class with only one minute to spare. I picked a desk in the back of the classroom. My only hope was to go unnoticed for the rest of the day.

At lunch, I sat by myself as usual. I thought of Amy and how much fun we would be having right about now. Girls and boys whispered around me, looking over at me from time to time. I even overheard a girl say, "Look at her shirt! Looks like my grandmother's!" followed by giggling. I noticed a few kids from summer camp but was too embarrassed to approach them. Without Amy, my confidence had dropped like a rock.

I finished my meal and walked to the library with my head down, ready to spend the rest of lunch recess alone, hiding behind a book.

Doris brought my bike to school, just like she promised. It was perfectly clean and shiny. She had also washed and dried my shirt and placed it in a bag that hung from my handlebars. I made a mental note to return her blouse the following day.

As we rode home, I told Gavin what had happened. He felt terrible for not noticing the accident and apologized several times.

I was anxious to get back and check on Amy, but when I rode into my driveway, I noticed there weren't any cars parked next door. When I walked into the house, my mom had a somber look on her face. She hardly ever stopped smiling, so it immediately made me nervous.

"Sit down, Alina. We need to talk," she said.

I sat down at the kitchen table. "Amy is in the hospital; she is very ill. I spoke with her mother this morning, and it turns out she has Leukemia. It's a type of cancer. They thought she was improving, but this morning she took a turn for the worse."

The world around me spun and tilted. It felt like I was on one of those spinning rides at the fair. I felt nauseous.

Amy has Leukemia? I was confused. *Why didn't she tell me she was sick?*

She had seemed fine until a week earlier. A deep sense of sorrow overcame me. It penetrated the depths of my soul and made itself a home there.

"Can we go see her?" I asked, barely able to get the words out.

"Yes, Amy's mother said we could visit her at the hospital today. Alina, you need to prepare yourself. She doesn't look good, Baby." Mom didn't know that I had peeked in Amy's window two days ago.

"I'll change and be ready in five minutes," I said.

"Hey, where did you get that shirt?" she asked, as I ran down the hall.

"It's a long story. I'll tell you later." I looked over at Frank, who was snoring loudly on the couch. Anger rose up inside of me. *How can he sleep at a time like this?* I wondered, wanting to go over there and punch him in the face. Instead, I told myself to calm down and quickly changed my shirt.

We hustled to the hospital and found out what room Amy was in. When we got to level three, the nurses provided protective gear and told us to wear it at all times. I quickly glanced into several rooms as we made our way to Amy's. I wondered why there were so many children on this floor. I didn't realize until later that we were in a children's hospital. I had never been in a hospital before. I didn't like it; a weird smell hung in the air.

Amy looked worse than she had only a couple of days ago. Her lips were chapped, her hair was greasy, her face was yellow, and she had dark blue circles under her eyes. She was hooked up to three different machines that beeped and flashed continually.

Amy's parents both sat stone-faced next to her bed but stood up to greet us upon our entry. I noticed her brother Christopher sitting quietly in the corner. Gavin walked over to him, but I hesitated at the door. Everyone was wearing masks and gloves.

"Come on in, Alina. She has been waiting for you," her mother said and reminded me again to keep my mask on. Then, my mom, Gavin, Christopher, and her parents quietly left the room so I could have some alone time with Amy. I reverently approached her bedside and whispered her name, choking back tears. She opened her eyes.

"Alina, you're here," she croaked, her voice just a whisper. She gave me a weak smile and sounded relieved.

"Hi, Amy." I tried to return the smile but I was so overwhelmed with grief, I could no longer hold back the tears and started crying hysterically. It took a few minutes for me to be able to speak. "I'm so sorry you're ill," I cried. Tears ran down my sweet friend's face. "You didn't tell me you had Leukemia, Amy," I said. "I would have done something to help you."

"I'm sorry, I didn't tell you. When we moved here, I wanted to have as normal a life as possible. We weren't sure how much time I had left." She took a break for a minute. It was as if each word took great effort to speak. "I didn't want to be known as the sick girl. I was so tired of having people feel sorry for me. You are my best friend, Alina. I love you, and I'm sorry I didn't tell you. You have been my favorite thing about moving here. Being my friend was the best thing you could have done for me." She closed her eyes for a minute. I thought maybe she had fallen asleep, but after a few moments, she opened them again.

"You're going to get better, right, Amy?" I pleaded. I knew the answer to the question but refused to face reality. *She had to get better*. She smiled again but declined to answer my question. Instead, she took my hand in hers. I couldn't stop crying. "I love you, Amy," I told her, returning her affection. I willed her to get better.

"Now that you are a Christian," she said weakly, "we will get to be together again one of these days." Another tear rolled down her cheek, and I gently wiped it away.

"I just can't do it without you," I said, sobbing again. "You have been the best friend I have ever had. I don't know how to go on without you."

Amy patted my hand. "I had a dream last night. Jesus told me you would go on and accomplish great things, Alina. You will be a light in dark places."

Just then, my mom, Gavin, and Amy's family returned with a nurse in tow. I tried my best to stop crying and wiped my face.

"We need to let her rest now, Honey," the nurse said as empathetically as possible. Amy looked as though she was exhausted and had a hard time keeping her eyes open.

"I'll be back tomorrow," I reassured her. She nodded, mouthed goodbye, and closed her eyes.

I went home and prayed as I had never prayed before. I begged God to heal Amy. I prayed and cried until I finally passed out from emotional exhaustion. Buddy didn't leave my side. He licked the tears from my cheeks and laid his head on my chest. While I slept that night, Amy left this world. When I woke up the next morning, I instinctively knew she was gone.

I couldn't get out of bed for a week. Buddy only left my side to use the bathroom and devour his dogfood. I couldn't eat or sleep. Mom finally threatened to take me to the doctor if I didn't get back into my routine. I reluctantly obeyed.

I attended Amy's funeral on a bright and sunny Sunday afternoon. It might as well have been a dark, dreary day. I was mad at the sun for shining on such a sad occasion. I felt hollow inside and numb to the world around me. Mom and Gavin did their best to try and cheer me up. I ignored their efforts. Nothing would ever be the same again.

CHAPTER 5
HEAVENLY ENCOUNTERS

The night of the funeral, I had a second dream about the garden.

Sometimes it's difficult to tell you're having a dream when everything feels and looks so realistic. I was back in the same place as the dream I had the first night of summer camp. What captured my attention this time was the variety of sounds I heard. A multitude of different species of birds chirped, squawked, and sang. The melodies were hypnotizing. A woodpecker hammered on a tree above me. A conversation was going on between two parrots perched on a branch overhead. They could have easily been mistaken for human voices.

"Hello," one spoke.

"Hello," another responded.

"How are you?"

"How are you?"

"What's your name?"

"What's your name?"

This exchange went back and forth for a while. I laughed out loud; the birds copied me. I closed my eyes and concentrated, giving my full attention to nature's orchestra.

A creek was bubbling nearby, and I could hear the water rushing over smooth river rocks. There were buzzing insects and croaking frogs. From not far away, an elephant trumpeted, and animals of all kinds called to each other in their unique languages. I thought I could hear singing far off in the distance. A breeze rustled the leaves from hundreds of trees that made their home in the garden.

I finally opened my eyes. White, fluffy bunny rabbits stirred the grass around the base of a pine tree that reached so high into the sky I couldn't see the top. Two squirrels rushed up its trunk, chirping loudly. The garden reminded me of summer camp, and summer camp reminded me of Amy. I waited for the sadness to hit as it always did when I thought of her. A minute went by. I felt fine. Better than fine; I felt wonderful.

Suddenly, to my surprise, laughter filled the air. I recognized it immediately; I would know Amy's laugh anywhere. I froze and listened carefully. She was talking to someone. I couldn't make out what they were saying, but it sounded like they were having fun.

I started searching for her, yelling her name. I tried to pinpoint exactly where the laughter was coming from, but the other garden sounds were so loud that it was hard to tell. I decided to climb a tree with low hanging branches. Maybe, I could locate Amy from higher up.

I found the perfect one. It had a bunch of different types of fruit hanging from it. Most of them, I had never seen before. I picked one that looked like a pear and carefully bit into it. It was unlike any pear I had ever eaten. My taste buds lit up. I felt like I had some type of tasting superpower. I detected everything that made up the pear-like fruit, the natural sugars, the minerals, the water, and even the Earth from which it was grown. I wanted to try all of them, but I was on a mission to find Amy. Having always been afraid of heights, I decided not to look down and very carefully started making my way up, branch by branch, gripping each one so tightly, my fingers ached.

I almost made it to the top when something peculiar happened. The branch below my right foot moved out from under me. I thought at first that I had imagined it. I was barely hanging on when the branch below my left foot did the same thing. At that moment, I knew I was going to fall. *Can you die in a dream?*

I closed my eyes tightly, waiting for the pain to start as I hit the original limb on my way down. But, to my surprise, it didn't hurt at all. I remembered my first dream and how soft and bouncy the ground was. I instinctively braced myself anyway and closed my eyes. The ground, however, was pillowy, like it had been covered in a deep pile of snow. Instead of a thud, it sunk in around me and then shot me flying back up into the air. I laughed with delight and floated like a feather back down to the garden floor.

When I opened my eyes, a man was standing over me. A brilliant light shone from within Him. He had a rainbow that encircled His head like a crown, and He wore a bright white robe with a golden sash. His hair was dark and matched His mustache and beard. His eyes twinkled, and the colors mysteriously shifted as He stared deep into mine. His beauty was astounding, and His presence breathtaking. I sensed that I had seen Him before but couldn't remember where.

"Hello, Child," He said with a slight Middle Eastern accent.

The very sound of His voice gave me goosebumps, and my heart skipped a beat. What I noticed most about Him was how He made me *feel*. I was suddenly the most important person in the solar system. His eyes drew me in like a moth to a flame and I experienced total satisfaction.

"Did you fall out of that tree?" He asked with a smile.

"The branches moved out from under my feet," I answered.

He looked up at the tree and made a "tsk" sound. The tree swayed from side to side and its leaves shook.

"Am I dead?" I asked.

"No, you are very much alive," He answered.

"Am I dreaming?" I asked.

"Yes and no," He said and helped me to my feet.

"Where am I?" I inquired.

"Where do you think you are?" He asked me.

I thought about it for a couple of minutes. Amy is in Heaven. If it was Amy's laughter I had heard, I must be in Heaven.

As if He could read my mind, He answered, "You are perceptive, I've always said so."

"Who are you? Have we met before?" I questioned.

"Yes, we have!" He exclaimed.

In my mind's eye flashed a memory of the stained-glass window inside the chapel at camp. The man before me looked very similar to the shepherd who had been walking amongst a flock of sheep. Amy had revealed to me who the shepherd in the artwork represented after chapel the first night at camp. *My heart almost leaped out of my chest!* The man standing beside me was Jesus. He smiled at my realization.

"Jesus," I whispered.

He was slightly glowing, and there was something majestic about Him. Jesus was God, but He talked like a human, and besides the ever-shifting color of His eyes, he looked like one too.

"Do you have something to ask Me?" He spoke. That was a loaded question; however, I immediately knew that He was talking about Amy.

"I was wondering if you know where my friend Amy is?" I inquired. "She has dark brown hair. I heard her laughing a few minutes ago. I'd know that laugh anywhere." I wasn't sure how long this dream was going to last, and I needed to find her as soon as possible.

"Yes, I know, Amy. She could not be with us today but wanted me to tell you hello and that she will see you very soon," He said gently. I waited to feel disappointment, but it did not enter my heart. Jesus met every need at that moment in time. I wanted nothing more than to be with Him.

"If I am not here to see Amy, why am I here?"

Jesus said, "You are here because you have a question that needs answering." I had a million questions racing through my mind right then. Only one stood out, though — a pressing one.

"You may ask, Daughter." *Daughter?* I remembered something important from church camp. They taught us that Jesus was our Father. I had always wanted a father.

"Why did Amy have to die? She was my best friend. She didn't do anything wrong, but you took her away from me."

Usually, I would begin to cry at the mere mention of Amy's early, unexpected death. But there, in that place, not a single tear made its appearance. I wasn't angry either, only curious.

"There are several things I want you to try to understand," Jesus began. "First, is that I love you and I always will. Second, I have a plan and a purpose for your life. That plan is for good, not for evil." He looked deep into my eyes as if reading my mind again. "And, yes, I love Amy too. Lastly, life and death have nothing to do with my love for you or anyone else for that matter."

Peace filled my heart. Just then, out of the corner of my eye, I saw it running toward me. I gasped at the sight of a lion quickly closing the distance between us. I waited to feel fear, but just like the tears, it was nonexistent. Instead, I felt pure excitement and love as the lion flew through the air and pounced on top of me, knocking me to the ground where we somersaulted our way down a small hill. When we finally came to a stop, he licked my face repeatedly with his large, rough tongue.

Even though I had never seen a lion outside of a zoo before, it felt like I had known him my whole life. I hugged him tightly and buried my face in his mane. I could hear Jesus laughing from on top of the hill.

It was at that moment when I heard thunder rumbling across the sky. The ground beneath me shook and started to break apart. The lion and I made eye contact again, and I was filled with warmth of friendship. His brown eyes stared at me with affection one last time. The ground shook again, cracked open wide, and I closed my eyes as I fell through.

I woke up in a panic, sat straight up in my bed, and grabbed my head between my hands. It hurt so bad, like someone had hit me with a baseball bat. I had already missed almost a week of school, so I knew Mom was not going to let me stay home.

I got up and headed to the bathroom, looking for the bottle of Tylenol. I thought about last night's dream; how utterly fantastic it was. I recalled every smell, sight, sound, and emotion. I was feeling more like myself again until I bumped into Frank while he was exiting the bathroom.

"What are you up to, Squirt?"

I hated the new nickname. It made me feel self-conscious about my size. I didn't need a reminder of how short and skinny I was.

He stood in the doorway, hovering over me, getting way too close for comfort. He had a strange look on his face, which made me feel uneasy. I could smell his foul breath as he moved even closer.

"Frank, I need your help with the car," Mom yelled from across the house.

He slowly moved past me, making sure he brushed up against me in an inappropriate manner. I hurried into the bathroom and shut and locked the door. My head was pounding. I fumbled around until I found the Tylenol.

When I looked in the mirror, I was shocked at what I saw. My hair was tangled, and I had dark circles under my eyes. I should have expected it. After all, I had been in bed all week, crying over the death of my dear friend.

I finished getting ready for school and ate breakfast with my head down. Breakfast used to be full of laughter and entertaining discussions. Since Frank's arrival, most days, our meals were eaten in silence. Even my mother, who was usually happy and silly, had become very quiet and withdrawn. Gavin barely spoke either. He kept his eyes on his food and was the first to be excused. I noticed a big bruise on his arm and made a mental note to ask him about it, even though I knew what the answer would be. I felt like a failure, unable to protect my little brother.

Mom came in from the garage. "Oh good, you're finally up," she said in a tone that I felt was a little too flippant, considering the circumstances.

There was a rumor that Amy's parents would be moving back to Tucson in a few weeks. Gavin was losing someone, too. I wanted to comfort him and started to say something about it but stopped myself. No one was the same after Frank's arrival and Amy's passing. Nothing I could say or do would change that. The feelings of peace and happiness from my dream were fading all too quickly.

Gavin got up from the table and quietly placed his plate in the sink. I followed suit, grabbed my lunch, said goodbye to Buddy, and walked out the door with my brother.

On the way to school, I thought about my dream of Heaven and the encounter I had with Jesus. *If Jesus loved me so much, why would He allow so much pain?* My dream had left me with more questions than answers.

Gavin and I rode our bikes in silence. I wanted to ask about his arm, but I really wasn't in the mood to talk. I was worried about missing a week of school. I happened to be a pretty good student. I spent my recesses and lunches doing extra credit work to keep my grades high. I didn't have any friends, so what else was there to do?

As I approached the spot where I crashed my bike, I stayed to the far right to avoid another mishap. I looked up at the house where Doris lived. She had been so caring and compassionate that day.

Just then, Doris burst out of the front door and waved us over. She probably wanted the blouse I borrowed, but in a rush to leave the house, I had forgotten it. Gavin and I parked our bikes as Doris strolled down the driveway with something in her hand.

"Hello, Honey. How are you today?" she asked. "And who is this with you?"

I introduced Doris to my brother, and they shook hands.

"I haven't seen you for a week, and I wanted to see how you were doing after that nasty crash. I admit I was a little worried about you."

"Her best friend died," Gavin blurted out. I shot him a dirty look and immediately regretted it when he hung his head down. He was so sensitive these days.

"I'm fine, thank you, Ma'am," I said softly, holding back tears at the mere mention of Amy.

"I sure am sorry to hear that," she said sincerely. "Losing someone you love is tough."

I saw something more than sympathy flash across her face. *Was it pain?* I wasn't sure.

She opened her hand to show me a giant blueberry muffin.

"Maybe this will cheer you up a little. I made these special for you, but now that I see there are two of you, why don't I go grab another one for your brother."

Gavin smiled for the first time in weeks and licked his lips. We didn't have a lot of time before school started, but Mom always taught us to be polite.

"I'll be right back in a jiffy," she said and walked toward her house.

I took a bite of the muffin; it was delicious. My stomach growled to remind me that I had barely eaten all week. Doris returned with the second muffin, and Gavin ate it in a matter of seconds.

"Well then, you both better get going. You don't want to be late. I'll be having muffins and tea tomorrow morning if you want to stop by again on your way to school," she said. Her kindness was so overwhelming; I had to bite my lower lip to keep from crying.

"Okay, thank you," we said in unison. I put the muffin in my lunch box, grabbed my bike, and peddled the last few blocks to school.

When I got there a few minutes early, I pulled out the muffin and shoved half of it into my mouth. It was the best tasting muffin I had ever eaten in my life. I immediately devoured the other half.

✟

Days turned into weeks, and the one thing that made life bearable were the mornings I spent with Doris before school. Sometimes Gavin stopped with me, and sometimes he didn't.

Doris's blueberry muffins were addicting. Sometimes she made biscuits and gravy or pancakes. She was the most gentle, thoughtful adult I had ever met. Her husband, Herman, was just as caring and loving as his wife. He always greeted me with a smile and would call me half-pint. I didn't mind when Herman would tease me about my height because I knew he liked me and said it with affection.

Slowly, Doris began to earn my trust. She would always listen attentively, never pressing or asking too many questions. I opened up about Amy and how devastating the loss of her was. I told her about school and how alone and awkward I felt. I let her in on the Frank situation. However, I didn't mention the times he would stand in my bedroom door at night and stare at me when he thought I was sleeping or about the drinking and fights late at night with my mom. Nor did I inform her that he was hitting my little brother or how my mom had changed into someone unrecognizable, and I chose not to say that I had stopped praying to Jesus and doubted everything I had learned at camp. I don't know why I didn't tell her these things. Maybe I thought she wouldn't believe me. Perhaps I thought she would be ashamed of me and not invite me over for tea and muffins anymore. Whatever the reason, those things I kept a secret.

In the spring, I was sitting in class when an officer and the principal walked in. The room went dead quiet as they spoke to our teacher, Mr. Roland who then looked straight at me and said, "Alina, Officer Strand and Principal Higgins would like to have a word with you."

The entire class turned around simultaneously and looked straight at me. I prayed the floor would crack open and swallow me up. Attention like that would most likely cause relentless gossip and additional ostracizing that would last the remainder of the year. I was scared and angry at the same time.

"Please take your things and go with them to the office," the teacher added.

I gathered my belongings and quietly exited the classroom. No one said a word as we walked together down the hall. A thousand thoughts and questions came to mind. *What did I do? Am I in trouble? Is my brother, alright?*

We walked into the office, and Mr. Higgins closed the door behind us. Gavin was sitting in a chair, head bowed. *What was he doing at my school?*

When Gavin saw me, he jumped up and threw his arms around my waist. After a quick embrace, we sat down. I was about to ask him what was going on when the officer cleared his throat. Mr. Higgins took a seat behind his oversized desk, while the policeman leaned against it, preparing to address us.

"I know you both are wondering why we brought you in here. First off, you're not in trouble."

I sighed with relief, letting out the breath I had been holding.

The officer continued, "We got a call this morning from the hospital. Your mom was taken to the emergency room with some injuries."

I took my brother's hand in mine. These were words neither of us were prepared to hear.

"We suspect her boyfriend; Frank Williams caused them." Gavin started crying. I bit my lower lip to refrain from joining in.

"She is going to be alright but," he hesitated for a moment, "she has a broken jaw, a broken arm, and three broken ribs."

I gasped as Gavin's crying turned into wails. All I could do was stare straight ahead in disbelief. The fighting between my mom and Frank had been getting worse, but I had no idea it would go that far.

"I'm going to ask you both some questions, and I need you to be honest with me," the officer said firmly but gently.

"Where is Frank now?" I managed to get out.

"He is in custody, pending assault charges. We have reason to suspect there has been additional abuse going on in your home."

I swallowed the lump that was developing in my throat. *Do I disclose everything?* Fear and hesitation filled my mind, and I started panicking. I wasn't sure if they could see me shaking. I didn't want to break my promise to Gavin, but this was a police officer. I took a deep breath.

"He's been hitting Gavin, too," I said almost inaudibly.

"Gavin, we need to hear it from you." Officer Strand went to put his hand on my brother's shoulder out of concern and sympathy, but Gavin instinctively jerked away. The police officer moved back a few inches out of consideration for him.

After several minutes, Gavin finally said, "Yes, he has been hitting me."

"Can you be more specific?" Officer Strand pressed.

Gavin went on to tell his story to the officer, our principal, and me for the first time. When I heard about the physical abuse my brother had suffered, tears flowed unchecked down my face.

I had no idea how bad it was until my brother lifted his shirt. Everyone in the room fell silent, except for me. After my initial gasp, I started bawling. Bruises, both old and new, covered his torso. My baby brother had been a punching bag for this monster. Sadness turned into pure hatred that rooted itself deep inside me. I wanted Frank to pay for what he had been doing to our family. The things he did to me seemed very unimportant compared to what he had done to my mom and brother.

The officer took several pictures of the bruises that ran across Gavin's stomach and back. Then he turned to me and asked the same question.

"Alina, you have a courageous brother right here." I nodded and squeezed Gavin's hand. "We need you to be brave as well." I couldn't help but wonder if they knew what Frank had been doing to me.

"He hasn't ever hit me," I said flatly. The officer nodded.

"There are other types of abuse," he said softly. My mouth went dry, and I could feel my face turn red. I knew he could tell I was holding back.

Mr. Higgins stood up and said, "Gavin let's go get a drink of water, alright?" Gavin looked over at me with fear in his eyes and begged to stay with me.

"It's alright, Little Bear." I reassured him that I would stay right there as Mr. Higgins led him out of the room.

Officer Strand sat down next to me. I gulped again. "I know you are scared, Alina," he stated. "I want to protect your family, but if I am going to do that, you will have to trust me."

"I haven't told anyone," I said, staring at my hands. "I'm not sure where to begin."

"Start wherever you want."

I couldn't stop myself from crying again. When my sobbing subsided, I told the officer everything. I told him about the times Frank would try to catch me without my clothes on, the sexual comments he made about my changing body, the nights Frank would come into my room and try to touch me while he thought I was asleep, and the times Frank would brush up against me in a way that made me feel dirty and humiliated. I cried until there was nothing left. By the end, I felt like a wrung-out dishrag.

"He did a lot of horrible things to you and your family, Alina. I don't want you to think any of this is your fault."

Then, the officer did something unexpected. He asked if he could pray for me. I hadn't talked to Jesus since Amy's death. I nodded my head yes as he knelt next to me and said the most beautiful prayer I had ever heard. He prayed for healing, not just for me, but for my brother and mom, then for wisdom and that God would hold Frank accountable for his actions. The last part surprised me the most. He asked God to find His way into Frank's life, to save him. I did not like that part of the prayer. I didn't want Frank to have one single moment of peace or forgiveness. *He deserved to go straight to Hell,* I thought. I certainly would never forgive him, no matter what.

When the prayer was over, Officer Strand asked me if we had any other family in the area. I told him, no, it was just the three of us.

He thought for a moment, then asked, "Is there anyone here in town that you trust?" I immediately thought of Doris and Herman.

"Why do you want to know?" I asked.

"Your mom is going to take a bit to heal. She will be in the hospital for at least a week. You and your brother will need to stay with someone for a little while."

I told him about Doris and how Gavin and I spent our mornings before school at her house, how it all started when I had crashed on my bike, and how kind she had been to me. I provided their phone number and address.

Gavin and Mr. Higgins returned, and Gavin rushed over and hugged me tightly. He looked up at me, seeking comfort. I squeezed his hand and tried to reassure him.

"I'm so proud of you, little brother. You are so brave." I looked over at the officer and asked, "Can we go see our mom now?"

"Yes, as soon as I make a couple of calls, I will take you to the hospital." I was suddenly hopeful and relieved for the first time in months. I wondered if Gavin felt the same way.

CHAPTER 6
NEW BEGINNINGS

When Gavin and I arrived at the hospital, Mom looked a lot worse than I imagined she would. Both of her eyes were black and blue, and the left one was swollen shut. I could tell she was both happy and embarrassed to see us. I was beginning to hate hospitals.

My brother and I carefully climbed onto the hospital bed and laid next to her. We sobbed and held each other until there weren't any tears left to shed. I could see the apology on Mom's face, and at that moment, I completely forgave her. I may never really understand why she stayed with Frank for so long, but I loved her more than anything and desperately wanted us to go back to the life we had before his arrival.

The hospital room door opened and in walked Doris and Herman Locke. Gavin and I carefully got up from Mom's bed and ran into their open arms. Herman and Gavin had become very close over the past few months. He had been teaching my brother all about fixing cars, which Gavin found fascinating. Doris was teaching me how to bake. I even learned how to make her award-winning blueberry muffins.

I could see Doris doing her best to hold back tears as she introduced herself to my mother. At first, I felt a little self-conscious. Doris and Herman probably knew about the secrets my brother, and I had been keeping. I wondered if they were disappointed with us for not telling them. I questioned if they were still going to want to spend time with us now that they knew our indiscretions.

My anxiety quickly diminished as Doris turned to us and said, "I'm so proud of you both."

Gavin took Herman by the hand, walked with him over to our mother, and said, "Mom, this is Herman. He's our friend. Sometimes we eat breakfast at their house in the mornings before school. Doris makes the best blueberry muffins on the planet." I was afraid that my mom would be angry at us for stopping at a stranger's house; however, if she was mad, she never acted like it. Mom nodded and tried to smile despite her jaw being wired shut.

I recounted my bike wreck on the first day of school to explain how we had met the Locke's. I left out the part where Frank had hung up on me.

A social worker named Peggy came into the room and explained to Mom that Doris and Herman had agreed to take care of Gavin and me while she recovered from her injuries. Mom motioned for a piece of paper and pen. She scribbled, "Thank you very much," on it and held it up.

It was difficult leaving Mom, but Doris promised to bring us back for a visit the next day. Herman drove us to our house to pack some clothes and pick up Buddy.

Poor Buddy was huddled in the corner when we got there. No doubt that morning's events had frightened my young puppy. I laid down and wrapped my arms around him. "Everything is going to be alright now," I whispered softly. He licked my face and then jumped up as if anxious to get out of the house for a while. I looked around and saw some of Frank's belongings still strewn about. Empty beer cans covered almost every surface. I went straight to the kitchen and grabbed a garbage bag from under the sink. Doris and Herman watched patiently and with understanding as I walked around from room to room, removing everything that had been his. Gavin even pitched in. It all went into the garbage bag. When I finished, it was as if Frank had never lived there. I took that bag straight out to the trash, washed my hands, and packed a suitcase of my own.

Doris and Herman had made up the bed in their guest room and tucked us in. It had been a long and emotionally draining day for everyone. Buddy took his place on the pillow by my head, as usual.

Doris knelt beside us, bowed her head, and prayed for our family. It was a touching one about healing, forgiveness, and restoration. Gavin closed his eyes, but mine remained open. I wondered if I would ever feel like praying again. Camp Pine Rock seemed like a million years ago. *Where is God?* I wondered. *Doesn't He love us?* I kept these thoughts to myself. After the prayer ended, I did finally close my eyes, beyond exhaustion. That night, I dreamt of the garden again.

This dream was a little different than the other two. I had a pressing feeling I needed to find something or someone, and it was causing a bit of apprehension. Even though the garden looked similar to the last two times, there was something off about it. I listened carefully. I didn't hear one single animal sound. There wasn't any rushing water, or singing, and nothing moved — not a blade of grass or a single leaf on a tree. My anxiety increased slightly when I also noticed that I felt weird, too. Gone were the overwhelming sensations of love and happiness that were becoming familiar with my visits to the garden. Instead, I was uneasy.

I walked around, searching for someone or something for what felt like hours even though I couldn't be sure what it was. I started to panic a little because I sensed that time was running out.

I happened upon a grazing herd of elk. One of them spotted me and sounded an alarm. They took off running, and the ground shook from the stampede. I ran to hide behind a tree trunk, but on my way, tripped over what I initially thought was a stick. I quickly jumped to my feet as it started moving. A giant snake slithered out in front of me. It rose up high into the air, its head facing mine. Fight or flight took over as I prepared to run. Then, unexpectedly, it spoke to me.

"Daughter of Eve," the snake hissed. "I have been looking for you." Its tongue whipped in and out, tasting the air around us. The fear dissipated, and curiosity got the best of me.

"Why have you been looking for me?" I replied. "I'm nobody important."

"I want to be your friend," came the answer, the forked tongue flicking from side to side.

"You do? Why? No one else does?" Pity rose up inside of me. Sadness filled my heart, and I felt like crying.

"You are a special girl and don't deserve to have so much pain in your life," the snake continued, lowering its head back to the ground. Slithering through the grass and winding up the tree next to us, it hung down on the lowest branch and faced me again.

"What can you do about it?" I questioned. Alarm bells went off inside me, but I ignored them.

"Unlike God, who makes everyone suffer, I can bring relief," it promised. "I can help you enjoy your life again."

"God says He loves me," I countered.

"That is interesting. Are you sure about that?"

"Yes," I lied. I was interested to know how this creature had information about me. "How do you know who I am?"

"Let's just say I am well informed." the snake said. "I know everything about you, Alina Gabrielle Sheridan." Goosebumps covered my skin, and the hair on the back of my neck stood straight up.

I was deciding if I was going to ask more questions or get the heck out of there when, from the corner of my eye, I saw movement. Out of nowhere, a massive lion leapt through the air. With a ferocious roar, he landed directly in between the snake and me. The lion opened his mouth and grabbed the serpent, shook it back and forth, and tossed it into a nearby bush. I could hear it slither off, wounded but still alive. I was frozen with terror as the lion turned and looked directly at me. His eyes were a multitude of colors, and I realized this was not the same lion from my previous dream. This one was the biggest lion I had ever seen in my life. He towered over me. Then, the lion spoke too.

"Alina! Stay away from that snake; he is not your friend."

"Am I in Heaven again?" I asked.

"No, Child. Lying serpents have no place in Heaven." I was about to ask another question when thunder boomed overhead. It was so loud; I instinctively covered my ears and ducked down. The dense garden floor shook violently, and I tried to steady myself. As before, the ground split open, and I felt myself falling.

I woke up with a headache again. This time, I welcomed the pain. It was better than going to school and sitting at recess or lunch by myself. It was better than remembering Amy was gone and that Mom was in the hospital with a broken jaw. And it was better than facing rumors after being escorted to the office by a policeman.

Despite those things, I needed to go and wasted no time getting ready. I had a test the first hour that I had studied hard for and was anxious to get it over with. Hopefully, everyone would continue to ignore me, like usual. After my embarrassing departure the day before, however, I had a bad feeling that would not be the case.

The prettiest girls in school were nicknamed "The Fabulous Four." They were always together, laughing obnoxiously at each other's jokes, and often wore matching clothes, purchased out of the most popular magazines and shops. Even though they were pretty on the outside, their insides were ugly. They enjoyed harassing anyone they saw fit. I avoided them at all costs. They were mean, rude, and downright devious. Most of the year, they had left me alone until today.

It was a few minutes before my math class, and I wanted to get into the room to review for the test. Gavin and I were opposites when it came to school. I excelled at English and he was better at math. He always helped me, including studying for the test on fractions I had that day. I would never hesitate to return the favor and help him with

English assignments.

The tallest one of The Fabulous Four was blocking the door into the classroom. "Excuse me," I whispered as I went to move past her. Thinking I would get by unnoticed, she surprised me when she spoke.

"Hey, Alina."

"Hi Vicki," I answered. She sounded friendly so I wondered if maybe things wouldn't be so bad that day, after all.

"No," she snickered, "I said hay. Like 'Hay is for horses.' You kind of look like a horse with those buck teeth." Vicki made a horse sound, and The Fabulous Four started giggling along with several other students who happened to be within earshot. I didn't know what to say. I had never been good at comebacks. I wasn't witty like my brother, so I chose not to respond. I tried to move past her again without success.

"My mom told us that you like older men," the shorter one named Beth said in a sarcastic tone. "I could set you up with one of my dad's friends." They laughed in unison again. *Do they know about Frank?* I wondered. *How is that even possible?* I had not told anyone but the police officer.

Then it hit me. I remembered Beth volunteered in the office sometimes and wondered if she could have been listening through the door. The bell rang, and the "Not-So-Fabulous Four" went into the classroom along with everyone else. I wanted to run away, but I had already missed too much school, and it was important that I took this test. I lowered my head and took my seat at the back.

During the test, I noticed The Fabulous Four whispering to each other when the teacher's back was to us. One of them, named Melissa, turned and threw a wadded piece of paper at me. It struck my arm and fell to the floor. When they giggled, the teacher turned around and started walking in my direction. When he came down my row, he noticed the wadded-up paper on the ground by my foot. He bent down to pick it up and proceeded to unfold it.

"What is this?" he asked. "This looks like the answers to the test. Does this belong to you, Ms. Sheridan?"

Before I could protest, Melissa immediately raised her hand and said, "I don't want to be a tattletale, but I did see Alina wad it up and drop it on the floor as soon as you started walking around the classroom." She batted her long eyelashes, attempting to look as innocent as possible. My mouth gaped open. I had never cheated in my whole life.

"Alina, you care to explain?" he asked.

"It isn't mine," I said, barely audible. I wanted to argue and point my finger at Melissa, but I knew it didn't matter. He didn't believe me. *Dang it!* I needed to get a good grade on that test, and now I was probably going to get a zero and be in trouble on top of it!

After the bell rang, my math teacher walked me to the principal's office. I followed behind him with my head hung low and my desperate thoughts keeping me company. *Fantastic, the principal's office twice in one week.* I could hear the whispers swirling around me. The school couldn't even call my mom because she was still in the hospital.

We walked into the office. "I'll see you tomorrow, Ms. Sheridan," my math teacher said before turning to leave.

See me tomorrow? I wondered in confusion. *There's still a full day of school left today.*

Principal Higgins called me into his office and said, "Alina, I know you have had a rough couple of days, but as you are aware, we have zero tolerance for cheating. Mrs. Locke is on her way to pick you up. Come back tomorrow, refreshed and ready for a new day."

He didn't even ask me if I had cheated, I screamed inside. *What a joke. I hate school.*

Doris signed me out, and we both walked to her car in silence. The last thing I wanted was for her to think I had really done this.

"Those answers weren't mine," I finally said in the car. "I don't cheat. I'd never do that." I told her about The Fabulous Four and that they had set me up.

"I believe you, Honey," she responded gently. I held back the tears that were threatening to make an appearance and instead plotted ways to get back at them. Fantasizing about it made me feel a little better.

"How about we go out for lunch today?" she asked me. "What sounds good?"

Maybe I should get sent home more often, I pondered.

"I love that Italian place down the street from my house," I suggested. I smiled for the first time in a while.

"Done deal," she said. "They have the best-unlimited breadsticks and salad."

After ordering our lunch, Doris said, "Alina, I want to talk to you about something."

Uh oh!

"Forgiveness," she said in a solemn tone. Doris lowered her voice so only I could hear what she was saying. "You have shared your stories with me; now I want to share mine with you. I had a son."

I thought I remembered a picture of a young man in uniform on the mantle above their fireplace. He looked like he might have been in his early twenties. Doris had never mentioned anything about having children, so I just thought maybe it was her brother or another family member.

"Our only son, David, came back from the war a very different man than when he left. We tried everything to help him with his depression. We tried counseling, medication; we even hospitalized him once. We prayed for him, encouraged him, and took him to church. It's such a hopeless feeling to see your child in so much pain and not be able to do anything about it." Doris took a drink of her soda, and paused for a moment, looking out the window. I could see it was still a struggle for her to talk about it all these years later. I knew the feeling; I couldn't talk about Amy without tearing up.

"He became addicted to drugs," she suddenly continued. "We were not aware of it for quite some time. Drugs can make you do crazy, impulsive, dangerous things. He was in and out of treatment centers for several years. We thought he was doing better, but one morning, when he didn't get up for breakfast, I went to check on him and found he had died sometime during the night. We were told that the cause of death was an overdose." Tears slipped down her face, but she courageously went on.

"Death does a number on the people left behind. Herman and I faced a mountain of questions. What did we miss? What else could have been done differently? Why our son? Everyone handles grief differently. I felt guilt; Herman felt anger. Things can seem very unfair when you don't learn to let God heal your hurt." Doris stopped to wipe her face as the waiter brought out our food.

I thought about Amy and how angry I felt at God for taking her away from the people that loved her so much. I thought about how unfair it was that people like The Fabulous Four got pleasure out of being mean to others. I also thought about my brother and mom. I felt guilty about keeping our secret for so long. Maybe if I had told someone sooner, Mom wouldn't be in the hospital, and my brother wouldn't have had to suffer so much physical abuse.

Doris continued, "I know that you have a lot of grief over the loss of your best friend and anger at the man who did unspeakable things to you and your family. And I am sure you are angry about being accused of cheating. You have every right to feel that way. But God wants you to forgive the people who hurt you, Alina. He doesn't want you to live with anger and sadness in your heart. This scripture helped me in my own journey to forgiveness. It says in Ephesians 4:31-32, 'Let all bitterness, and wrath, and anger, and clamor, and evil speaking, be put away from you and be kind to one another, tenderhearted, forgiving one another even as God for Christ's sake has forgiven you.'"

I remembered Pastor Steve talking about the great forgiveness of sins through Jesus. I thought about my many conversations with Amy and how she said that God loves everyone, even awful people, like Frank. I could feel the ice around my heart starting to melt a little. I guess God also loved The Fabulous Four.

"How do you forgive people?" I asked. "I feel so hurt and angry; I don't know how to forgive them."

"You do it little by little, Honey," came Doris' soft reply. "It doesn't mean you are okay with what people have done to you. It just means that you give that hurt to God and let Him make those wrongs right." I didn't know how God could ever make what Frank did right.

"It's just as important, if not more, that you forgive God, Alina. We don't always understand why God allows things to happen, but I know He has a good plan for our lives. He is not the one that made Frank do those terrible things to your family. Satan is responsible for that. He is behind all the evil in the world and is described in the Bible as the great deceiver. He deceived Adam and Eve in the Garden of Eden with a simple piece of fruit, and he will try to deceive you too. He convinces people that his ways are better than God's ways."

"How did he deceive Adam and Eve in the garden?" I asked.

"He appeared to them in the form of a serpent and convinced them to sin against God," Doris answered in between bites of a breadstick.

My fork stopped midway to my mouth as I remembered the snake from my dream the night before. It happened in a garden as well. *Had that snake been Satan?* I wondered as the dots connected. *The enormous lion with the rainbow-colored eyes mentioned something about a 'lying serpent.'*

"Well now," Doris sighed. "I think that's enough for today." She smiled and patted my hand. "What are we ordering for dessert? Do you want a cannoli or ice cream?"

"Cannoli!" I answered, returning her smile with one of my own. I felt a weight lift from my shoulders, and the knot in my stomach began to shrink. The somewhat radical thought that God just might care about my family and I, began to creep its way into both my head and my heart.

When Gavin got home from school, we went to see Mom in the hospital again. I told her all about what had happened that day. She scribbled notes to me and shook her head yes and no in response to my questions. It turned out to be a pretty good one, after all.

I did not want to go to school the next day and face The Fabulous Four. I thought about my forgiveness conversation with Doris. *Could I forgive people as Jesus does?* I wondered why Jesus would want to forgive us, and why He loved people so much? I sure wasn't fond of a lot of them. Doris said that we needed to be like Jesus and to love people the way He loves us. *Is that even possible?* I continued to ponder. Clearly, I still had my doubts.

I got to school a little earlier than usual, which gave me plenty of time to use the restroom. I drank almost a gallon of orange juice that morning and thought my bladder might burst by the time I entered the bathroom stall. Suddenly, I overheard someone crying in the one next to me.

I didn't know what to do. I had cried so much in the last year, my heart hurt for whoever it was. I hesitated for a minute, and finally whispered, "Are you okay?" The girl didn't respond at first.

"Beth, Vicki, and Melissa are so mean," finally came a voice. "I didn't wear a matching sweater today because my mom forgot to wash it. The only clean shirt I had was the one my grandmother got me for

Christmas. Beth said she wouldn't be caught dead in this sweater. They all know my grandmother passed two months ago!" More sobbing echoed off the bathroom walls. "How could she say such a horrible thing? I was very close to my grandmother, and she knows that! Oh my gosh, there is no toilet paper in here!" the girl moaned.

I had seen someone enter the bathroom before me, but I didn't realize it was Katie. She was one of The Fabulous Four. I was suddenly scared she didn't know it was me she was confiding in.

Without saying a word, I passed a giant wad of toilet paper under the stall. Katie continued, "I'm so sick of them. All they do is make fun of other people." She blew her nose. I couldn't believe how much she was telling me. Then she said something that stunned me, and I knew my cover was blown.

"That was a terrible thing they said and did to you yesterday, Alina. I had nothing to do with it." She must have recognized me somehow. "In fact, it really made me mad. I talked to Principal Higgins after class and told him that Melissa was responsible for the wadded piece of paper, but he dismissed it. I let the girls know I thought that they were way out of line, saying those nasty things to you before class. That's probably why they were so mean to me today." After a few more sniffles, she followed up with, "I'm sorry, Alina. I should have stood up for you sooner. Did you get in big trouble?"

We both exited our stall at the same time. I avoided eye contact with her and kept my head down. "That's okay. I forgive you." I surprised myself with that statement. *I forgive her! Wow, I underestimated how good it would feel.* "No, I didn't get in trouble; I got taken out to lunch."

I dared to peek up at her, and to my surprise, she was smiling. She had a perfect set of teeth, lucky girl. I smiled back, pursing my lips so she wouldn't see mine.

"Thank you, Alina. Both for the forgiveness, and for the toilet paper." Katie let out a little chuckle. "Do you want to eat lunch with me today?"

I almost fell over. *Stay calm*, I silently insisted to myself before answering a little too quickly. "Sure!" *What is going on here?* I couldn't help but wonder. *Did one of The Fabulous Four just ask me to eat lunch with her? This better not be a trick.*

"Ok, great! I'll save you a place next to me." It felt like I was in another dream. "I can't believe you didn't snitch on Melissa. And you got lunch out of it!"

"Did I mention I got dessert too?" A giggle escaped. Amy would be so proud of my blooming confidence.

To my surprise, Katie started giggling too. Once we started, we couldn't stop. I laughed so hard I almost peed my pants again. "Man, drinking all that orange juice before school was a bad idea," I said and ran back into the stall.

"I'm an apple juice fanatic, myself," Katie said, still laughing. I could not believe this was happening. *Thank you, God,* I thought. The first bell rang, and we headed off to class together, talking like we had been friends forever.

Katie and I had a blast at lunch. The Fabulous Four were now The Terrible Trio. Katie loved my new nickname for them. They huddled together, whispering and snickering as usual. We ignored them entirely.

That next Sunday, Gavin and I attended church with the Locke's. It was the first time I had been since Camp Pine Rock. It felt invigorating. I forgot how much I had missed it. Sunday's message was exactly what I needed to hear, and I mulled it over in my head for a while afterward.

The pastor said that God doesn't allow anything to happen that He can't bring something good out of. We don't always see it right away, but you can bet He is working behind the scenes. He said that is why faith is so important. When bad things happen, we have a choice. We can get angry and lose our faith in God, or we can pray about it and trust God's purpose for our life. Pastor also talked about kindness and how powerful it is. "Mountains can be moved, and chains can be broken by showing kindness, especially to people who we feel don't deserve it," he said.

A week and a half after being admitted to the hospital, Mom came home. Her jaw was still wired shut, but she communicated with us through paper and pen. Sometimes Mom talked to us by drawing pictures instead of writing it out in a sentence. Gavin and I would take turns trying to guess what she was saying. She slowly started getting her sense of humor back, and our family of three grew by two as Doris and Herman came over frequently to help around the house and spend time with us.

Summer was in full swing, and another birthday came and went. This birthday was completely different from the previous ones. Katie and I celebrated in style. We went to the mall to do some shopping and see a movie. We even got our nails done. In the evening, Doris and Herman brought over a German chocolate cake, my favorite.

It was already a hundred degrees in Phoenix. Luckily, Katie had a swimming pool at her house, and we spent several days a week playing in the cool water. Then we would watch our favorite cartoons, look at fashion magazines on the floor of her bedroom and talk about boys.

Mom healed completely, and things went back to the way they were before Frank. Meals were full of stories and laughter once again. Mom threw herself into her crafts and joined a Bunco group with Doris. Amy was never far from my mind but thinking of her no longer hurt.

That summer, Gavin and I taught Buddy how to do a bunch of tricks. He could sit, roll over, play dead and speak, along with a dozen others. Buddy was the smartest dog I had ever seen. He followed me everywhere and slept by my head each night. Katie and I would often walk him around our neighborhood or take him to the park so he could run. Buddy had turned into a handsome looking dog. He was medium-sized with reddish, brown hair. He had the face of a Collie and his body was covered in short hair except for his tail, his neck and the back of his legs. We often said he looked like a little lion. I had developed a real love for those majestic creatures. Mom had even gotten me a new bedspread for my birthday with the head of a lion embroidered on it.

Days turned into weeks and weeks into months as another school year finished out. Katie and I were inseparable and the best of friends. Doris and Herman became like adopted grandparents, and we spent a lot of time with them. Mom was able to save enough money to pay for me to get braces and contact lenses. I pitched in for the cost by earning cash from cleaning Doris's house every other week and helping mom sell her crafts.

It was the summer before my freshman year in high school, and I was not afraid to look in the mirror any longer. Katie showed me how to put on make-up and style my hair. My teeth were getting straighter by the day. Gavin and I attended church every Sunday with Doris and Herman. Eventually, Mom started accompanying us, as well. She accepted Jesus into her heart that summer.

A new family with a son named Dalton moved into Amy's old house. He was Gavin's age. It had sat vacant for a long time and it was nice to see it finally occupied. It didn't take long before Dalton and Gavin became best friends. One late afternoon, Gavin asked Mom, "Can I have Dalton over for dinner tonight? His parents have to work, and he will be all by himself."

"Estamos teniendo delicioso comida Mexicana esta noche," Mom stated, in her best Spanish accent.

"Mom, you can't speak Spanish when Dalton comes over; he is going to think you're crazy or something, and I don't know what you are saying," Gavin said, annoyed.

"She said we are eating delicious Mexican food for dinner tonight." I translated.

"No estoy loco!" Mom said, laughing.

"She said she's not crazy," I commented again, trying to suppress laughter because I knew Gavin was getting frustrated.

Gavin continued with, "Mom, when are you going to get rid of all these Santas? It's so embarrassing!" Gavin was now in the "Mom is so weird" stage. I had entered back into the "Mom is hilarious" phase. A giggle escaped, which only encouraged her.

"Nunca!" Mom exclaimed. "Amo a mi Papá Noel."

"She said never. She loves her Santa's." Gavin continued arguing with Mom, and I watched out of amusement.

"I can't understand Spanish, Mom!" he said, exasperated. "Please don't humiliate me when Dalton comes over, or he's never going to want to hang out with me!" Mom continued speaking Spanish, and Gavin stomped off to his room. I wondered when Mom had learned Spanish but didn't want to interrupt with a question. The whole exchange was quite amusing.

Mom was very creative. She spent most days working on projects like stained glass windows or mosaic coffee tables. She would then sell them to neighbors, people at church, or right out in our front yard. At any given time, Mom would have paint on her face, hands, or in her hair. Trying not to trip over her on-going projects became quite the task.

Her favorite place to work was under an old oak tree in our backyard. On bearable days, when the heat wasn't too bad, she would be out there for hours, singing to herself or humming a catchy tune. Mom made money in all kinds of ways. She cleaned houses, took care of the elderly, and made homemade dog treats, which she sold to pet supply stores all over town. She was creative and resourceful. I had not inherited her creativity, but I was definitely resourceful. I had also missed out on her beauty , her sense of humor, her love for art, as well as her ability to make friends wherever she went. My mom was the most loving, generous creature on the planet, and I thought the world of her.

"Come here, Buddy, it's time for a walk." Buddy ran over, retrieved his leash, and dropped it at my feet. Another neat trick I taught him a few months ago. "Good boy," I said and nuzzled the long, soft hair around his neck.

It was a beautiful sunny day. As we walked down the street in our neighborhood, Buddy took his time smelling every mailbox post and bush, peeing on each one, marking it with his scent.

Rob Dunham's house was on my street. He was going to be a junior that year, and I'd had a crush on him for as long as I could remember. He was probably the most popular guy in school and well-liked by everyone. He played football and was a good student.

That day, he happened to be in the driveway, washing his dad's truck. I watched him hard at work as Buddy finished his business on their hedge. He must have heard us and turned around to catch me staring at him. *How embarrassing.*

"Hi, Alina," he said as he walked toward me. "Hey, Buddy." He bent down to scratch Buddy behind the ears. "He is a handsome boy." I nodded in agreement as Buddy licked Rob's face. So, you'll be a freshman next week, huh?" His skin was tan and smooth around solid muscles. With his shirt off, you could tell he worked out. My heart skipped a beat, and I could feel my face flush.

I finally found my voice. "Yes, I'll be a lowly freshman this year," I answered with a grin. I was feeling a bit more confident.

"It's not so bad. We were all freshmen once. Well, I'll see you around school, then," he smiled. His teeth were perfectly straight, and his eyes were the color of the ocean. He had light brown hair with blonde tips, most likely bleached from the intense Arizona sun.

He went back to work on the truck while I turned to head home. I could not wait to tell Katie about my encounter. Even though we had lived in the same neighborhood our entire lives, Rob had never had a conversation with me. He had always been polite and said, "hello" whenever he was outside, and I would walk by; however, this was the first time we'd had had actual dialogue.

Mom said I could invite Katie over for dinner since Gavin had company. I told Katie about Rob, and her reaction was exactly how I imagined it would be.

"Oh my gosh, Alina, how exciting! Maybe he likes you! I heard he broke up with his girlfriend a few weeks ago." We giggled and enjoyed boy talk over dinner, while Gavin and Dalton discussed video games. Mom cleared the table and sent us kids off to enjoy our company. Knowing there were only a few days left of summer fun.

Once we were back in my room, Katie commented on Dalton. "Dalton gives me the wrong vibes." Katie loved the word "vibes." I think she used it almost every time we were together. "Keep an eye on him," she added with a frown. I took note of what she was saying but thought he looked innocent enough to me.

After our friends left for the night, I was exhausted. The summer heat had a way of draining you throughout the day. I was in bed and asleep by 8 p.m. That night, I finally had another dream about Heaven, and it was by far the coolest one yet.

I was walking down a winding path towards a city on a hill. Golden light emanated from somewhere within it. I could see a multitude of people entering and exiting enormous gates. As I approached the entryway, I noticed the gates were made of pearly white, round, bead-like structures the size of houses, stacked on top of one another. Two enormous angels sat high upon pillars. Their faces were beautiful and radiated with light. Their wings were pure white and spread out for hundreds of feet, in a protective stance, watching over the passageway. Thousands of rainbows spanned from one side of the city to the other. The path changed as I entered the gate. I couldn't be sure, but the ground looked just like solid gold; it sparkled where the light touched it.

Negative emotions such as fear and discontent were absent in every way. I searched for them, but it was as if they never existed, and I was overwhelmed by feelings of love, kinship, wonder, and joy as I entered into a new region of this mysterious kingdom.

The buildings and towers were comprised of a translucent substance I did not recognize and were covered in dazzling jewels. Katie's father worked at a jewelry store, and I had learned the names of several precious stones. I recognized diamonds, rubies, black opals, onyx, jasper, and blue garnets. Hundreds more covered the city's buildings, bridges and structures.

There was a thriving culture, and I noticed everyone was young and healthy looking. I saw no one with any sign of weakness or sorrow. Instead, I saw pure joy and an endless reservoir of fascination evident on every face. Colorful lights encompassed them and shot out of their chests like beams. They were talking with each other, and even though people spoke in different languages, there seemed to be no communication barriers. No one looked like they were in a hurry or stressed out. No one seemed lonely or sad or frustrated.

Their bodies looked changed, too, like the ones on Earth but different somehow. They were wearing spotless robes of white with colorful sashes, scarves, and jewelry. Some people even had small crowns on their heads. Everyone was laughing and talking with one another. They were eating and drinking food I had never seen before. It honestly looked like a celebration was taking place. People were cheering, laughing, and embracing each other. I had the warmest feeling of affection for all of them.

I witnessed indescribable art and heard beautiful music that came from all directions and had notes and melodies I had never heard before. The city streets were bustling with activities but I didn't see one traffic light, stop sign or even car. Nor did I hear any sirens, or sense any waste or pollution. There were parks and gathering places full of such magnificence, grandeur, and extravagant elegance, no words could describe them.

The things I could see, however, were unimaginable and inconceivable. There were rivers in the sky and trees that grew upside down with their roots shooting up into the heavens. I saw many species that humans on Earth had never encountered and witnessed people traveling in the most unconventional of ways.

In the middle of the metropolis was a giant throne. On it sat a being that I had never seen before, but knew instinctively was God the

Father, my king, and I was in His kingdom. Water, clear as crystal, flowed out from the bottom of the throne, producing a massive waterfall that poured out, creating streams and rivers that wound their way throughout the city. Trees, flowers, and green grass lined these streams on both sides. Each tree bore multitudes of fruit, and not one was rotten, nor was one leaf withered. I felt profoundly at home here. Surrounding the throne were people of every nationality. They were worshiping the being who sat on the throne. They sang in perfect unison:

> "Let us come into his presence with thanksgiving;
> let us make a joyful noise to Him with songs of praise!
> For the Lord is a great God,
> And a great King above all gods.
> In His hand are the depths of the Earth;
> The heights of the mountains are His also."

I dropped to my knees in awe and marveled at God. He was beyond what my mind could comprehend. A radiant light burst from His countenance, and it lit up the entire kingdom with an intensity brighter than the sun. Gold crowns rested upon His head, encasing exquisite jewels and precious stones. Radiance surrounded the whole throne, and seven flaming torches were burning in front of it.

His voice was like the roar of many waters. He was neither man, nor spirit, but a supreme, unworldly being, incomprehensible to the human mind. There were no words in the English language that could describe God. Near the throne were four living creatures covered with eyes in both the front and the back.

They repeated over and over, "Holy, holy, holy is the Lord God Almighty."

I bowed my head in reverent humility, undeserving of God's holy gaze. My spirit compelled me to worship Him, for His glory covered Heaven like a blanket. His purity and goodness showered over me like rain. He held the Earth and the cosmos in the palm of His right hand. His wonder and splendor were unmeasurable.

Suddenly, a loud, recognizable thunder crashed overhead. No one but me seemed to notice. The ground shook, and I looked down to see the golden arena I was standing in crack open. I immediately closed my eyes, prepared myself, and said goodbye to the City of God.

CHAPTER 7
UNEXPECTED KINDNESS

I woke up from my dream of Heaven with another massive headache. It was the first day of high school, and I didn't have time for it. I found the Tylenol and downed a couple with my orange juice at breakfast. Gavin was trying to talk Mom into taking us to school on our first day. I barely listened. I was deep in thought. There was something extra special about the dream from the night before.

Oh, to live in a place like that! I repeatedly thought.

I tried to hold on to every single detail of what I experienced. I concentrated and walked myself through it from beginning to end over and over again in my mind. That was the day I decided I would start recounting them in a journal.

Mom said she would take us to school, and Gavin exploded with happiness and gratitude. I didn't want to ride my bike anymore, either. I was excited and nervous to start high school. Grade school and been terrible, and although most of junior high had ended up great, it had a rough start. Hopefully, that was all behind me.

Luckily, I had Katie as a best friend. Socialization seemed effortless for her. We had a few other friends that hung out with us from time to time, both in and out of school, but for the most part it was just Katie and I that did everything together. I was the most content with one close friend. Besides, juggling a sizeable social calendar wasn't really my thing.

"We need to leave a few minutes early today. I have to stop by the store on the way to school," Mom said. I snapped back to reality and hurried to clear my dishes and gather my backpack.

"I don't want to be late on my first day," I whined.

"We won't. It will only take a second," Mom reassured me.

As Gavin and I sat in the car waiting at the store, I observed a homeless man sitting on the corner near our parking spot. He looked like he was a little younger than my mom. He held a sign that read:

Veteran

Lost Everything

Anything Helps

Something pulled at my heartstrings, and for some reason, I felt drawn to him. The feeling was so compelling that I opened my purse and pulled out a ten-dollar bill. I was supposed to be saving my money, but instead, I opened the car door and walked over to him.

"This is all I have," I said and held out the bill. He looked up at me with surprise, then gratitude as he glanced down and noticed the money. He gently took it from my hand and looked back up at me.

"You have a rainbow around your head. I can see it clear as day," he said.

Is this guy on drugs? I wondered but kept it to myself. I didn't know what to say, and before I could come up with something, he continued.

"Thank you for your kindness."

Compassion for a man I didn't know rose up so intensely I had to bite my lip to keep from crying. He held out his hand to shake mine.

"My name is Cameron."

I shook it and said, "You're welcome; my name is Alina." We stared at each other curiously. There was a magnetic quality to our encounter, and I wondered if he felt it too. "I have to go now. My mom is taking us to school. It was nice meeting you. Goodbye." I turned and walked back to the car. *There's a rainbow around my head?* I continued to ponder. *And why am I so emotional? What the heck was I thinking, talking to a homeless man? Mom is going to kill me.* Just as the thought was complete and I started to put on my seatbelt, she came hurrying out of the store.

"Nia gave that homeless man some money," Gavin told Mom as soon as she shut the car door. I shot him a dirty look. He smiled mischievously and shrugged his shoulders.

"Alina! Don't go around talking to men you don't know!" she yelled, completely exasperated. "My goodness! And a homeless man? He could have kidnapped you!"

I thought the comment was kind of funny, so I giggled.

"Why are you laughing?" she immediately asked. "I'm serious!"

"Where is he going to take me? He's homeless, Mom!" I responded and stared out the window at him as we drove away. It looked like he was praying. Mom continued lecturing, but I didn't listen. I was busy saying a quick prayer of my own.

"He doesn't have to have a home to kidnap people, ya dork," Gavin quipped.

That I heard loud and clear. "Don't call me a dork!" I shouted at him, a little too loudly, and then quickly regretted it.

"That's enough!" Mom turned around and gave us her best dirty look. I covered my mouth to keep from laughing. When she turned back around, Gavin and I elbowed each other in the ribs and mouthed "ouch" to each other.

School was a madhouse the first day. Trying to figure out the combination for my locker, location of my classes, and navigating the campus took up most of my time and attention; however, the homeless man was never far from my mind. I told Katie about him at lunch.

"We should help him!" she exclaimed.

I thought about it for a minute and said, "What if we raised some money for him? We could have a bake sale or something."

"We have three giant bags of chocolate chips at my house," Katie responded enthusiastically. My mom was supposed to make cookies for a potluck but ended up getting sick and didn't go. Everyone loves chocolate chip cookies!" I was entirely on board with the idea, so we spent the rest of our lunchtime planning how and where we would sell them.

"We could set up a stand or even sell them here at school," I suggested.

Katie and I went to the office to get permission first. We were disappointed to find out that the school policy stated nothing non-school related could be sold on campus; however, the secretary said it would be fine if we wanted to sell them before or after school, off-campus. She even suggested hitting the bus stops.

I was so excited that I could barely concentrate on my afternoon classes. I called Mom from the office to ask if I could go to Katie's after school because we had an important project to complete. I mean, it wasn't a lie. She agreed but said I needed to be home for dinner.

Katie and I worked for hours on those cookies. After they cooled, we wrapped them in cellophane and put a little red bow on each package. We made one hundred chocolate chip cookies that night. When I got home, I barely had enough time to eat dinner and complete my homework before bed.

The next day, after school, Katie and I rode our bikes to every bus stop we could find. We didn't limit our route to just our school, either. We biked around for hours selling our delicious chocolate chip cookies. We were astonished at how many kids were willing to give up fifty cents for one. The demand was so high we met up at Katie's house again the next day to bake some more.

For two weeks, in our spare time, we made and sold cookies. We raised three hundred and twenty-six dollars. Neither of us could believe it. We were exhausted by the end of the second week, but it was well worth it. Don't ever underestimate kids and their addiction to sugar.

Friday, after selling our last cookie, we rode to a local bank and cashed in our coins for dollars.

Katie had volleyball practice the day we had planned to take the money to Cameron, so I went alone. My mom would have killed me, but despite knowing that, I rode my bike to the corner store where I had last seen him. He was sitting down and still had on the same dirty jeans and t-shirt he was wearing two weeks before. He stood up when he saw me coming.

"Hello again, Rainbow Girl."

"Hello again," I replied and handed him the envelope full of money. "My friend and I had a bake sale. We made quite a bit of money. As it turns out, kids love chocolate chip cookies." His jaw dropped as he pulled out the cash and he shook his head.

"I can't accept this," his voice broke as he attempted to hand the envelope back to me.

"Sure, you can!" I put my hands behind my back. "We did it all for you."

"Thank you so much," he said, still in shock. "This is the kindest thing anyone has done for me in a very long time." He wiped his eyes. "I haven't always been homeless, you know. When I came back from my time in the military, I got an excellent job. I married my high school sweetheart, and God blessed us with two handsome twin sons. When the economy declined, I lost my job. I tried to find another one but had a tough time." Cameron paused reflectively before continuing.

"One evening, my wife was driving home from the grocery store with the boys when a car smashed into their vehicle, killing all of them instantly. I had to use the last of our savings to cover the costs of their funerals. The driver fled the scene, and the police never made any arrests. It turns out the vehicle he or she was driving had been stolen. We didn't have car insurance; it was one of the many things we had to cancel when I lost my job."

He paused again for a moment. "I suffered from so much depression that I couldn't have held a job even if I had been lucky enough to find one. Lost our house shortly after. The accident happened almost two years ago." A tear rolled down his face. He abruptly brushed it away, suddenly appearing self-conscious. I knew he could tell that I had been crying too. "I should not have burdened you with all of this. I'm so sorry. It's just that I was praying that morning you pulled into the parking lot. I asked God to please send me some help or bring me home to be with my family in Heaven."

Everything made sense at that moment. God had sent me to Cameron. "I lost my best friend two years ago," I told him. "She died of Leukemia. She was the first person outside my family to accept and love me for who I am. And she's the reason I am a Christian. It took me a while to recover from her loss. I was mad at God for a long time." I couldn't believe I was telling a total stranger about Amy. "I learned that God has a purpose for things. I don't always understand what that purpose is, but I finally believe it. Well, most of the time anyway," I added.

"I'm sorry for your loss," he said compassionately.

"Thank you. I'm sorry to hear about your family as well." We sat quietly and watched cars as they drove by. Suddenly, I had a thought.

"Well, I've got to head home, or my mom is going to send the police out looking for me."

"That wouldn't be good," he said with a smile. I stood up and jumped on my bike.

"Listen, I'd like to be of more help," I told him. "Please stay close by so I can find you."

I took off before he had a chance to argue with me and rode home as fast as I could. As soon as I ran through the door, I grabbed the phone to call Doris and asked if I could come over the next day to discuss something important with her. She of course agreed.

Buddy was excited to see me, and I laid on the floor with him, scratching his belly and reviewing the crazy events that had taken place over the last two weeks. I closed my eyes and said another prayer for Cameron.

Saturday morning, after chores, I rode my bike over to the Locke's house and rang the doorbell.

"Come in!" Doris yelled. "Look what I made!" She set down a plate full of freshly baked chocolate chip cookies. I started laughing. What I would give to never see another chocolate chip cookie again.

Nevertheless, I sat down, picked one up, and ate it. *No use in being rude,* I thought. It was much better than the ones Katie and I had baked. *These might be the best chocolate chip cookies I have ever tasted in my life,* I realized before helping myself to another one.

Doris sat down and picked one up for herself, "What's so funny?" she inquired.

I told her about Cameron and our extraordinary encounter. I told her about his tragic loss and the bake sale. I even told her about the rainbow comment and how Cameron didn't want to take the money Katie and I had raised for him.

"He begs on the corner down the street from my house and barely makes enough to eat. He doesn't have anywhere to shower or the extra money to buy new clothes, so he isn't able to look presentable for job interviews. He prays to God and seems very kind-hearted. I know if someone gave him a little help, he would be able to get back on his feet again. Short of holding another bake sale, there's not a lot I can do. I was hoping maybe you guys might have a better idea."

"You have such a giving heart, Alina." Doris patted my leg affectionately. "Let me talk to Herman, pray about it, and see what God leads us to do."

I felt relieved and exhausted at the same time. It had been a long couple of weeks. I rode my bike home, yawning the entire way but also managed to say a quick prayer, "Dear God, please let Doris and Herman help Cameron, and thank you for bringing him into my life." It was at that very moment I knew in my heart what I wanted to do with my life. I planned to help as many homeless people as possible. I wanted to be a light in a dark world, a rainbow after a storm. I smiled as I thought about Cameron's nickname for me.

I had seen Cameron on Friday, and now it was Sunday morning. I was anxious to talk to Doris and Herman and find out what they had decided. I waited for their arrival by the church's glass doors while Mom and Gavin found seats for us.

I could hardly believe my eyes when I saw Doris and Herman walking towards the church from the parking lot. *Cameron was with them!* Only he didn't look like the Cameron I had talked with on Friday. He was clean-cut and wearing new clothes. His beard was gone, and his hair was nicely trimmed. He looked like an entirely different person.

My heart overflowed with joy and felt as though it would burst. When they walked in, I hugged both Doris and Herman as tightly as I could. Then I turned and made eye contact with Cameron. His eyes sparkled and teared up a little. He didn't have to say thank you because it was written all over his face. I had touched his heart, and he had touched mine. No words could describe how good it made me feel.

"Hello, Rainbow Girl," he said.

"Hello, Cameron." I looked over at the Locke's again and shook my head in disbelief. Herman winked at me. I knew there would be no time for questions because I could hear the congregation starting to sing worship songs.

"It's a great day to worship the Lord," I heard the pastor say as we took our seats. I agreed. It was a *great* day.

The news about Cameron was even better than I had imagined. Herman and Doris had invited him to live with them until he could find a job and a permanent home. I was overjoyed when I heard the news. Doris and Herman joined us for dinner that week and Cameron came with them.

Herman had connections all over the city and helped Cameron get a job at a local hardware store. Doris helped Cameron apply for Veteran's services, including counseling and job skills development.

After a few months, we couldn't help but notice how close Mom and Cameron were becoming. Anytime Cameron was set to come over; Mom would put on extra make-up and spend a little more time doing her hair. It was no surprise to any of us, then, when sometime later, Mom announced that she and Cameron were dating.

We began to see a lot more of Cameron once that was out in the open. He and Gavin spent time outside playing ball or inside watching sports on television. My time with him was special, as well. Cameron had been a chef in the military. He and I spent hours in the kitchen together, and he taught me how to cook and follow recipes.

Things at school were going alright most of the time. Girls were still mean for no reason, but that year, I finally learned how to stand up for myself. The Winter Formal was at the end of November, and I hadn't given it much thought until Rob Dunham approached Katie and I at lunch.

"Hey girls," he said and sat down next to me. I looked up to find his face less than a foot away from mine. He smiled and stared straight into my eyes. My face immediately flushed, and a thousand butterflies took flight inside my stomach. Katie's sandwich stopped half-way to her mouth. She slowly set it down and cleared her throat.

"I've got to get something; I'll be back," she said, leaving us alone. *Come back,* I thought. My palms got sweaty, and my heart beat a million miles a minute. *Why is Rob sitting next to me?* I gave myself a mental pep talk. *Alina, breathe and act normal for goodness' sake.*

"So, I was wondering, are you going to the Winter Formal with anyone?" he asked, smiling. He could've broken a thousand hearts with that smile.

I wonder if I have food in my teeth. I had to get out of my head and say something. *Find your inner coolness, Alina!* "No," I finally started to say, "I didn't think lowly freshmen could go to the formal." I returned his smile with a grin.

"They can if an upperclassman takes them. Do you want to go with me?" Rob asked. I could see people watching us out of the corner of my eye. I was determined to get through the conversation without any social catastrophes.

Trying to act nonchalant, I said, "Sure, that sounds fun."

"Cool. Brad, Jesse and I are splitting the cost of a limousine. We want to arrive at the dance in style." I had never been in a limousine before, and it all sounded so exciting. Katie was headed back over so Rob started to get up. "I'll talk to you later then," he said.

I nodded, and he shot me that award-winning smile one more time before heading back over to his buddies.

"Oh my gosh!" Katie exclaimed as she sat down. "Did Rob Dunham just ask you to the Winter Formal?" I did some more nodding.

"Keep cool, Katie," I warned softly. "There will be plenty of time to freak out later when we're alone. Let's get out of here; everyone is staring at us."

"They are staring at you! Out of jealousy, no doubt!" she whispered. "I cannot wait to go dress shopping with you." We threw our trash away and walked out of the cafeteria. I reached down and squeezed Katie's hand, trying to release some of the excitement I felt. "Ouch!" she said, laughing.

I was so anxious to tell Mom and Gavin what had happened. "Mom, where are you?" I yelled as soon as I got through the front door. Buddy greeted me joyfully. I bent down and gave him some much-needed attention. I grabbed a dog treat from the kitchen, and he promptly started running through all his tricks without being told. I giggled at his antics and tossed his treat up in the air. He jumped and caught it on the first try.

"I'm in my room!" she yelled back. Buddy followed me to Mom's room, where she was folding towels on her bed and listening to music on the radio. "Hey, Sweetie. How was school?"

"It was probably the best day of my life," I said and grabbed a towel to pitch in. She raised her eyebrows as she shook her hips to the music. "I got asked to the Winter Formal."

"What? Really? How exciting, Honey! Wait, are freshmen allowed to go?"

"They are as long as an upperclassman invites them. You are not going to believe this, but Rob Dunham asked me!" Mom stopped dancing.

"Isn't he a junior this year?" she probed, even though I was sure she knew the answer. We've lived in the same neighborhood our entire lives. I could feel Mom's hesitation from the look on her face.

"Yes, what's the big deal?" I asked, challenging her.

"Isn't he a little too old for you?" This wasn't the reaction I had expected.

"Mom, we aren't boyfriend and girlfriend. He just asked me to the dance." I was beginning to get annoyed. I had spent my entire life as an outcast and didn't understand why she couldn't just be happy for me.

"I think, maybe, he's a little too . . . experienced for you."

"Mom, we are going with two other couples, as a group," I tried to reassure her.

She paused for a minute. "I will have to think about it." I rarely argued with my mom, but she was being ridiculous.

"Mom, I already told him yes. Everyone was watching us. I can't tell him no. I'll be laughed right out of school!" I felt like crying. I exited her bedroom and went straight to mine, closing the door a little too hard. I sat down on my bed and tried to come up with a convincing argument. Buddy jumped up and put his chin on my leg. I couldn't bear the thought of going to school and telling Rob that my mom said "no."

There was a knock at the door. "Yes?" I said and readied myself for the bad news as Mom walked in.

"Honey," she started as she leaned forward and put her hand on my shoulder. "I'm only trying to protect you. Boys can be persuasive."

"You don't trust me?" I asked in frustration. I had never given my Mom a reason not to.

"That's not it; I do trust you. I don't trust teenage boys." She hesitated for a minute then said, "Well, I guess since you're going as a group, I suppose I can't refuse." I jumped up and threw my arms around her neck.

"Thank you, Mom!" I squealed.

"You're welcome. Just promise me you will stay as a group the entire time."

"I promise!" I assured her.

"When is it?" she asked, a little defeated.

"In two weeks. I need to find a dress! When can we go shopping? Katie wants to come too!" I was so excited; I jumped up and down on my bed. Mom cracked a little smile.

"We'll go this weekend. I have a little extra money. I can buy your dress, but you have to buy your shoes, and I expect you home by ten o'clock." *Fair enough*, I thought and nodded in agreement before calling Katie to tell her about the upcoming shopping trip. We screamed together out of excitement.

"Girls are crazy," Gavin said to no one in particular but still put on a show with an exaggerated roll of his eyes.

"Las chicas no están locas." I retorted.

"Mom, will you two please stop speaking Spanish all the time?!" he shouted.

Mom and I started laughing hysterically as he stomped off to his room.

CHAPTER 8
RESILIENCE

We picked up Katie to go shopping on Saturday morning, and after visiting four different stores, I found the perfect dress and matching shoes. The formal gown was canary yellow with a big bow in the back. It was slim fitting, not too short and not too long, with a lace neckline and sleeves. Mom agreed to let me borrow some of her favorite jewelry. Katie went on and on about how pretty I looked and how the color complimented my skin tone. She promised to help me style my hair and apply my makeup for the event.

When the day of the Winter Formal finally arrived, I was a nervous wreck. Doubt filled my mind in the hours leading up to the dance. *What if Rob regrets asking me? What if I trip in my new high-heel shoes? What if I make a fool out of myself dancing?*

Katie could tell I was panicking and tried to talk sense into me. "It's going to be great. You look beautiful, Alina. Rob's the lucky one here." She pumped me full of compliments and assurances. When the last bit of mascara was applied, Katie finally let me look in the mirror to see her completed work. I couldn't believe my eyes.

"Well, what do you think?" Katie asked.

"I can't believe it's me," I responded, incredulously, as Katie beamed with pride. My mom walked in and gasped.

"Honey, you look stunning." Mom teared up a bit. Gavin even commented.

"Nia, you look pretty."

"Thanks, Little Bear," I said.

Rob and his parents arrived half-an-hour before the limousine was scheduled to come by the house and pick us up. There were flashes from cameras and exchanges of compliments. The other couples arrived, and before long, it was time to go. Mom gave me one last hug and quietly told me to be careful. We piled into the limousine and headed to the local community center, where the event was taking place. To my disappointment, things started going awry almost immediately.

I noticed a small, silver flask being passed around on the way to the dance. I had seen enough movies to know what was in it. When it came around to me, I passed it on without taking a sip. Brad's date Sarah noticed and gave me a hard time.

"Hey, Goody Two Shoes, it's only a little alcohol." Then she warned me, "You better not tell anyone." Sarah leaned over to whisper in the ear of a girl named Lisa. I was sure it was about me. I looked to Rob for support.

Instead, he said, "Come on, Alina, it's just a little drink to calm the nerves and loosen things up." Everyone laughed.

I didn't know what to say, so I just shrugged my shoulders and looked out the window. They continued to pass it around and pretty much ignored me for the remainder of the drive. I was crushed. This was not how I had pictured the night going.

We pulled up to the community center and everyone outside stared at us as we exited our fancy transportation. Rob helped me out and kept ahold of my hand. I began to relax. Maybe things would improve after all. I smiled at Rob as we walked into the Winter Formal together.

The decorations inside were stunning. There were white and silver balloons, streamers, and banners. A large disco ball hung down in the center and cast dancing sparkles all around the room. Christmas lights twinkled brightly from every wall, fixture, and table, and giant paper snowflakes dangled down from the ceiling. The uncomfortable drive there was all but forgotten as Rob led me to the middle of the floor and started to dance. He was great and a lot of fun. It quickly became clear this was not his first time.

After about an hour though, I caught a glance of another flask being discreetly passed around. I continued to decline it but Rob seemed to get more intoxicated as the night went on.

After a while, I went looking for the girls' restroom and found it located down a long, dimly lit corridor. When I exited the bathroom and started walking back to the central area, someone opened a random door, grabbed my arm, and pulled me into an empty room.

I started to scream, but a hand covered my mouth. "Shh, it's only me," Rob whispered.

"What are you doing? It's dark in here!" I laughed nervously but had a bad feeling about the situation.

"That's the point, silly. You look so pretty tonight," he said, slurring his words. I started backing away from him but had nowhere to go. It was pitch black, and I couldn't see anything. He pressed me up against a wall and kissed me, mouth open. I had never kissed a boy before. I turned my head after a second, disgusted with the taste of alcohol. Then he started kissing my neck. I tried to wriggle free.

"No! No, Rob! I don't want to do this!"

"It's alright, Alina, it's just a little kiss. I'm not going to hurt you." Every time I would push his face away or turn my head, his lips would find their way back with increased resolve. I was getting more nervous by the second and was running out of options.

I said a quick prayer to God, asking for His help. Then I did something I had never wanted to do to a boy; I kneed him in the privates.

I heard him crumble to the floor. "What did you do that for?" he managed to say, in-between moans.

I hurried and felt for the doorknob, turned it, swung the door open, and ran out as fast as I could. I sprinted down the corridor and straight for the exit, which was not an easy task in high heels. There was no way on earth I was going to stay there a minute longer.

I couldn't find the limousine anywhere. I threw off my shoes and ran down the street until I saw a house with lights on. I was afraid to call Mom. I couldn't bear the thought of the police getting involved, and I definitely didn't want to hear, "I told you so." I called Doris, and within fifteen minutes, was picked up.

"Are you alright, Honey? You look a mess!" Doris exclaimed as I shut the car door. All I could do was nod yes. I couldn't speak; it took everything I had to hold back the tears.

"Should we take you home?" I shook my head no; and looked out the window. I was so disappointed with the whole night. My first high school dance, and he ruined it. Doris and Herman exchanged glances in the front seat and headed to their house.

When we arrived, I went straight to the bathroom. I could hear Doris reassuring my mom on the phone. I didn't understand most of what was said because I finally allowed myself to cry. I looked in the mirror and was shocked at what I saw. My hair, which had been neatly pinned up, was now hanging around my face, disheveled. My makeup had smeared, and mascara ran down my cheeks. My dress was torn along the neckline, and the bow on the back was hanging on by a thread.

Doris softly knocked. "I laid a change of clothes by the door. I told your mom you had a rough time and asked if you could stay the night. I assured her that you were okay. You are okay, right?"

"Yes," I lied. I ran a bath and soaked in it for about half an hour. Doris knocked on the door every ten minutes to check on me. When I finally emerged, Doris, Herman, and Cameron were sitting around the table, quietly talking amongst themselves, concern written all over their faces. I sat down with them to offer an explanation, but there was no way I was going to tell them exactly what happened.

"The group of kids I went with snuck alcohol into the dance," I started matter-of-factly, deciding to go with a half-truth. "Then they got drunk, mean, and out of control. I didn't feel safe or want to get in trouble, so I left early." I prayed they wouldn't ask me for more details.

After a short pause, Herman said, "Well then, you made a good choice." Doris looked a little skeptical but didn't pressure me for more information.

Cameron asked, "Did you tell an adult?"

"No, I don't need any extra drama at school. I'm so exhausted, do you mind if I go to bed now?"

"Of course not, Honey," Doris said. "You want me to pray with you tonight?" I shook my head, no. "Alright, the couch is made up for you," she said, concern still evident on her face.

"Thank you for picking me up and letting me stay over. Good night." I tried to sound as normal as possible.

"Sleep tight," Cameron said.

I appreciated the sentiment but knew I wouldn't sleep much that night. I kept replaying the whole evening over and over again in my head. Doubt filled my mind, and I wondered what was going to happen next. *What am I going to tell Mom? What's going to happen next week at school when I have to see Rob again? What do I tell Katie?*

The phone rang all day on Sunday. I knew it was Katie, wanting to hear all about the dance. I wasn't prepared to tell her what happened yet, so when Gavin finally answered, I pretended I didn't feel well and couldn't come to the phone. When I saw her Monday, before the morning bell, she was furious with me.

"Are we still friends?" she asked with attitude, her hands on her hips.

"Of course, we are. You're my best friend." I reassured her before feigning confusion. "Why? What's wrong?"

"Really? Best friends? Because I called you on Sunday like a thousand times but you wouldn't talk to me. Then, I get to school, and

I hear all kinds of rumors about you and Rob."

"What rumors?" I looked around and noticed several people staring at me. A girl named Tammy walked by us and called me a slut under her breath. Her friends burst out laughing.

"The rumor is that you and Rob had sex at the dance. I'm not judging you, but I'm hurt because you didn't tell me about it first. I had to hear about it from everyone else."

"What are you talking about?" I asked panicking. "We did not have sex."

"Well, several people saw you coming out of a storage closet down the hall from the restroom at the dance. They saw Rob come out a few minutes after you. Everyone has heard the rumor, and I do mean everyone." The bell rang, and before I could tell Katie my side of things, she turned and stomped off. I went straight to the nurses' office and called my mom.

"I don't feel good, Mom. Can I come home?" I begged.

"Do you have a fever?" she inquired.

"No, but I feel like I'm going to throw up." That was true. I could feel my breakfast threatening to make an appearance.

"Okay. I'll be there in a few minutes." I hung up the phone and stayed in the nurse's office until I could hear my mom talking to the receptionist.

Mom reached up to feel my head. "Well, you don't feel warm," she said, her forehead wrinkled with concern as we walked to the car. "Do you need to go to the doctor?"

"No, I don't think so," I murmured.

"Well, alright, then. When we get home, I'll make you some soup. I want you resting in bed for the remainder of the day."

Buddy snuggled me as I sobbed into his soft fur. Every so often, he would lick the tears from my face. As soon as I would hear Mom coming down the hall to check on me, I would wipe away the tears, close my eyes, and pretend to be sleeping. I didn't want her to see me so upset and start asking questions. After school, Gavin even peeked in a couple of times, but I would always pretend I was asleep. The dance had reopened all the wounds of rejection and loneliness from years earlier and I was having a hard time coping with it.

That evening, I asked Mom if Katie had called. The answer was "no," and my heart sank. She had been my best friend for two years, and the thought of losing her was more than I could endure. She was hurt, and I understood that, but so was I. *How can she assume the rumors are true without hearing my side of the story?* I wondered over and over again.

Feelings of embarrassment and betrayal weighed so heavy on my heart that I closed my eyes and said a prayer. *Dear Jesus, You said, You love me, and You said You'd never leave me, but I sure feel alone right now. I try to make good decisions, and I try to be a good person. I even try to forgive people who hurt me. I could really use Your help. . . .immediately. Amen.*

I still didn't feel better. Sometimes I wondered if God cared about the little things we go through. I thought about the stories of Jesus and His disciples. They experienced some difficult times, too. But they always seemed to endure. *Can I make it through this?*

At dinner, Mom served chicken and dumpling soup. It tasted delicious. I realized I hadn't eaten anything for lunch.

"Oh, by the way, Alina, Rob called this afternoon." Luckily, Mom didn't see the look on my face. "I told him you weren't feeling well. He wants you to call him when you're better." I hadn't told Mom everything that happened at the Winter Formal. I made up a story about mean girls and alcohol. That seemed to satisfy her. Doris had kept my dress so that she could repair it. Mom changed the subject and lectured Gavin about school. He had gotten a warning letter from one of his teachers for being disrespectful, so Mom was giving him an earful. He'd been getting in more trouble lately, and I had a feeling it was in part due to his friendship with Dalton.

I thought about calling Rob back and giving him an earful of my own. *How dare he call me after spreading rumors that we had sex!* I screamed inside my mind. *Now he's harassing me at home?* I pushed the soup away. I had lost my appetite.

That night, I dreamt of the snake again. He was trying to convince me that he could solve all my problems. This time, I knew him for who he was and told him to stay away from me. After a while, he slithered off, making some very serious threats as he left. They sent shivers down my spine.

"I'm not afraid of you!" I yelled.

"You should be," he warned.

The giant lion with rainbow-colored eyes appeared out of nowhere and said, "I am the Lion of Judah; King of kings and Lord of lords. Behold, I am doing a new thing. Now it springs forth, do you not perceive it? I will make a way in the wilderness and rivers in the desert."

Even though His words brought comfort, I still didn't trust them.

"I'm afraid. I don't want to return to school and face everyone," I said.

"Fear not, for I am with you; be not dismayed, for I am your God. I will strengthen you; I will help you; I will uphold you with my righteous right hand," He said. At that moment, I knew that the lion with the rainbow-colored eyes was Jesus. Thunder rolled and told me it was time to go. I closed my eyes as the ground cracked open and swallowed me whole.

I woke up with a terrible headache again. It was so bad it made me nauseous. I used it to my advantage and convinced Mom I was still sick. It worked for three days. On day four, detecting no fever, Mom insisted I return to school or go to the doctor. Knowing my doctor wouldn't find anything besides a broken heart, I relented and reluctantly returned to school. I thought I had given the rumors enough time to fizzle out. Unfortunately, teenagers have great memories when it comes to drama.

Katie made herself scarce, but I finally tracked her down. "Listen, Alina," she said curtly, "we just don't share the same values any longer." Two girls, we both knew, stood on each side of her, arms crossed. I could tell by the look on her face that there was no use trying to argue my side. Her mind was already made up.

Before heading to the cafeteria, I went by my locker to grab my lunch. There was a note taped to it. I unfolded the piece of paper and found a crude sexual drawing. I turned and saw several girls giggling. *How many people have heard this rumor?* I wondered, somewhat naïvely. The girls watched as I crumpled up the picture and threw it in the trash. *Gross!*

I ate my lunch in the bathroom stall, crying softly in between bites of my peanut butter and jelly sandwich. Afterward, I went back to my locker to find another note taped to it. I almost threw it away without opening it, but curiosity got the best of me. It read:

> Alina, I really need to talk to you.
> Please call me.
> Rob D.

Yeah right! I instantly thought. *There is no way I'm calling you!* I tore up the note and threw it away. I didn't want to hear anything he had to say to me. What I didn't realize at the time was that I was doing to Rob exactly what Katie was doing to me.

After school, I spotted him waiting by my locker so, I hid behind a tree until he gave-up and walked off. I stopped by Doris' house on my way home. Cameron was outside working on the sprinkler system.

"Hey, Rainbow Girl," he said with a big smile. When he saw the look on my face, he put his tools down.

"What's wrong, Sweetie?" Cameron and I had become very close. Now that Mom was dating him, he was one of the two men in my life that I actually trusted. "Sit down here next to me. Let's talk."

As I did so, the tears streamed down my face. It took me a while before I could speak. Cameron waited patiently, his arm around my shoulder. His presence was comforting, even in the silence. I rested my head on his chest, and when the tears subsided, I finally spoke.

"Kids are so mean, Cameron. I wish I never had to go back to school again. Katie isn't talking to me anymore. And people are spreading rumors about me that are not true."

"I know this has something to do with what happened at the dance. I also know that you haven't told us the entire story yet," Cameron said gently. Some things are just too embarrassing to tell a man, but my silence spoke volumes.

"I was not a very nice teenager when I was your age. I did a lot of things that I truly regret. I hurt people. My dad was an alcoholic, and I had to witness him hitting my mother night after night. It made me extremely angry. I didn't know what to do with the emotion that was building up inside me, so I took it out on others. People who are hurting, hurt other people, Alina."

I felt sympathy for Cameron. He had been through a lot of pain and sorrow in his life. My problems were nothing compared to what had happened to him.

"What do I do, Cameron? I'm humiliated, embarrassed, angry, and alone again!"

"There are worse things than being alone and embarrassed," he responded. I saw emotion flash across his eyes, and I knew he was thinking about the loss of his family. "They humiliated, beat, and lied about Jesus too. His best friends denied they even knew Him, and even though Jesus was innocent, He died a horrible death on a cross next to two criminals. And He was the Son of God!"

I had heard all of this before, but it impacted me in a new way. It made Jesus relatable.

Cameron continued, "Little did His enemies know that Jesus would triumph in the end. Not even a sealed tomb could keep Him from His destiny. Alina, have faith that you have an important purpose. Satan doesn't want you to believe there is hope. He wants you to harbor unforgiveness in your heart. He is a snake in the grass, waiting to bite you any chance he gets, but Jesus crushed Satan when He died on the cross. That means you and I win in the end." Cameron squeezed my shoulder and said, "Hold your head up, Alina. This is not how your story ends."

That night, I finally had another dream about Heaven. I was in the garden, laying in a field of soft grass. I watched an eagle soar overhead and heard horses whinny nearby. A slight breeze sent dandelion seeds floating up into the air, where they eventually scattered in the wind. If I listened carefully, I could hear a chorus singing in the distance. I wondered if it was coming from the City of God.

I suddenly felt a presence to my left and turned my head. Amy was lying next to me. I shot up. "Oh my gosh, Amy!" She stood up, and we embraced tightly. I wanted to scream, laugh, and cry all at the same time.

"Hello, my friend! There are no tears in Heaven, silly." She always knew what I was thinking.

"Oh, Amy; I've missed you so much! You have no idea how hard it has been without you. Can't you come back?" I asked.

"You know the answer to that," she responded patiently, again reading my mind.

Amy looked rejuvenated. Her face no longer carried the signs of cancer, and a dazzling blue light radiated out from within her chest. Blue was her favorite color. I wondered if I had a light emanating from me. I looked down but didn't see anything.

"I wish I could stay here with you. Things are a mess right now." I glanced around at the magnificent garden and felt a longing for it. Even though I knew Amy couldn't leave, I also knew she didn't want to. I admitted to myself that, if it were me, I wouldn't want to leave either.

"Alina, listen, I need to tell you something important, and we don't have much time together. There are still many crucial things for you to finish on Earth before you join me in Heaven. Don't get distracted by caring what people think or say about you. Care about what *God* thinks of you. It is easy to focus on your pain and get stuck. Remember what God has told you. 'Let not your heart be troubled, neither let it be afraid.' And remember, you are a light in a dark place, Alina."

"But it's so difficult," I said. "I don't want to be alone again."

"Yes, having cancer was difficult for me as well, but God was with me and He is with you, too. He will strengthen you in your time of need. You are not alone."

"Did you accomplish your purpose, Amy?"

"Yes, Alina." She smiled widely.

"But how? You were too young to die!" I protested.

"Age has nothing to do with purpose," she retorted.

"What if I miss my purpose?" I asked with concern.

"You won't," Amy replied firmly. "I have enormous faith in you!" She smiled and embraced me again.

Thunder exploded, like fireworks on the fourth of July, and the ground trembled. I looked at Amy one last time. Her face glowed more brightly than ever, and she winked at me. The grass and dirt beneath us fractured. I closed my eyes, crossed my arms, and fell through cracks in the floor of Heaven.

"Ouch!" I held my head in between both hands and massaged my temples. I reached for the Tylenol bottle that now had a permanent place on my nightstand.

I couldn't believe I got to see Amy again. "Thank you, Jesus," I whispered, knowing in my heart that He had orchestrated the reunion. I said a quick prayer as I got ready for school. I asked for the ability to withstand the bullying and to be able to forgive the perpetrators. Knowing I had a unique, God-given purpose gave me enough strength to face the day.

It was Monday, four weeks after the Winter Formal, and the beginning of a new semester. I glanced at my schedule. Choir was my first class of the day. I had forgotten that I chose it as an elective. Cameron had told me at church several weeks ago that I had a beautiful voice. I wasn't sure I believed him but singing was better than physical education any day. Being picked last for teams due to having absolutely no natural athletic talent was not my idea of enjoyment.

I made it to Choir before the bell rang and took my seat in the back of the class, as usual. Several students saw me and exchanged glances with each other. I tried to ignore them. I also recognized several kids from my church; a couple of them even smiled at me. I smiled back.

I took an instant liking to our choir teacher, Mrs. Kendrick. She was kind, funny, quirky and a fantastic singer. But the fact that she made us stand up and introduce ourselves in song was a brief set-back. *Great,* I remember thinking, *P.E. is sounding better by the minute.* Almost everyone sounded like they belonged in there. When it was my turn, I said a little prayer and sang, "Alina Gabrielle Sheridan."

"Wonderful, Alina! Great job! You will be with sopranos!" sang Mrs. Kendrick. I wondered if she was going to sing everything.

I got up and moved over to join my assigned group. One of the girls in my soprano group said to me, "I love your voice."

Mrs. Kendrick told us all about the local competitions with other high schools, and if we got first place, we would have the chance to compete nationally.

The rest of the morning flew by, and when lunch approached, I expected I would be eating by myself again. Even though I didn't look forward to it, I would never eat in the bathroom again.

I sat down at a nearly empty table, close to the exit, just in case I needed a quick escape. To my surprise, five other students from my chorus class joined me, two of whom were from my church.

They sat down and started chatting about their day. A girl named Christy said, "Hey, Alina, how come you don't come to youth group Wednesday nights?"

I shrugged my shoulders, finished chewing, and replied, "I don't know why. I guess I never really thought about it."

"Well, you should come," she said.

Another boy added, "Yeah, you should come. We go on mission trips to Mexico, and in the summer, we take trips to the waterslides and the beach. I'm Nick, by the way." He reached out to shake my hand. *Where have all these kids been my whole life?* I wondered. Last week I thought I was destined to spend the rest of high school alone; today, I sat next to five friendly faces. I wasn't too sure what was going to happen once they heard the rumor about me. I pushed the thought out of my mind and decided to enjoy the company while it lasted.

Just then, a popular girl named Marlene walked by me and shouted, "Oh look, the slut found the nerds and the Jesus freaks." Laughter from her group of friends and nearby kids erupted.

Before I knew it, Christy jumped to her feet, got in Marlene's face and said, "I'm not so much of a Jesus freak that I won't slap you in the face, right now, in front of everyone." She smiled and inched a little closer to Marlene. Christy was very tall and towered over her.

Then, a guy from choir stood up and added, "Last I heard; you're not so innocent yourself. At least that's what Michael Jones said in history class last week." Someone yelled, "Burn," and Marlene's face turned bright red. She started to say something but decided against it and instead stormed out of the cafeteria.

Christy sat down, and everyone in my group burst into laughter. Nick high fived another guy sitting next to us. Christy looked at my surprised expression and said, "We nerds and Jesus freaks look out for each other." Everyone laughed again.

As we walked out together, I said a quick thank you to God under my breath. Jesus had answered my prayers and given me not one new friend but five. Everyone hugged me as the bell rang and told me that they would see me the next day and to make sure I got my butt to youth group that week. I could not wait to tell Cameron about it. I even said a little thank you to Amy, who I was sure could hear me all the way up in Heaven.

CHAPTER 9
UNFORSEEN CHANGES

The months that followed were the most fun I'd had in a long time. I was surrounded by a wonderful group of friends from both choir and church and did a fantastic job on my first solo in our school choral performance. I attended our youth group every Wednesday night, which taught me a lot more about Jesus than Sunday mornings. My freshman year was almost over, summer was around the corner, and I was signed up for several exciting trips. Katie eventually apologized to me, but our relationship was forever changed. We said hello in passing, but that was about it. Rob and I avoided each other; however, I tried my best to begin the process of forgiving him.

I was finishing up some homework in my room when Mom came in and announced she and Cameron were going on a date that night and wanted to know if I would keep an eye on my brother. I hadn't seen Gavin much lately and missed spending time with him. I made a mental note to dig out a board game and invite him to play with me. Mom looked stunning in a black dress with her hair pinned up.

"Mom, you look gorgeous," I said, admiring her. I wished I had one-tenth of her beauty.

"Thank you, Sweetie." She gave me a quick hug and kiss. "Your brother is in his room. I told him no company tonight. He needs to focus on his grades; they are slipping again," she added, heading out the door.

I nodded, said goodbye, and tried to focus on studying for my Algebra final. About twenty minutes after Mom left, I caught a whiff of something in the air. At first, I thought I imagined it; however, after several minutes, it became very noticeable. I recognized the familiar smell of cigarettes coming from somewhere outside my room. It was dark in the hall except for a little bit of light shining through the bottom of my brother's door.

I went to Gavin's bedroom and knocked. Even though I could hear movement, no one answered. There was no doubt in my mind that the smoke was coming from inside. I threw open the door and caught Dalton climbing out the bedroom window. The stench of cigarettes hung heavy in the air. I coughed dramatically.

"Gavin!" I yelled. "What the heck are you doing in here? Have you guys been smoking?" Dalton was already through the window and busting butt to flee the scene. Gavin had a guilty look on his face that quickly transitioned to defiance.

"You better not tell on me, Nia! It was just one cigarette anyway, and I wasn't even the one smoking." I knew he was lying to me.

"Let me smell your breath, then!" I dared him.

"No!" he yelled rebelliously. "And if you do tell Mom I'll tell her what happened at the dance." I could tell he felt bad immediately when he saw how that comment impacted me. I was devastated but covered it up with anger.

"What do you think happened at the dance?" I asked, my voice shaking from trying to hold back tears.

"I wasn't there, but I know what I've heard," he said in a lower voice. Gavin looked down at his feet. Both of us wore our feelings on our faces. My mom used to tease us about it and say how she could always tell right away when we were lying to her.

"YOU DON'T KNOW ANYTHING!" I screamed and slammed his door shut. I couldn't believe that my brother had heard the rumor too. How embarrassing. I was both wounded and offended that he believed what people were saying about me. I wanted to go back in there and tell him the truth, but I couldn't. I couldn't risk Mom finding out about the dance, so I had no choice but to keep his secret, for now.

"No more smoking, Gavin!" I yelled through the closed door.

Katie had been right about Dalton. Gavin would have never done anything like that on his own. The fact that Dalton lived next door, complicated things even more.

Mom came home around 9 p.m. and called us both into the living room. I didn't think much about it, but when I saw Cameron sitting there, I knew something was up. They were both grinning from ear to ear and holding hands. We sat down as they announced their big news.

"We are getting married!" Mom exclaimed and followed it up with a little high-pitched squeal. Cameron leaned over and kissed her cheek. "Before we move forward with setting a date, we wanted to get your blessing."

Gavin shrugged and said with little enthusiasm, "Fine with me." No doubt, he was feeling guilty for smoking and being mean to me. Cameron didn't seem to notice and patted his knee. Mom was more focused on my reaction.

I was in shock. Their engagement was out of left field. Once I collected my thoughts, I stood up, walked over to Cameron, and gave him a big hug. Gavin was quick to follow my lead.

"I'm so happy for you guys, really I am. Just a little surprised is all." I smiled at Mom and hugged her tightly. Joy welled up inside of me, and I did what I do best; I cried. For the first time in my life, we were going to have a father figure.

"We get to plan a summer wedding!" Mom said, full of enthusiasm. Cameron assured us that we didn't have to call him dad and that he wouldn't be moving in until after the wedding. I loved Cameron, and I loved Mom. Both of them deserved to be happy. I was starting to get a little annoyed at my brother for not acting more excited and shot him a look saying just that. He tried a little harder. Mom and Cameron didn't seem to notice the non-verbal exchange between my brother and me. They were focused on each other.

"We have so much to do! I don't even know where to start!" she said giggling. Mom looked at both Gavin and I, expecting a response. My brother just said goodnight and slunk off to his bedroom. "What's wrong with him?" Mom asked me quietly. I guess his attitude hadn't gone unnoticed after all.

"We got into an argument, so he's mad at me," I said.

Mom seemed satisfied and her attention quickly turned back to planning her wedding. I said goodnight as well and ducked out, so I could finish my homework and get in bed at a reasonable time. *What a night!* It was after 10 p.m. when I finally crawled into bed and I fell asleep within minutes.

I dreamt I was strolling down a winding path with a lake on one side and a line of trees on the other. A lion walked alongside me. This lion was much smaller in stature and had dark brown eyes. I recognized him from one of my very first dreams of Heaven. He was the one that had tackled me in the garden, licking my face with his sandpaper-like tongue. He seemed to know me; I instinctively rested my hand on his head as we walked.

The beautiful lake to my left glistened as the light bounced off its surface. The top of the water looked like it was covered in millions of sparkling diamonds. Hundreds of graceful, white swans and brightly colored ducks swam offshore, honking at each other and diving beneath the surface of the water. Lily pads with white and yellow flowers covered the lake's shallows, and thousands of dogwoods shot up around the shoreline. A blue-grey heron took flight from somewhere amongst the thick overgrowth. Every so often, a fish would breach the surface and make a loud splashing sound as it re-entered the water.

I could hear laughter in the not-too-far-off distance. I stopped and looked around; maybe Amy was nearby. I spotted a dozen teenagers standing on the edge of a cliff hundreds of feet up. I watched them jump, one by one, into the water and waited for them to resurface for air. Being afraid of heights, I could never imagine doing something so daring. All of a sudden, a strange sensation came over me. Even though I didn't feel panicked, I knew there was a serious problem.

"Help! Someone needs to rescue them! They aren't coming up for air!" I yelled, looking around frantically for help. I briefly considered jumping in but, luckily, I saw a man walking toward me. I immediately started sprinting directly at him.

"They're drowning!" I yelled and pointed at the lake. "We have to do something!" When I got close I noticed that I was not speaking to a normal human.

"No one drowns here," the brilliant creature said to me, matter-of-factly. He glanced in their general direction, and in an unconcerned voice, said, "They can breathe underwater." I looked over to where the kids had jumped in. A sense of relief and excitement rushed through me. *Cool*, I thought, *Heaven gets better every time I visit*. Finally, a head popped out of the water, and the others followed several seconds later.

"Did you see that?" one of them said.

"That was amazing," said another one. Then they disappeared back underneath the surface again.

I surveyed the angelic being standing next to me. He was magnificent. I couldn't help but stare at his glorious wings, neatly tucked behind his back. His face shone like the stars at night, and he was wearing a white garment covered in hundreds of jewels. I thought about the angels that decorated our dining room walls and chuckled at the comparison. Real angels look nothing like people on Earth think they do.

"What is your name?" I dared to ask.

"My name is Michael; I am the protector and the leader of the army of God against the forces of evil," he said. His voice sounded musical, almost like symphony. "We must go. *He* is waiting for you." I wasn't sure who *He* was, but I followed the magnificent angel anyway.

When we got to a thick grove of trees, Michael told me to follow the river and stay to the right until I spotted a large granite boulder under a tall oak tree.

"He will be there when you arrive."

His departure was a spectacular sight to see. His wings unfolded and spread out as wide as a small airplane. With one leap, he launched himself into the air, and the wind that his wings created when they flapped blew me back several steps. His beauty and radiance were something to behold. I would never look at our dining room decorations the same again.

As I followed his instructions, I took my time observing the scene before me. I stopped to watch a large cinnamon-colored bear skillfully climb up a tall pine tree. Monkeys swung overhead from branch to branch, grunting at each other. Moss grew on rocks and trees, and vines with leaves as big as an elephant's ear wound their way up and around everything. Lush, green grass covered the ground, and every plant sprouted a flower of some kind.

I saw a man in the distance. He was sitting on top of a large rock, dipping His feet into a little, round pond. A bright light encircled Him, and I immediately recognized Him as Jesus. I couldn't help myself; I started running in His direction. Every doubt, every care evaporated instantly. Joy, peace and love filled my heart and poured out of me like a river.

When I reached Him, I jumped into His arms. It was like coming home from an extended journey. After our embrace, He held me at arm's length and took a good look at me. His eyes were the color of many rainbows, the exact colors of the enormous lion I had encountered several times.

"You are growing up so fast!" he said and kissed my forehead. "We don't have much time, shall we talk?" I nodded yes as we sat down on the rock and watched the tiny fish swim over to greet us. "It is so good to see you, Alina. Oh, how I have missed our time together," He stated and squeezed my hand. "We need to talk more often."

"I try to, Jesus. But every time I want to make myself dream of Heaven, I can't. The dreams always happen when I least expect it," I explained.

"I am speaking about prayer, Daughter," He clarified lovingly. "Prayer is talking to me. I want us to communicate with each other about everything, not just in times of trouble."

"I know how to communicate with You but, how do You communicate with me?" I asked, a little confused.

"That is a great question! You always have such wonderful questions, Child. I have many ways that I communicate with people. The most important way is through My Holy Spirit." Suddenly, a dove appeared above His head, then flew over mine. "My Spirit is with you always but I may also use visions, angels, and other miraculous methods."

"Like dreams?" I asked.

"Yes, like dreams! You are so smart, Alina." He tousled my hair. "I also use My holy words written in the Bible. That means you have to read it!" He gently chided. "Communicating with Me daily brings us closer together. The more you know Me and the more connected we are, the more you will understand what I am leading you to do. It will always coincide with scripture and is described by many as a still, soft, small voice that speaks to you through thoughts and feelings. You must cleanse your mind every day from ungodly mental clutter, false beliefs, and attitudes. You must free it from unhealthy feelings and misguided plans. My Holy Spirit will replace all of that with true thoughts that reflect My purpose for your life."

There was that word again, "purpose." Just as I was about to ask Him what my purpose was, Jesus continued.

"I need you to remember something essential. I am your Shepherd, and I will supply your every need." I thought back to Camp Pine Rock and the stained-glass window of a shepherd, watching over his sheep. "In times of pain and trouble, take into account that I am the only One who can deliver you. In all things, remember that you are My child, and everything will work out for your good."

"Yes, I will remember, I promise," I assured Him.

I had so many questions, but before I could organize my thoughts, thunder sounded, and the ground beneath us shook and began to break open. I toppled off the rock, rolled straight into the open crevice, and fell through this world and back into to my earthly home. I woke up to the all-too-familiar throbbing pain in my head.

"Headache, headache, go away and don't come back another day," I said out loud as I grabbed my glass of water and two Tylenols before heading toward the bathroom. I couldn't help but wonder why my dreams always ended so abruptly. There never seemed to be enough time in Heaven to get all my questions answered.

When I got back to my room, I pulled out my notebook and recorded the details of my latest dream. Then, I tried to say a well thought out, extended prayer and found it very challenging. After the first two sentences, my mind started wandering. I thought of what I needed to do for the day and wondered what Mom was doing. I remembered the math final scheduled for that day and contemplated what other school projects I needed to finish. I wondered how to pray when my mind went every which way? Just then, I got an answer, almost like a small voice in my head.

I grabbed an empty notebook, and for the first time, I wrote down my prayer. I approached it like a journal entry. When it was complete, I closed my bedroom door and read the prayer out loud. This method made it much easier to concentrate on what I wanted to say. Success at last, and it felt so good.

I hid both notebooks in my closet. I had not yet told anyone about my dreams of Heaven and the time I spent with Jesus. I was afraid if I did, the dreams would stop. I couldn't imagine life without my heavenly trips. The garden was like a second home to me now and just as real as my life on Earth.

Despite the Tylenol, my headache didn't go away that day. It was a dull, vice-like pressure that wrapped around my entire head. It became somewhat difficult to concentrate or have conversations because it hurt so bad. I thought about telling Mom but hesitated; she was up to her eyeballs in wedding plans. By the following morning, I was finally free of it.

I left my room to find Mom buried in what looked like thirty different bridal magazines.

"Alina, come over here and help me pick out a dress. I can't decide on anything." She sounded desperate.

I sat down, crossed-legged on the floor, and helped Mom pick out the flowers, reserve the church, and narrow down the dresses. Doris was making the cake, and Herman had agreed to give her hand in marriage. Weddings were a lot more work than I had ever imagined.

The weeks that followed were exciting and full of fun. I completed my freshman year with good grades and helped Mom finish the last details for her big day. I hung out with my church friends on Wednesday nights and weekends. We went on a few trips to various places around and outside of Arizona. I wrote down and read out loud my prayers each day and watched God do some amazing things in my life.

Gavin and Dalton were no longer friends, and I was happy about that. He never told me what happened between them, but it must have been significant.

Mom and Cameron's wedding took place in late July at the church where we attend. It was intimate and beautiful. I was the maid of honor, wore a teal-colored dress, and mom paid for me to have my hair and make-up professionally done for the special event. Mom was gorgeous in an off-white, slim-fitting wedding dress with matching lace gloves and a fancy veil. Gavin looked handsome in his tuxedo, as

Cameron's best man. Buddy got in on the action and walked down the aisle as a ring bearer. He even had his own fancy outfit. Cameron couldn't stop smiling, and I watched several tears surface as our mom walked toward him with Herman on her arm.

The reception took place in our backyard. I had helped decorate everything. We took pictures and danced well into the evening to a live band.

I couldn't believe we were going to be a complete family for the first time in our lives. Gavin and I watched Mom and Cameron during their inaugural dance as husband and wife. All along, I had thought that God had brought me into Cameron's life to help him, but it was actually the other way around. God had brought Cameron into my life to help us.

I leaned over and rested my head on my little brother's shoulder. He wasn't so little anymore. One more year and Gavin would be in high school with me. Time seemed to be flying by, and I wanted to tell it to slow down a little bit.

Two weeks before school was to start, we were all eating breakfast together, laughing at something Cameron said, when Mom abruptly got up from the table, went over to the kitchen sink and vomited. Cameron jumped up and ran over to her. Even after her breakfast had been dispelled, she continued heaving uncontrollably.

"I'm ok, I'm ok," she said, in-between bouts of throwing up. Gavin and I exchanged concerned glances. I racked my brain, trying to think of the last time I recalled Mom being sick, but couldn't remember one single instance. When the heaving stopped, Cameron helped Mom to the living room couch, placed a cold rag on her head, and positioned a bowl nearby, just in case she had another bout of vomiting.

"Why don't you two clean up the kitchen for your mom?" Cameron suggested. We got up quickly and quietly started clearing the table. The stench of vomit hung in the air, and I immediately washed it down the sink.

Mom spent the day on the couch, trying her best to recuperate. But, after four days of a high fever, vomiting, and weakness, Cameron finally insisted she go to the emergency room. Mom reluctantly agreed. It was shocking and scary to see her so weak after only a few days of being sick. Cameron and Gavin had to help her walk to the car. She had not been able to keep any food down and lost a lot of weight in a short amount of time. I was a little concerned but sure she would be back home in an hour or so, diagnosed with some virus that was making its rounds.

Gavin and I had been lying around, watching television all day, when Doris and Herman suddenly showed up at the house. I jumped up and gave them both hugs.

"Hi, kids. I brought some leftovers for dinner and a cheesecake for dessert," Doris said in her usual cheerful voice, however, I noticed her face didn't match her tone. A small knot developed in my stomach. Gavin was excited about the cheesecake and went straight to the kitchen to cut himself a piece.

"Where's Mom?" he asked. "It's like six o'clock."

Herman broke the news as casually as possible, but we could tell something was going on. "They decided to admit your mom to the hospital for a few tests. She asked if we could come over and hang out with you two tonight since Cameron is planning on staying with her."

Seeing the concern on our faces, Doris added, "I'm sure it's no big deal, kids."

We ate our meatloaf and mashed potatoes in silence, then gathered in the living room after dinner to watch a little television before bed. The silence was almost deafening. No one was in the mood for dessert except for Gavin; he ate three pieces of cheesecake. I said goodnight and retreated to my room. I got out my prayer notebook and asked God for help. I don't know why, but the feeling of impending doom hung over me like a dark storm cloud. There was a knock at my door.

"Come in," I said. Gavin walked in with a pillow and blanket.

"Can I sleep in here tonight, Nia?" he asked. My little brother, now taller than me, looked vulnerable and afraid. I could tell he had a bad feeling too.

"Of course, you can," I said. I scooted over to make extra room. Buddy was nestled beside me with his head on my chest. When Gavin climbed in bed next to me, Buddy, feeling dejected, reluctantly moved down to the bottom. It was a tight fit with the three of us, but his presence was reassuring.

"What are you writing?" he asked.

"I am writing a prayer for Mom."

"Why are you writing it down?"

"My mind tends to wander, so writing my prayers down helps me focus and be more specific," I explained.

"Will you read it to me?" he asked, tearing up a little.

"Sure." My brother closed his eyes as I read my heartfelt prayer out loud, my voice breaking toward the end.

"That was beautiful," he said, tears streaming down his face. "I have a bad feeling, Nia."

"I don't think we have anything to worry about" I said with confidence. "Lots of people end up in the hospital because of the flu. Mom will be home in no time." I suddenly thought of Amy and felt uncertain about this statement. I could tell Gavin didn't buy it either.

"What's in this one?" he asked and picked up the other notebook. I hesitated for a moment; not sure I was ready to share my dreams with anyone.

"It's about my dreams of Heaven." I whispered reverently.

"What do you mean?"

"Well," I said, trying to find the right words. "I have dreams about being in Heaven. They started at Camp Pine Rock. I've seen and spoken with Jesus, walked around the City of God, and even met with Amy one time."

"Wow, that sounds amazing. Can I read it?" he asked. I nodded and watched him read each entry, witnessing his expression change from curiosity to fascination.

When he finished, he slowly closed the notebook and carefully set it down. "Nia, I can't believe you never told me about this. You seriously had all these dreams?"

"Yes," I answered softly.

"What's the story with the snake?" he asked curiously.

"I believe the snake is the devil, and I don't think those dreams take place in Heaven. It *looks* like Heaven, but it doesn't *feel* like Heaven. Something seems off about it; like it's pretending, you know what I mean?"

"No, I have no idea what you mean," he chuckled. "Do you think Heaven is real?"

"Absolutely," I said.

"What do you think it all means?"

"I'm not sure; there must be a purpose to it all. Maybe I am supposed to do something, but I haven't figured it out yet. The dreams don't last long and end abruptly," I explained, yawning. Gavin picked the notebook back up and started rereading. It had been a long and stressful day. Despite my best effort to stay awake, my eyelids became heavy, and I fell into a deep and dreamless sleep.

I woke up tired and cranky from a rough night of sharing a small bed with two people and one large canine. I could hear several adults talking in the kitchen. I quickly crawled out of bed, hoping that one of them was my mom. Buddy jumped down and stretched. Gavin woke within seconds and trailed behind me, also eager to see what was going on. I was disappointed to see Doris, Herman, and Cameron sitting at the kitchen table, drinking coffee.

"Hey, where's Mom?" Gavin asked, looking around.

"She's still in the hospital, Honey. Come sit down with us," Doris said gently and patted the empty seat next to her. My stomach dropped to the floor.

"Why don't I make you both some breakfast?" Cameron asked, trying his best to put a smile on his face and sound as normal as possible. "What would you like to eat? How about pancakes?" I saw right through him, but I couldn't get any words out, past the lump in my throat.

"Tell us what's going on with our mom, please," Gavin stated politely but firmly. He instantly appeared much older than thirteen.

Cameron cleared his throat and sat down. "Your mom is set to have more tests today but . . ." he trailed off, seemingly unable to finish.

Doris finished for him, "The doctors found a mass in her stomach, and they are doing a biopsy today to determine if it's cancer." She continued explaining, but I went into shock and blocked out the rest. Gavin put his head in his hands and started to weep; Herman put his arms around him. Doris turned to comfort me, but I brushed her off, stood up, and walked straight out of the house.

Once outside, I started running. I didn't know where I was going, and I didn't care. I didn't care that my hair was a tangled mess. I didn't care that I was barefoot. I didn't even care that I was still in my pajamas. All I knew was that I would not hear another word about Mom having cancer.

I had no clear direction in my travels, so it was quite by accident that I ended up at Rob Dunham's house. And it was pure coincidence that he happened to be outside mowing the lawn. I stopped and glared at him. Anger rose up inside of me and threatened to explode. The mower stopped when he saw me. He froze. We hadn't spoken since the Winter Formal even though he had tried many times.

I surprised myself when I walked straight up to him and slapped him across the face as hard as I could. He instinctively backed away from me. I didn't relent. Using as much strength as possible, I pushed him. He kept trying to back away from me, but I persisted. He finally backed into a thick bush that blocked his escape. That's when I began punching his chest, and by this time, I was sobbing. He put his hands down to his sides and let me hit him.

He finally grabbed my wrists and pulled me into his arms. I collapsed, as the adrenalin finally ran out. Then he did something that shocked me. He held me close, stroked my hair, and whispered, "I'm sorry." When the tears subsided, I collapsed to the ground. He sat down next to me and put his arm around me. I shrugged it off before he even started to speak again.

"I tried to call you. I wanted to apologize. I have never done anything like that before. I shouldn't have been drinking. I had convinced myself that you wanted to kiss me. But I'm not the one who started that rumor. In fact, I told everyone it was a lie."

My mind was swirling. "I would have never done anything to hurt you," he said gently. It was silent for a few minutes. "My mom might have cancer," I blurted out. I have no idea why I told him this. I looked down at my dirty, bare feet and suddenly felt self-conscious. What I should have said was, "You better be sorry, you jerk; I hate you." However, I didn't say anything about the Winter Formal or the rumors and bullying I had endured for months afterward.

"I'm so sorry to hear that," he said sincerely. Rob sat with me for over an hour, trying his best to comfort me. I told him about Amy and how difficult that loss had been. I told him that I was fearful something terrible was going to happen to my mom. He shared with me how he had lost his grandfather to cancer a few years ago and how difficult it had been for him. After a while, I finally looked up. In his eyes, I saw genuine concern, compassion, and vulnerability. The anger about our past melted away, and I knew it didn't matter anymore.

"Thank you, Rob," I said, embarrassed by my behavior. "I'm sorry I hit you."

"I deserved it," he replied. "Hopefully, we can start over and maybe even become friends." I wasn't sure what to say about that, so I just stood up, said goodbye, and headed home.

I took my time getting there. I stayed out front and looked at the home I had grown up in. Even the house looked sad. I walked in the front door, past everyone's concerned gazes, and straight to my room. I got out my notebook and started writing another prayer for Mom. Surely God would hear me.

CHAPTER 10
MASKING THE PAIN

Mom never made it back home from the hospital. She passed away on a Sunday. The doctors told us her cancer spread to her blood and liver before anything could be done to save her.

I felt a numbness beyond what I had experienced when Amy died. It was a terrifying feeling that threatened to suffocate me.

Not only did I have to deal with my own emotions, but I also had to watch what it did to Gavin and Cameron. It was too much to endure. I locked myself in my bedroom and cried myself to sleep off and on for days. At night, I would lay awake and think about all the "what if's" and regrets. Thoughts like *Why didn't I spend more time with her?* and *Why wasn't I nicer to her?* overwhelmed my brain. Like a slideshow, hundreds of memories, both good and bad, flashed through my mind.

Doris and Herman were at our house almost every day, caring for us, supporting us, cooking, and cleaning. Whatever we needed; they were there to take care of it. After a while, I almost resented it. I wanted peace and quiet. I wanted to be *alone*.

A week after the funeral, Cameron sat us down. He told Gavin and me that he deeply loved us, and Mom's dying wish was for him to take care of us. We loved Cameron, too; he was the only father figure we'd ever known. It would take a while, but he planned to start the legal adoption process after the funeral.

I also became very resentful toward God. So resentful, in fact, that I thought about tearing up both of my notebooks. All of those prayers meant nothing; neither did the dreams. There was no purpose for our lives or a loving God that cared about us. I threw them under my bed instead. The mere sight of them brought my blood to a boil. I heard a gentle voice assure me everything was going to be alright. I dismissed it and pushed that voice deep down inside.

Rob had brought flowers by the house on the day of the funeral. We started spending more and more time together. He was a big comfort to me and was slowly becoming my best friend. Even though we never officially discussed being a couple, we spent as much time with each other as possible. We both had acquired part-time jobs, and with Rob getting ready for college, our time together was limited. On our days off, we would go for walks in the park with Buddy or take a drive up to Flagstaff. I was quiet and a little melancholy most of the time. He did his best to try and cheer me up. Every once in a while, he would get me to smile or talk about my future, but those conversations were few and far in between. He was very patient, but I knew that one day he would get sick of me and move on. Eventually, I got better at pretending to be happy, but inside, I couldn't see my way past the pain and anger I felt.

I didn't know if I was in love with Rob. I couldn't feel any emotions outside of the painful ones. Sometimes I felt like I was falling in love with him, but my brain would tell me different. After all, he would be gone soon, too, away to college. In the end, everyone leaves, one way or another.

I stopped going to Wednesday night youth group the week Mom passed away. I wanted nothing to do with God. He didn't hear my prayers, and I hadn't dreamt of Heaven for a long time. Finally, I concluded that my dreams were just that, dreams. They were not real. God wasn't trying to communicate with me. I wasn't even sure that God existed.

Cameron still made me go to church Sunday mornings; however, I used that time to draw and doodle on the bulletin. Doris would often try to get me to sit down with her and discuss my feelings, but I would always pretend to be too busy. Cameron asked me if I needed to see a therapist. I declined that as well.

My entire sophomore year was a blur. I barely passed my classes, and, besides Rob, I didn't talk to anyone outside my family. I had no social life whatsoever, and that was fine by me. After all, I had trained for this. Being by myself was what I did best.

It was my junior year in high school when I had finally decided I wasn't going to mope around any longer. I still didn't feel happy, but I was bored and wanted to have some fun experiences before high school was over. Rob had started college in Tucson, but we frequently spoke on the phone. We had decided that we would remain friends but keep our options open. That was the year high school became less of an educational experience and more about having fun. After a few months had gone by, and with Rob gone, I became a little more interested in other guys.

One in particular, Troy Hicks, had caught my attention. He was a senior and transferred from another high school. Every girl was in love with him. Besides being good-looking, he was athletic, funny, and very outgoing. The rumor circulated that his parents were out of town frequently, and he loved to throw all-night parties at his house. He lived in a giant, two-story mansion in Scottsdale, the wealthy side of town. I heard someone whispering about the pool and jacuzzi in his backyard, and all the alcohol he could buy because he had a fake I.D. I got very good at flirting with him at school. Not caring about anything anymore was good for my self-confidence. I worried less about rejection.

After a few weeks, Troy finally invited me to one of his parties, and I was determined to go. I lied to Cameron about staying at my friend's house.

I got a ride to Troy's from a girl named Krista. She always hung out with the party crowd and I was new to this group. When we pulled up to his house, you could hear the music thumping. This was my first *real* party, and I started getting nervous.

Krista and I walked around the side gate to the backyard, and I couldn't believe my eyes. People were jumping off his roof into the pool; some were even doing flips. Teenagers were making out in dark corners everywhere, and red plastic cups and beer bottles were littered all around. There was an on-going game of beer pong on the patio, and several guys were arguing on the grass. I was convinced the police were going to show up at any moment and haul us all to jail.

An hour later, I was sitting on a lawn chair in the backyard with

Krista and Diane, laughing at something one of them said when Troy sat down next to me.

"Hey, ladies, what up?" he said, but only looked at me. Krista and Diane put on their best smile and quickly adjusted their hair and make-up, no doubt attempting to get his attention.

"Where's your drink, Alina?" he asked. Up to that point, I had never experimented with drugs or alcohol, but I obviously wasn't going to tell him that.

Trying to sound casual, I held up an empty cup sitting next to me and said, "I'm all out." I smiled at him, showing off my straight teeth and tossed my hair a little to the side like I had seen other girls do. None of this came naturally to me, but I was putting on a pretty good show. "I was waiting for you to refill it," I added.

"Oh, really? Well, if I had known that I would have come over here a while ago. Here, you can have mine; I just topped it off." He handed me a full cup of beer. I was at a crossroads, and I knew it. I could hear a voice from deep down, warning me against it. I pushed that voice back down where it belonged, tossed my head back, and swallowed the entire drink in three gulps. Wrenching guilt ran through me, twisting my insides. I ignored it.

"Look at you!" he said, clearly impressed. "I'll get you a refill." He stood up and walked to the beer keg.

"Dang girl, slow down," Krista cautioned. Diane giggled and gushed over Troy's looks.

Within minutes, warmth flowed through me. It felt like someone turned on an internal heating pad. My mind got a little fuzzy and worry and guilt disappeared *almost* completely. Troy returned with two cups and handed me one.

"Thanks!" I said and took another giant gulp. I admit I didn't like the taste of beer, but after finishing the second one, my taste buds surrendered.

"So, Troy, do you have a girlfriend?" *Did I just ask Troy Hicks if he had a girlfriend?* I took another sip. I felt like I was speaking in slow motion.

"No, I like to keep my options open," he teased, smiling. He leaned in and gently plucked an eyelash off my cheek.

"Make a wish," he said. Tingles ran up and down my spine. At that moment, Rob crossed my mind. I missed him. I closed my eyes and wished Rob would not fall in love with someone else at college.

"Well, what did you wish for?" Troy asked.

"How about I keep you guessing?" I didn't even know what I was saying.

"You're funny, Alina. I like your name; it's different. What does it mean?"

"Who cares! It's a stupid name!" I blurted out while throwing my arms in the air. I thought about Mom for a moment and waited for the pain to hit, however, all my emotions were dulled and blunted. It felt good. "My brother calls me Nia, which isn't any better," I said, slurring my words. "What does Troy mean?" I asked sarcastically.

"I don't know either!" We laughed as he held his cup in the air. "Here's to our names and not caring what the hell they mean. Cheers!" We tapped our plastic cups together, then Troy leaned over and kissed me. It felt good, maybe *too* good. I kissed him back.

Just then, someone interrupted us and said, "Troy, you got to come inside, man. Joey is fighting some guy, and they're tearing up the place." Troy shot up, mouthed an apology and took off.

"Bathroom break," I said and stood up a little too quickly. People and things in Troy's backyard started spinning. It felt like I was riding a merry-go-round going one hundred miles per hour. *Woah!* I sat down for a minute. Troy sauntered back over and joined me.

"You are staying at my house tonight, right?" he asked. Krista and Diane got up to mingle. I couldn't believe they were able to walk right now.

"Sure, I told my stepdad I was staying at Krista's house tonight." I saw Krista sit down on the other side of the pool and flirt with a guy named Adam. "Krista told her parents she's staying with me."

"Classic," he said and leaned over to kiss me again. That's when everything went dark.

"Wake up, Sleepy Head!" Krista shouted and splashed me with pool water. My head ached so badly I could barely move. "We need to get out of here before my parents and your stepdad suspect anything." Troy sat down next to me.

"You passed out on me last night," he teased. I realized that I didn't remember anything past our second kiss. *Did I sleep in this lawn chair?* I wondered as I tried to piece the puzzle back together.

"Sorry about that," I apologized. I was suddenly very self-conscious about my appearance in the morning light.

"No big deal." He smiled and offered me a cup of water and two round pills. "Here's some Tylenol. I figured you might need them."

Krista dropped me off at my house, and I did my best to smooth down my hair and fix my make-up from the night before. Gavin was suspicious immediately.

"Where is Cameron?" I asked, trying to act casually.

"He went to the store. You smell like a brewery, Nia." I shot him a look that said you better not say a word. One of the things I loved about our relationship is that he wasn't a snitch, and neither was I.

After a long, hot shower, I brushed my teeth for ten whole minutes, trying my best to get rid of the smell. When Cameron got home, he asked if I had a good time at my friend's house.

"Yes, it was fun," I said. I felt bad for lying to him. He didn't deserve it, but there was no way I was telling him the truth.

"Good," Cameron replied. "I'm glad you're getting out of the house."

This became my regular, Saturday night routine. Pretend to stay the night somewhere but, instead, stay up all night drinking and partying with friends. Troy and Krista were not the best influences, but they were fun, and I was finally enjoying myself for the first time since my mom died.

Deep down, however, I felt guilty and ashamed a lot. I had nightmares at least once a week. I was in the snake's fake garden. He would slither around my feet and tell me what a terrible person I was and how I was letting everyone down. He even told me it was my fault my mom died. He threatened to ruin my life if I didn't pledge myself to him. The only thing that would stop the nightmare was the roar of a lion in the far-off distance. I always woke up shaking and covered in cold sweats.

Rob continued to call me once a week, but I never mentioned Troy or the drinking. I felt dreadful about lying, but secrets were my specialty. I was becoming an expert at burying things and people. I wasn't ready for anything serious anyway. That's how I justified my behavior.

Troy Hicks was my Saturday night fling. Neither of us officially claimed to be dating, but any time we were at a party together, we would end up kissing. Sometimes we ate lunch together at school, but most of the time, we hung out in groups instead of as a couple. Girls were always hanging on and around him. He was good looking and friendly enough, but my heart wasn't into it.

One warm summer night, two weeks before my senior year was to begin, I was partying at Troy's house, as usual. A group of us were playing a drinking game, and I was losing big time. Troy was continually trying to get me to sleep with him in his bedroom, but I always refused. That night, against my better judgment, I took him up on his offer. I thought we would kiss a little, then cuddle-up and fall asleep.

Drinking too much alcohol can be a dangerous game and a recipe for disaster. I lost my virginity that night, and I barely even remembered it.

Troy stopped pursuing me soon after that night and the following weekend took another girl into his room. I was devastated. I gave him the one thing that I should have saved for someone I truly loved. It filled with so much shame that I started avoiding Rob's phone calls altogether.

It was a scorching Sunday afternoon when Krista invited me to go inner tubing down the Salt River with her and a large group of friends from school. I was excited to wear my brand-new swimsuit and get out of the house for the day. Cameron had started pressuring me about college. It was only the beginning of my senior year, and I wasn't ready to make career plans yet.

Phoenix is still blistering hot in September, so the water felt wonderful. About twenty-five inner tubes were tied together, and our crew of rowdy teenagers set afloat down the cool desert river. An ice chest of alcohol had its very own inner tube, and as the day wore on, things started getting crazy. There were chicken fights and people getting overturned. Girls would scream when splashed and empty beer cans and glass bottles were chucked to shore, some exploding upon impact.

I untied my tube and let it float just far enough behind to enjoy a little peace and quiet. I laid my head back and closed my eyes. Sounds of rushing water and chirping birds reminded me of my dreams of the garden; it felt like such a long time ago. I would give anything to have one more dream of Heaven. I wanted to feel something besides sadness and self-loathing.

I failed to notice my inner tube had floated out of the center of the river and to the far right into an area where the water became deeper and faster. I struck a protruding rock and bounced into a thick bush hanging over the side of the riverbank. My hair got tangled around a branch and caused me to fall out of my inner tube.

I managed to get my hair untangled and started swimming as fast as I could toward my tube. Just as I was about to catch up to it, my right foot got caught in a mess of branches beneath the water, and the current pulled me under, trapping me just below the water's surface. No matter how hard I kicked and pulled, I could not break free.

Eventually, as the last amount of oxygen absorbed into my lungs, I stopped struggling. *Well, I guess this is it for me,* I thought. No one will even know what happened to me. It was a surreal feeling, letting go like that. I said goodbye to the people I loved and thought about my mom; maybe I would see her again.

Then, a small, soft voice spoke to me. It came from a place I thought I had closed off. It was a voice I recognized, and it said, "In times of pain and trouble, take into account that I am the only One who can deliver you. In all things, remember that you are *My* child, and everything will work out for your good."

Peace washed over me, and I prayed for the first time since Mom died. I was on the verge of passing out when I felt a hand grab my arm and somehow pull me free. I burst through the surface and sucked in air as fast and hard as I could, coughing in between gulps of oxygen. It took me several minutes before I realized I wasn't going to die in the river that day.

A married couple saw me go under, and the husband had come to my rescue. His wife was able to grab my inner tube, which had rested on the opposite bank. I thanked them with sincerity and climbed onto it. Then I did what came natural to me; I cried.

When we reached the exit point, I realized no one had even noticed I was gone. Krista and Lisa were complaining about their sunburns, and drunk teenagers were piling into a big, yellow bus that would take us back to our vehicles, several miles upriver. I sat in the back, by myself, and stared out the window. I played the incident over in my head, the soft voice and the last-minute rescue. *What was I doing with my life?*

That night, I wasn't feeling very well. I wondered if the incident in the river combined with too much sun had gotten the best of me. I crawled into bed and was asleep within minutes. And for the first time since Mom died, I dreamt of Heaven once again.

I was walking down the winding path, the garden on one side and the crystal-clear lake on the other. The City of God was off in the distance, and I could hear the music coming from within it. I suddenly felt a presence next to me and expected to see the lion with brown eyes. Instead, Jesus was walking beside me. He smiled at me affectionately and took my hand in His. He radiated with brilliance, and His beauty was beyond comprehension.

"It's been a long time since we've talked," Jesus said tenderly. "I have missed you more than you'll ever know." He led me toward the garden.

Rabbits, squirrels, chipmunks, and many other animals greeted us. Jesus stopped, sat down, and took the time to stroke each one lovingly. A variety of birds starting landing all around us. The word must have gotten out because the larger animals joined in. Leopards, zebras, pandas, foxes, and kangaroos, all came to see Jesus. So many animals, in fact, that I lost count; many of them I had never seen before in my life.

"Do you know that I have numbered every animal on Earth and in Heaven?" He asked me. I shook my head, no. "I know them all by name." He reached over and softly caressed the hawk that had landed on his shoulder. "I know when a single sparrow falls from the sky and perishes." I thought about the time I accidentally stepped on a lizard and killed it. *Did Jesus know that lizard?* I briefly wondered. Then, Mom came to my mind.

"Nothing that dies on Earth stays that way. Not sparrows or lizards or even mothers," He said, reading my mind. Jesus opened his hand, and I saw a small lizard resting comfortably in it. It looked up at me and tilted its head to the side.

"Nothing is lost, My child." He gently placed the lizard on the ground, pulled up His sleeve, and ran His index finger over the scar on His wrist. "Do not be afraid. I have paid the price. I have conquered condemnation, fear, sin, and death. When you lose your faith, I will stand in the gap until you are totally restored. I will help you find your way again."

"I did lose my faith, Jesus." I could not look at Him. "I feel ashamed. I have strayed so far away from You. I don't know what to do or how to find my way back." Jesus stopped and gently put His finger under my chin and lifted my head. He peered into my eyes, and I could feel Him reach into my soul.

"I forgive you," He said. "I will help bring you back onto the right path again. Even when you don't understand why things are happening, know that I am the Lord your God, I hold you in the palm of my right hand. Nothing is impossible with Me. Do not fear; I will help you."

"But why is there is so much pain and loss? Can't you prevent it?" I needed some answers.

"Dearest one, there are many things that I do prevent. Satan is responsible for pain and suffering, but that doesn't mean I can't use it for your good. From the beginning, man has been given free will. Since Adam and Eve used that free will to choose sin, evil was planted in the hearts of man, and it still reigns on Earth today. Paradise has been lost due to human moral shortcomings, and as a result, you live in a fallen, broken world. Hatred, war, rebellion, and selfishness lead to despair, hopelessness, and eventually death, but fear not, I have conquered sin and death."

"But there is *so much* suffering. Even by those who believe in You and choose to do what's right. *My mom suffered, Amy suffered, I am suffering! You said you would be here for me. I have said many prayers asking for help, asking for healing; I don't understand why they were not answered.*" Finally, the truth came out. Jesus did not get angry at my questions. He didn't scold me or make me feel bad.

Instead, He wrapped His arm around me and said, "Sometimes the answer is, no. Suffering is temporary, and if you allow it, it will draw you apart from the world and bring you closer to Me. Restoration, love, kindness, and faithfulness can all be by-products of tribulation. I can take those times of trouble, times of suffering and pain, to produce a beautiful piece of work, something stronger and more productive.

Also, sometimes, I allow tests. If your faith is weak, it may not be obvious when life is going smoothly, and you aren't challenged in any way. But, when hard times come, a weak faith will be revealed for what it really is: shallow and unable to help you through life's difficulties. I don't allow tests because I don't know how strong you are; instead, I allow tests because *you* don't realize how strong you are. Asking Me to help your faith grow and make you spiritually stronger is the key to passing these tests."

"I will try harder to understand; it's just challenging sometimes. Losing someone you love so deeply is devastating and," I looked for the right word, "final."

"If you could truly fathom the answers on your own, what need would you have for Me? What need would there be for faith? Trust in Me with all your heart and lean not on your own understanding. Don't forget that My ways are not your ways. My plans are for your good, not for your destruction," He said tenderly. "Death is inevitable and unavoidable. Death doesn't destroy us but liberates us from the horrid conditions that result from sin. If you believe in Me, then to die is to gain and to be absent from the body is to be present with Me."

I thought about this for a few minutes, as Jesus waited patiently for me to process the information. My mom had always dreamt of going on a cruise. Instead of sick in the hospital, I imagined her on a large vessel, getting ready to depart on some extraordinary voyage. I could see her waving wildly from the front of the ship, blowing goodbye kisses to us. I could picture her face aglow with excitement and anticipation for the journey ahead to a destination better than any island of paradise Earth could offer.

Jesus bent down and kissed my forehead and whispered in my ear, "I have a gift for you." As He did this, I heard a familiar rumbling overhead. The ground began to split open, and I closed my eyes, waiting for the fall, this time, with a smile on my face.

I woke up with a headache so severe it almost made me vomit. Nausea swept over me with such intensity that I could not move.

When it finally subsided, I reached underneath my bed and pulled out the notebooks that had laid dormant for almost two years. I read through them both, shed a few tears, and wrote down my dream from the night before. Next, I wrote a prayer asking for forgiveness and guidance. I laid there, thinking about my dream and what Jesus had said. For the first time in a while, I wanted to change. I needed to change. I wanted to be a person of faith again. I wasn't sure how, but I knew God would help me.

Fear tugged at the corners of my heart, though. *Would I be strong enough to change my behavior? Would my church friends accept me back into their lives? If not, could I handle being alone and isolated again?* Deciding to be more faithful and obedient seemed easy when you're dreaming of Heaven and talking with Jesus, but real life has a way of throwing wrenches into the best-laid plans.

CHAPTER 11
AN UNCONVENTIONAL GIFT

My nausea subsided for a bit but returned full force later that day, and the day after that, and the day after that. I felt miserable. I didn't have a fever, chills, or cough, just nausea and vomiting. It even woke me up in the middle of the night.

I think Cameron thought I was faking it at first. Then, he was convinced I had the flu or some other kind of virus that would eventually run its course. By day four, I could see deep anxiety develop on both Cameron and Gavin's faces as we all started worrying there might be something very wrong with me. I feared it might be similar to what Mom had, and I knew they were thinking the same thing.

"You have to go to the doctor, Nia," Gavin demanded.

Doris had been taking care of me while Cameron was at work. I could hear them arranging a doctor's appointment first thing in the morning. I didn't protest; I had zero energy left.

The ride to the doctor was quiet and solemn. I held onto a bowl, just in case I needed it. There was nothing in my stomach to dispel because I hadn't eaten anything in days. In the prior twenty-four hours, I had even struggled to keep water down. Cameron, Gavin, and Doris all insisted they go with me. I lay in the back seat with my head in Doris's lap while she gently stroked my hair.

"It's going to be alright, Honey," she would say every few minutes when I would start to heave. I think she was trying to convince herself more than me.

I was so darn sick that, I thought about death for the second time. Little did my family know, I had faced what I thought was the end almost a week ago at the Salt River. Being reunited with Jesus, Amy, and Mom didn't seem all that bad.

We arrived at Dr. Steven's office, and after examining me from head to toe, he gave me a shot of anti-nausea medication and ordered labs.

"Well, it doesn't look like it's the flu," he said. "With your family history, we need to rule out some other more serious diagnosis." He didn't come out and say the word "cancer," but I knew what he meant. His next question surprised me the most. "Are you sexually active?" he asked casually. *Oh no.* I looked down at my feet as everyone waited for my response.

"Um, no, not currently but I . . . uh . . . ." I didn't get to finish the sentence before the doctor interrupted me.

"I'm going to order a pregnancy test, just in case." I couldn't look up; I was too embarrassed. I didn't want to see the disappointment on everyone's face.

"It's been a rough couple of years for her," Cameron said to the doctor, trying his best to make me feel more comfortable. It worked a little.

"Understandable," the doctor remarked. "We can do that test right now. That way, we can rule it out before sending you off for more." He handed me a cup, and his nurse showed me to the restroom. "Just leave it right there on the counter, Sweetie," she said as she closed the door behind me.

It was unbearably awkward and humiliating. *How am I going to face my family?* I remember thinking as I went back to the room and sat down, refusing to look anyone in the eyes. Gavin tried to make small talk with Cameron, and Doris put her hand on my knee. It was her way of telling me she was there for me. *Oh God,* I silently asked him, *I couldn't be pregnant after having sex one time, right?*

After what seemed like an eternity, the doctor and nurse returned to the room. I held my breath. "Well, we have the results. Alina, you're pregnant." He paused after breaking the news, letting it sink in. It was so quiet; you could hear a pin drop. I was mortified.

After a minute of silence, the doctor continued, "The reason you're so sick is that you most likely have Hyperemesis Gravidarum. Your body is having a tough time with the changes in your hormones, which can lead to excessive, severe morning sickness that comes and goes throughout the day. Now, some people do get better after a month or two, but other women can experience these symptoms throughout their entire pregnancy. I have given you some medication to help with the vomiting, but due to the lack of water and food intake, I'm going to make a referral for a Home Health Nurse. You'll be on intravenous fluids with anti-nausea medication twenty-four hours a day. You will feel much better, and the IV will keep you hydrated and nourished until you can start eating and drinking again." The nurse handed me a pamphlet.

"I also want to make sure you understand all your options. This pamphlet has information about abortion and adoption if you choose *not* to keep the baby." I couldn't concentrate on what the doctor was saying because I was still processing the fact that I was pregnant. The rest of the information was just background noise. I could feel the anti-nausea medication starting to work.

"I'll write it all up and be back in a few minutes with the paperwork. A Home Health Nurse will contact you today to get things rolling." The doctor and nurse exited the room. Tears rolled down my face. I couldn't believe this was happening. I waited for my family to chastise me, but what they said next made me cry even harder.

"Well, we are going to have a baby!" Doris said and took my face in her hands. She lifted my head gently so that I was forced to look her in the eyes. "Babies are a gift from God, Alina."

Cameron walked over and put his arms around me. "It's going to be alright. No matter what, we are here for you. No one in this room is judging you."

Gavin joined him and said, "I'm going to be an uncle! You *are* keeping the baby, right, Alina?" I couldn't speak. I was in a state of shock from the news and their reaction. Combined with my own feelings of guilt and shame, I didn't know what to say. The one thing I did know was no one was condemning me. No one was telling me what a mess I had made of my life. All I felt was love, acceptance, and forgiveness.

After a few minutes of processing everything, I looked up at Gavin and whispered, "Of course I'm keeping my baby." I couldn't imagine having an abortion, and adoption wasn't an option for me, either. My mind had been racing and I seemed to be missing the brake pedal. *Could this be the gift Jesus referred to in my last dream?* My brain took a detour of all the gifts I'd rather have instead of a baby before arriving at, *How will I figure out my purpose now?*

Cameron could tell I was struggling and tried to reassure me. "All things work together for our good because we love the Lord," he said, quietly.

The doctor and nurse walked back in with a stack of paperwork and explained a few more details to Cameron, then sent us on our way.

I felt better on the ride home and was able to sit up and look out the window. All I could think about was how I was going to tell Troy Hicks he was going to be a father. Doris kept a close eye on me, no doubt watching to see how I was handling everything. To be honest, I felt numb.

Gavin broke the silence and asked, "By the way, who is the father?" Cameron shot him a dirty look that reprimanded him. At that point, Gavin was a sophomore and attended the same high school as me, so he would no doubt find out anyway.

"Troy Hicks," I said flatly. It was at that moment; I wished more than anything I could have answered, "Rob Dunham." The news of my pregnancy would break Rob's heart. It was breaking mine. It was then that I realized how much I loved Rob. He most likely would never speak to me again, and I prepared my heart for the loss. I felt like crying, but I didn't want to concern anyone more than they already were.

"Troy Hicks!" Gavin exclaimed. "I didn't even know you were

dating him! Didn't he graduate already?" This time Cameron elbowed him in the ribs. "Hey! Ouch!" Gavin rubbed his side.

Gavin turned around and looked at me. "Sorry, Nia," he said and scowled at Cameron.

"Now, now," said Doris. "Let's give Alina a little time before we start asking questions." She squeezed my hand.

When we got home, I went straight to my room. After about two hours, I could feel the medication wearing off and nausea returning. I had managed to get a couple of crackers and a glass of water down, but it was quickly finding its way back up. Doris was still at our house, and when she heard me vomiting, came rushing in to care for me. I was so weak; I could barely lean over the bowl.

"The Home Health Nurse is supposed to be here anytime," Doris said, worriedly looking at her watch. I wretched again while Doris held my hair back. I loved this woman so much and was very thankful to have her here. She was doing the job Mom would have done.

I wondered how Mom would have handled all this. I felt like she would have been disappointed in me. I could imagine her shaking her head and saying, "Look what you've gotten yourself into now, Alina! What were you thinking?" She would have been mad at me in the beginning; I was sure of it. Then, she would have forgiven me, and anger would have given way to excitement.

She would have enjoyed helping me choose the baby's name, most likely trying to convince me to name him or her something weird. She would have loved buying the first tiny outfit, and no doubt, would have been an amazing grandmother.

I bent over and expelled the remaining water and crackers. *How long is this sickness going to last?* I wondered as my mind seemed to pull out of the garage and back onto the race track. *What am I going to do about school? It's my senior year! What about college?* I instantly felt overwhelmed and anxious.

Then, a recognizable, soft voice spoke to me and said, "Trust in Me with all your heart and lean not on your own understanding. Don't forget that My ways are not your ways. My plans are for your good, not for your destruction." A wave of peace washed over me, and I fell into a deep sleep.

Cameron met with the school principal and was able to get several weeks' worth of school assignments, so I could complete them from home and not fall too far behind. The IV was a pain in the butt. I had to drag the pole it hung on everywhere, but it made administering the anti-nausea medication very efficient. I began to think that I didn't need the IV anymore, but as soon as I was taken off of it, I started vomiting again.

The house became like a prison cell. Cameron and Gavin were at work and school all day, which left me alone a lot. There were many times that I had to fight off depression and loneliness. My only company was Buddy and Doris. Buddy was an ever-present source of comfort. Sometimes I would put my IV bag in a backpack and take him on a short walk around the block, always avoiding Rob's parents' house. Doris came over for a bit each day to look in on me. Then, the Home Health Nurse would come by, check my IV, and administer my anti-nausea medication. When Gavin and Cameron came home, I would talk their ear off; excited to have more human contact.

It had been six weeks since I found out I was pregnant, and I still hadn't told Troy. I wasn't sure if he was still living with his parents or had gone off to college. I tried to figure out what he would say. Sometimes I imagined him excited and supportive, and other times I imagined total rejection. Cameron had been pressuring me for weeks to tell him. "He deserves to know, Alina," he would say.

It was a late Friday afternoon, and no one was home when I finally decided to call Troy. I wished I had enough courage to meet with him face to face, but I didn't. My hand shook as I dialed his number. He answered on the second ring.

"Hello?"

"Hey, Troy, it's Alina." I tried to sound calm and natural.

"Hey, girl; what's up? I haven't seen you for a while."

I realized that was basically confirmation he didn't know yet and I started to feel like I was going to have a heart attack. "I've been sick. I have something called Hyperemesis Gravidarum."

"What's that?" he asked alarmed.

My mouth went dry. "It's a sickness caused by," I paused for a moment, trying to get the words out, "pregnancy," I whispered. There was dead silence on the other line for a long time. "Hello?"

"Well, it can't be mine," he finally said. "I mean, Alina, we only had sex that one time."

"It only takes one time." I could hear my voice breaking. *Do not cry on the phone with Troy*, I told myself.

"How do you know I'm the father?" he said flatly. I had a bad feeling this was not going to end well.

"You are the only guy I have been with, Troy," I countered.

"Are you going to have an abortion? I could help pay for it." And, there it was. His reaction cut me like a knife. I took a deep breath in and let it out, attempting to calm myself down again.

"No, I'm not getting an abortion, and I'm not putting him or her up for adoption. I've decided I'm going to keep the baby."

I expected him to argue with me and attempt to talk me out of it. Instead, he did something unexpected; he hung up on me. I listened to the dial tone for a full minute before replacing it. *Well, I'll be doing this alone,* I realized. *Alone. A familiar word to me.*

God's voice whispered into my soul, "You will never be alone. I will always be with you." It was then I realized I was not by myself. I had a wonderful family that loved and supported me. For the first time, I gently rested my hand on my belly and looked down. I was going to be a mom. Time to accept it and move on.

Gavin walked through the door; I was still standing by the phone. He must have sensed something and asked, "What's wrong, Nia? Are you alright?" He walked over and put his hand on my shoulder.

"I finally called him. He wanted me to get an abortion, and when I told him I was going to keep the baby, he hung up on me."

Gavin turned around and headed for the front door. "I'm going to kill him."

I tried to go after him, but I was attached to a pole. "Oh my gosh, oh my gosh!" This time, my mind was clipping along at such a fast pace, I couldn't keep my thoughts inside. I paced back and forth, dragging the stupid IV pole with me. "What do I do?" I called Cameron at work, but he was unavailable. I left a message. Then I called Doris and Herman and told them what happened and that I was afraid Gavin was angry enough to do something foolish. I gave Troy's address to Herman and hung up.

It felt like hours before a car pulled into the driveway. Doris, Herman, and Gavin walked in the front door. I examined my brother and found that he was in one piece. *Shew!* First, I hugged him; then I punched him in the arm.

"Ouch! What was that for?" he said, rubbing it.

"You scared me! Why did you do that?" Now that I knew Gavin was fine, curiosity got the best of me. "So, What happened?"

"His mom answered the door. I told her right then and there that Troy got my sister pregnant. I told her I wanted him to come out front because I was going to kick his butt; however, I didn't use the word butt." My heart overflowed with love for my brother. "Then Herman and Doris showed up and went inside to speak to his parents. They made me wait outside by myself. Troy is lucky because I would have beat him to a pulp." I could see Gavin was still furious.

"Well, thank you for standing up for me, but I'm glad you didn't fight him. He isn't worth it." At almost six feet tall, Gavin probably could have held his own, especially with all that extra adrenaline pumping through his veins.

Cameron came through the front door in a panic. "What's going on? Alina, are you alright?" I got a message that you called. I called back, but no one answered, so I rushed home." I reassured him as

Herman explained what had happened.

"What did his parents say?" Cameron asked.

"Well, I think they were in a state of shock," replied Herman. "His dad asked if there was any chance someone else could be the father."

Everyone looked at me simultaneously. "No, there is no chance," I reassured them.

"That's what I said," Herman added. "They are going to talk it over with their son and get in touch with you, Cameron." *What a mess*, I thought. *I don't know what I expected to happen; a marriage proposal? A commitment to raising this child together?* I shook my head in disbelief. I started feeling tired and a little weak, so I excused myself. I went to my room and laid down next to Buddy, cuddling him tightly.

We never heard back from Troy or his parents. Cameron called them multiple times without success.

Three months later, I was finally able to get off the nausea medication and the IV. I had kept up on my assignments, but if I was going to graduate, I needed to get back into school. Luckily, our high school had a unique program for kids who were not able to attend regular classes. The principal told me if I was to finish out the year, I had to enroll in this program.

There were fifteen students in the special class, but only three, including me, who were pregnant. Three of the students had seizure disorders of some kind. It was quite frightening at first to see someone have a seizure, first-hand. Two others had something called Tourette's Syndrome. They would often have obscene outbursts off and on through the day. After a while, you got used to it and learned to tune it out. Four of the twelve had cancer and were in various stages of radiation and chemotherapy. The classroom had a private restroom, and the four of them would often abruptly get up and run to it. My heart hurt for them as I tried to block out the sounds of vomiting and concentrate on my classwork. The last three were in wheelchairs. One was paralyzed from the neck down, and the other two had Muscular Dystrophy.

We didn't change classrooms like the rest of the school. Instead, the teachers came to us. We had five different teachers who rotated in and out, depending on the subject. Most of the students were very open about their struggles, and the teachers allowed us time to talk and support each other.

At the end of the first week, on the last day, I made sure to learn each person's name. When I got home, I wrote every one of them down in my notebook and made a conscious effort to say a prayer for them every night before going to bed.

In my second week, our English teacher asked us to write a two-hundred-word paper about something that had made a profound impact on our life. Then she announced we would be reading it out loud to the rest of the class. After careful consideration, I decided to write about my dreams of Heaven. I had already done most of the work at home in my notebook. The hard part was condensing it all into two hundred words.

After I read my essay, before I had a chance to take my seat, half of the hands in the class went up. The other students wanted to ask me questions. No one else had been asked questions after their presentation. I looked over at the teacher, and she nodded in approval.

They wanted to know all about Heaven. They asked questions about Jesus, the garden, the City of God, and the lions. Their questions continued for over twenty minutes. Finally, the lunch bell rang, and even though we could leave for lunch, most of us stayed inside. I am sure everyone had their reasons.

It wasn't until a couple of weeks later that one of the girls in my class told me she had heard Troy's parents had sent him to live with his grandparents in California. I can't say I was surprised. Even though I was still hurt, occasionally, before I fell asleep, I would pray for Troy.

The two other pregnant girls in my class remained curious about my dreams of Heaven and would often ask me follow-up questions. One day, I decided to bring the Bible Amy had given me to school. I'm not sure why I did that, but before long, the three of us had formed a small Bible study during our lunch hour.

Then three students turned into five. After several weeks, all fifteen of us spent our lunch hour reading the Bible and discussing spiritual issues. There was something special about this group of teenagers. We were bonded by the fact that we all had more important things on our minds than parties, popularity, dating, or college. Some of these students were just trying to stay alive. We were a close-knit family, supporting each other, praying for each other and lifting each other's spirits with kindness and love. All in all, it was one of the most fulfilling times in my life.

CHAPTER 12
HAVING FAITH

It became evident to me that Gavin was struggling. Since Mom's death, something had shifted in him. It happened gradually over time. First, he withdrew from our church and would only attend when Cameron insisted. Then, my brother started pulling away from the family. Gavin would make excuse after excuse as to why he couldn't spend any time with us. I tried to get him to talk about his feelings, but he refused. He was rarely home, and when he was, he spent most of his time in his room with the door closed and locked. He always stated he was studying or playing video games; however, his grades proved that only the latter was true.

I admit I had been so busy with my own problems that I hadn't made the time for him as I should have. At first, I thought it was only depression; God knows we had all gone through it. More recently, I had a feeling that something darker was taking hold of him which made me think about the time I had caught Dalton sneaking out of his bedroom window, the smell of cigarettes lingering in the air. I wondered if that was the start of it all.

I missed the good ole days, and I longed for things to go back to the way they were. My brother and I used to play games and climb the old oak tree in the backyard. We would make forts on the grass and pretend to have to hunt for our food. At one point, we had an above-ground pool. We would always play mermaid versus shark or race each other to the opposite side. During monsoon season, we would dare each other to stand outside in the pouring rain and lightning. Mom would get so mad and tell us how dangerous it was.

Gavin rarely let me in his room anymore. When I knocked, he would open the door just a crack and say, "Hey Nia, what's up?" Sometimes a strange smell would find its way into the hallway. I recognized it from my partying days. It smelled like a skunk, but I knew it was marijuana. I wasn't sure how to confront him.

Cameron did his best to try and bring Gavin out of his funk. They used to go to baseball games and watch sports on television, but Gavin eventually became totally disinterested. I could tell that it hurt Cameron; they had always been so close.

He had always been skinny; both of us were. Gavin had shot up over the last year, thinning him out even more, but now there was a gaunt, sunken-in look to his face, and his clothes were two sizes too big.

I would often pray for Gavin. I also prayed that God would give me the courage and strength to talk to him about whatever was going on. One day, after school, he rushed into his room as usual and closed the door behind him. I followed him and stood right outside for a full ten minutes before gaining the confidence to knock. As expected, he cracked the door open slightly and asked me what I wanted.

"Can I come in, Little Bear?" I asked carefully. He hesitated and told me to hold on a minute and closed the door. I could hear him shuffling things around before opening the door wide enough for me to walk in. His room was a mess. Not only were clothes and video games strewn about, but it was also downright filthy. Plates of old food and half-drunk cups of soda covered his dresser. Papers, no doubt incomplete school assignments, were piled high.

"Gavin, your room is gross!" I exclaimed.

"Well, if you don't like it, you can leave," he retorted with a curtness I rarely heard from him.

"Sorry," I said softly, "I am just surprised. Usually, you keep your room so neat."

"How would you know? When was the last time you even cared enough to come in here, *Mom*?" I winced. He saw the pain on my face and looked down.

"Sorry, Nia," he offered with sincerity. My brother and I rarely fought or said mean things to each other. It was very unusual for him to be so defensive. Something was definitely wrong with him.

"I just wanted to check on you, see how you are doing? Been hanging out with anyone interesting lately?" I was getting more nervous by the minute. I didn't know how to handle this kind of stuff.

"I'm going to the skate park in a while to meet up with some friends from school," he answered flatly. Herman had given him a skateboard for Christmas, but I had never seen him use it. I saw it propped up against the wall. The wheels looked brand new.

"That sounds cool. Maybe I could come to see you skate sometime. Are you any good at it?" I asked, trying to sound nonchalant.

He shrugged his shoulders and said, "I'm okay, I guess." I knew he was lying. He observed my reaction. I wasn't sure if he was gauging my responses, but it seemed like it. Alarm bells were going off inside me. It all felt wrong, but I wasn't sure where to go from there.

He looked at the time and said, "Oh, hey, I have to meet up with my friends. I'm going to be late." He ushered me out of his room and shut the door behind us.

"Can I come and watch you?" I asked timidly. He acted shocked at the idea and looked down at my big belly. I knew what the answer was before he said it.

"Maybe next time. Wait until I get a little better at my tricks," he answered. Then my brother did something that surprised me. He hugged me tight and said, "Love you, Nia," and walked out the front door.

I stood outside his bedroom, trying to figure out what to do next. Part of me wanted to go into his room and turn it upside down. I had a feeling he had hidden something he didn't want me to see. But I was afraid Gavin would notice something out of place and know I had gone through his stuff. He would never forgive me.

I decided to follow him. I let him get a five-minute head-start and then wound my way around the neighborhood in the direction of the skate park, trying my best to stay out of sight. I felt like an undercover policewoman, ducking behind cars and hiding behind trees. It was almost impossible to conceal myself with my enormous, pregnant belly.

I squatted behind a small shrub across the street from the park and observed him talking to a couple of guys I had never seen before.

There were half a dozen teens, grinding on cement blocks and rails, making jumps, and trying out new tricks. Gavin remained outside of the fenced skate park, talking with three sketchy-looking teenagers.

What happened next transpired so quickly, I almost missed it. Gavin discreetly handed one of the teens what looked like money, and after surveying his surroundings, that teen then placed something small into my brother's hand. They all looked around again, making sure no one was watching them. It took me a few minutes to realize that I had just watched my brother participate in a drug deal.

Seconds later, the two teens walked off and left Gavin by himself. My brother shoved whatever it was he had bought in his pocket, looked around again, then just stood there, messing with his board. He never joined in with the others; he just put one foot on the board and moved it back and forth. It was apparent to me that he had never ridden it before. He sat down on it and watched the other skaters from a distance.

In that instant, my heart split into a million different pieces. It broke in a way that it had never broken before. The innocence of my little brother was gone. The reality of the situation became crystal clear to me, and I turned around and headed home, crying the entire way.

When I got there, Cameron was in the kitchen, cooking dinner. To distract myself from what I had just witnessed, I offered to help. He planted a kiss on my cheek and asked about my day. I had taken the long way home, attempting to let my eyes dry out before facing anyone. I had no clue as to how I was going to handle the situation with my brother.

Cameron put his hand on my belly and said, "Not long now, huh? We are going to have ourselves a little rainbow baby here very soon. I managed to get my hands on a used crib. It's out in the garage. I'm going to sand it down and repaint it."

"Thank you so much, Cameron," I said, trying to sound upbeat.

"Take a load off; I can finish this up by myself. Where's your brother?" He bent over and opened the oven, checking on the lasagna. It smelled delicious. I sat the salad on the table.

"He's at the skatepark," I answered.

"He's been spending a lot of time there lately. I'm glad he's getting out of the house. I hate seeing him isolated in his room, playing video games all the time." I tried to think of a response to this statement, but my mind was replaying the scene from the skatepark. I bit my lower lip to keep from crying again.

"I'll do the dishes tonight," I offered.

"Thanks, Sweetie. Dinner should be ready in about fifteen minutes. I hope your brother gets home in time to eat it while it's hot."

I went to my room and grabbed my prayer notebook. I wrote a long prayer for my brother. I asked for God's guidance on my part, as well. I had no idea how to approach the issue, who to talk to about it, or how to help him. I knew God was just as concerned about Gavin as I was and had the ability and desire to heal him. I read the prayer out loud as usual, and by the time I finished, I heard Cameron calling my name.

Gavin walked through the door just in time for dinner. Cameron didn't notice Gavin's eyes like I did. He was busy talking about his plans to refurbish the crib. Gavin quietly ate his dinner, barely looking up. I understood why he didn't want to make eye contact with anyone; his pupils were massive. He caught me staring at him suspiciously, pushed his plate aside, and excused himself from dinner, saying he was full.

"You didn't eat much, Gavin," Cameron commented, "Hope you're not getting sick." He looked concerned and a little disappointed.

"My friends and I grabbed a cheeseburger at McDonald's on the way home." I knew he was lying, of course. Mom would have known too.

I wanted to lift Cameron's spirits, so I ate a double portion of lasagna. "My appetite is out of control right now. This lasagna turned out perfect," I said.

He smiled, and we chatted about things that still needed to get done before the baby arrived. My due date was approaching rapidly, and my ever-growing belly was a sign that he or she was coming soon.

"By the way, I almost forgot to tell you, Doris said that our church is throwing you a baby shower." I couldn't believe it. Our wonderful, kind, and generous congregation was going to help me celebrate the birth of my baby, despite the unconventional circumstances. "It's next Saturday at two o'clock." I smiled at the thought of receiving tiny little socks, outfits, and bibs. I had been reading as much as I could about infant care and exchanging tips with my pregnant friends at school.

"Have you picked out a name yet?" Cameron asked as we cleared the table.

"I've got a few in mind," I said. I had decided that I didn't want to know the gender until the day he or she arrived.

That night, I dreamt about the snake again. We were in a house with hundreds of rooms. The snake slithered around, looking everywhere for Gavin. I did my best to distract the evil reptile by pretending I found my brother, luring him away from Gavin and into a vacant area.

Then, I saw a lion about to enter one of the rooms. He looked over at me with His rainbow-colored eyes and motioned for me to follow Him. The snake saw me run toward the lion and hurried to catch up. I rushed into the room and slammed the door shut to keep the snake out. I could hear the serpent trying to get in, but the lion leaned against the door and kept it closed with ease.

When I turned around, I saw Doris kneeling by a bed, and she was crying. *What is she doing in here?* I wondered. A young man lay on the bed. He looked like he was sound asleep. I noticed him from the photos Doris kept above her fireplace. It was her son, and he was not sleeping. I could hear her praying softly next to him. Then, I noticed my brother standing there in the corner. He was staring at Doris and her son, tears rolling down his face. Suddenly, thunder quaked and a loud cracking noise began as the house shook. *No!* I silently screamed. I didn't want to fall; I needed to help my brother.

I woke up and realized I was holding my breath. I let it out, relieved to be awake. *What an awful dream,* I thought as my head started to pound. It was early in the morning, so I quietly walked down the hall to my brother's room and slightly opened the door to check on him. I could see his chest moving up and down. *Shew!* I knew what I had to do. It was time to break our pact and get some help. After all, Gavin's life was at stake. I got dressed, left a note for Cameron, and began the long walk over to Doris and Herman's house.

Doris answered the door and looked towards the curb. "Did you walk all the way here at five in the morning?" she asked, alarmed. I nodded. "Well, get in here and sit-down, Honey. I have some blueberry muffins, hot and fresh out of the oven." Then she said something that stunned me, "I had a dream last night about you, your brother and my son," she hesitated for a second, "I saw a snake, a lion, and you were there. It was quite startling."

I was schocked when I heard this statement.. Did Doris and I have the same dream? Is that even possible? I desperately wanted to tell her about it; however, I decided to get straight to the point. "My brother is using drugs," I said matter-of-factly. "I followed him to the skatepark and watched him buy them off some guy. His eyes have been looking strange, and he has lost a lot of weight. You are the only person I could come to." I looked over at her son's picture, and sadness for their loss filled me with grief. She followed my gaze. "I've never told on my brother before," I continued. "I feel like I'm betraying him, but I don't want something to happen to him." I couldn't say the word "die," but I didn't have to.

"You came to the right place, Alina," Doris replied as she squeezed my hand. "This must have been really difficult for you. I know how close you and your brother are. He is most likely going to be very angry at you, but this is the best and most loving thing that you could have done for him. It might even save his life." I nodded.

I asked, "How do we confront him? What do we say? I'm petrified."

"I totally understand; we will sit down as a family and address it." Doris scooted closer to me. "If he has been using drugs for a while, he will have to go into a treatment program. He may deny it at first. I have a feeling this has been a problem for quite some time. Everyone has their own way of dealing with grief and loss. This is how your brother has dealt with it."

I thought about my own life and looked down at my belly as the baby kicked inside. "Yes, we both had our way of coping with my mom's death."

"This matter cannot wait. I will speak with Herman and Cameron today after work, and, most likely, we will sit down with your brother tonight."

She told me how proud of me she was, and we talked about the baby shower and ate her delicious blueberry muffins. She gave me a ride home, and I quietly walked into my house. It was still early, and Cameron and Gavin were sound asleep. I looked in on my brother again and watched his chest move up and down for several minutes. I slowly and softly closed his door.

Then something odd happened. Fluid ran down my leg and onto the floor. I knew it wasn't urine, but it took me several seconds to realize that my water had broken. An excruciating contraction took hold of my abdomen, and I moaned.

No, no, no, no! It's too early, I thought. *I'm not due for several more weeks! I haven't had my baby shower, and the crib isn't ready!* These thoughts and more rushed through my mind as another contraction hit. I let out a scream, and both Cameron and Gavin came running out into the hallway where I stood doubled over in pain.

Cameron shouted at Gavin, "Gavin, get dressed, grab a towel, and the car keys! I'm going to get my clothes on; help your sister to the car!" Gavin just stood there, frozen in terror.

"Gavin, help your sister!" Cameron shouted again, more loudly this time. My brother jumped and sprang into action. He threw on pants and a shirt, then ran into the bathroom and grabbed a towel.

Gavin did his best to wipe off the liquid that was dripping down my legs. He grabbed my jacket, draped it over my shoulder and helped me to the car, in-between contractions. I laid down in the backseat as another one hit me. I cried out in agony. Never in my life had I ever experienced that kind of intense physical pain. *Weren't contractions supposed to be five minutes apart?* I was starting to feel the urge to push. *That can't be right.*

"We have to hurry, Gavin; the baby is coming!" I managed to say.

Cameron came running out of the house and jumped behind the driver's seat. "Hold on, Honey! Whatever you do, don't push."

I'm pretty sure Cameron broke every traffic law in the books. He blew through red lights and stop signs and took corners like a NASCAR driver. All I could do was hold on for dear life and do my best to keep from pushing. I was determined not to have my baby in the backseat of our car. We arrived at the emergency room, and Cameron told Gavin to run in and grab a nurse and a wheelchair.

Everything became a blur. The pain was almost more than I could bear. I was wheeled directly to a room, where nurses rushed in and out, preparing for a quick delivery. When I could finally push, it was both a huge relief and an entirely new kind of agony. At that moment, I missed my mom so much. The emotional pain of not having her there to hold my hand was just as intense as the physical pain.

When my baby finally made its appearance, I waited for his or her newborn cry, but it did not come. I immediately started freaking out. *Weren't babies supposed to cry when they're born?* The doctor rushed my baby over to a table where he hooked him or her up to monitors. Finally, after what felt like an eternity, I heard a loud wail.

The doctor brought over my newborn and said, "Meet your new baby girl. She is a little early and had trouble breathing at first, so we are going to keep a close eye on her." He laid her down gently on my chest.

She was the most beautiful thing I'd ever seen. Her cries abated as soon as she touched my skin. Her blue eyes opened and stared right into mine. I spoke to her, softly cooing and stroking her gently. I didn't even try to stop the tears from coming. *"I have a gift for you."* I remembered those words like they were knitted into my heart. The feelings of failure and guilt faded away, and a new spring of hope and faith filled my soul.

My little girl was so tiny and fragile; I was afraid to handle her. I wondered how easy it was to break a baby. She had my mother's nose and chin. She had a small tuft of dark hair that stuck straight up. I lightly smoothed it down. Not once did she take her eyes off me. Her tiny hand grasped my finger and held on tight.

I spoke to her softly, saying, "Hello, little girl. I'm your mama, and I will take good care of you. You are a gift from God." A love like I had never known filled my heart, and I knew instinctively that my life would never be the same again.

Cameron, Gavin, Doris and Herman all filed in the room, anxious to see the little bundle of joy, and expressed relief that she and I were in good health.

"The doctor said we barely made it in time!" Cameron stated, proud of his expert driving skills, which had gotten us there in one piece.

"Oh, Honey, she's beautiful," said Doris, with Herman nodding in agreement.

Gavin stood back a little. He looked nervous. I motioned for him to come and meet his niece. He still looked shocked and scared, poor guy.

"What are you going to name her?" he finally asked me quietly.

"Her name is Faith," I replied.

"You named her after Mom?" Gavin's eyes teared a bit.

"Beautiful choice," echoed Doris. Cameron was excited to get his hands on her. I carefully handed the baby over so everyone would have a chance to meet the new addition to our family; however, I didn't take my eyes off her the entire time.

"Your mom would be so delighted. I am sure she is smiling down on us right now." Doris squeezed my hand and told me how proud of me she was.

"Watch her head and be careful," I said, as Gavin took his turn.

One of the nurses came in and said, "We are going to take her to get bathed and weighed and recheck her vitals." Panic rose up inside of me at the mere thought of losing sight of her. The nurse must have read the look on my face and continued, "Don't worry, we will bring her back shortly. We need to work on breastfeeding in a few minutes, so take this opportunity to rest for a bit. You are going to need it." I watched her walk out with my baby girl.

Doris sat down next to me to lend some comfort. Cameron announced he was going home to get some things ready for our return and asked Gavin to help him. Herman offered to go along with them.

When everyone left, I looked over at Doris, and she had tears in her eyes.

"Sorry, I'm just so emotional. When our son died, I lost all hope of ever having a grandchild. God brought you into our lives to fill that void, Alina. Thank you for this gift. Thank you for allowing us to be a part of this joy. You truly are a light in our lives." Her sincerity sent me into tears again. She bowed her head and, between the two of us, said a lovely prayer of thanksgiving. One day I hoped to be able to pray like Doris.

It wasn't long before the nurse brought Faith back in. She said, "Faith is healthy, breathing well, and all her vitals look good. She weighs six pounds, five ounces." The nurse worked with me for over half an hour on breastfeeding. At first, I was afraid I would never get the hang of it, but once Faith latched on, it was easy as pie.

"We are going to keep you both here for a couple of days to make sure that she doesn't lose any weight, her oxygen levels are normal, and breastfeeding continues to go well," she said. I was relieved to hear it.

The thought of bringing her home scared me a little bit.

Doris fawned over Faith, and we talked about the upcoming baby shower. "Now we can tell everyone that you had a baby girl. You are going to get so many pink outfits! Oh, I'm so excited! I'm sure that Cameron and Herman will get things ready for you and the baby. I wrote down a list for them while we were in the waiting room. Your brother was so worried about you. We had to reassure him everything was going to be fine." I thought about my brother and the things he was going through. We still needed to make time to address his issues, sooner rather than later.

That first night I was in the hospital, and unbeknownst to me, Cameron, Doris, and Herman sat Gavin down and confronted him about his drug use. Cameron had gone through Gavin's room and found his stash, so my brother was unable to deny it. Doris told me later that Gavin confessed to everything and, with tears streaming down his face, admitted that he was addicted to multiple types of drugs and had been using them for a while. They were able to get him into a drug detox center, and he would go from there to a treatment facility for a while. Doris waited until I was discharged from the hospital to tell me all the details.

"Is he mad at me?" I asked, knowing the answer was probably yes.

"No, Honey, he is not mad at you. He loves you and feels very guilty about the whole thing. Praise God he is willing to get the help he needs." I was so relieved; I started crying again. If I had a quarter for every tear I'd shed, money wouldn't ever be a problem.

While I was in the hospital, Cameron, Herman, and Doris had

worked hard preparing my room for Faith. The crib was still drying in the garage, but right next to my bed was a beautiful little bassinette with a tiny pink blanket. Several new outfits were draped on my bed with a package of diapers, along with the other items needed to care for a newborn. Thankfulness and love for what they had done to make this transition easy welled up inside me. I gently laid Faith in her bassinette and pulled out my prayer notebook.

I wrote my thanks to the Lord for the safe delivery of Faith and my supportive family. I thanked Him for the courage to reveal my brother's secret and asked Him to heal Gavin.

When I finished, I wrote a letter to Mom. I told her everything that had happened. I told her that Faith looked just like her and how blessed I had been to have an excellent example of a mother growing up. I cried as I told her how much I missed her and how one of these days, I would see her again. I promised I would do my very best to raise Faith in a way that would make her proud and vowed to look out for Gavin. I looked over at my precious baby and thought, *How could life get any better than this?* Little did I know, God had another gift in store for me.

CHAPTER 13
A SURPRISE REUNION

The baby shower came and went, and the beautiful crib Cameron finished was filled to the brim with everything I needed to care for Faith. Even my youth group friends were in attendance. It was a joyous occasion. Our church family had welcomed Faith with open arms.

I finished out the last few weeks of school at home and completed enough assignments to enable me to graduate with the rest of my class. Herman helped me enroll in the local community college, and Doris promised to watch Faith so I could attend a couple of classes a week.

Gavin had made it through the first several days of detox and was transferred into a local drug treatment facility. We spoke to him on the phone several times a week and visited every Saturday. He told me he was finally taking the time needed to work on his issues that stemmed from Frank's abuse and Mom's death. I missed him so much and couldn't wait for his return.

I started a summer English class at the community college. I decided to take one course at a time for now. Being a mommy to a newborn was a lot of hard work.

I was sitting at the kitchen table, focused on an English paper when I heard a knock at the door. I set down my pen and headed to the entryway, thinking it might be Doris stopping by to say hello. She did that often. I loved seeing the joy on her face every time she held Faith in her arms.

When I opened the door, my lower jaw hit the floor. The last person I expected to see was Rob Dunham. All my old feelings for him resurfaced in a matter of seconds. He had matured into a fine-looking man. It had been over a year since I'd spoken to him.

"Hi," he said. "Sorry to show up like this." He shrugged and smiled. "You stopped taking my calls, so you gave me no choice." I could tell he was second-guessing his decision because he added, "I just wanted to see how you were doing."

He was right. Over the past year and a half, I had refused to talk to him. I convinced myself that he was better off without me. I wasn't sure if he had heard about the baby yet. I knew once he found out, he would never forgive me, and any hope of a future with him would dissolve completely.

"What are you doing here?" I asked. Disappointment flashed across his face, so I corrected myself. "I mean, what are you doing in town?"

"It's summer, silly. One year of college left to go." He smiled. That darn smile of his could melt ice.

"I thought you had two more years left," I said.

"I've been taking extra classes every summer, so I'm graduating early. Are you going to invite me inside? It's blazing hot out here."

"Yes, sorry, of course." I opened the door wide enough for him and shut it quietly behind me. I didn't want to wake up Faith; I had just laid her down for a nap. I led him to the kitchen table and got us both a glass of water. I knew in my heart it wouldn't take long before the jig would be up. There was no way the diapers, baby bottles, and other items scattered around the house would go unnoticed. It was just a matter of time before he'd be gone. This made me sad, but I prepared myself for it.

We chit-chatted for a few minutes about school. I told Rob about enrolling in the local community college and did my best to steer the conversation away from the past. I told him about my brother, and he expressed his concern and relief that Gavin was getting the treatment he needed. It wasn't long before he got straight to the matter at hand.

"Alina, why did you stop talking to me? I thought we were...," he trailed off for a moment, trying to find the right words, "best friends. I called you a million times. Did I do something wrong?" He looked down for a moment. "I know what I did at the dance was unforgivable, but I thought we had moved past that. Was I mistaken?"

I shook my head, no. "A lot has happened in the last year, Rob. I didn't want to drag you into all of it."

"But that's what friends are for, I mean, I could have helped you through it. I deeply care about you, Alina." I had wounded Rob and misjudged his feelings for me. That was clear now.

"I'm so sorry I hurt you," I said softly and placed my hand over his.

He continued, "I told myself that when I got home this summer, I wasn't going to bother you. I figured you didn't want me in your life, so I needed to move on with mine. But then, when I got here, I don't know," he trailed off again for a moment and tears filled his eyes. "I just couldn't stay away." He looked down at my hand on his. I could tell sharing his feelings was difficult.

"It wasn't about you, Rob. I did care for you. I mean, I do care for you. When I lost my mom, I was so broken. Despite your best efforts, I couldn't find my way out of a very dark place. I figured you would be happier without me. I told myself that you would find someone at college, fall in love, and forget about me."

"Well, obviously, that is not the case," he said flatly. He toyed with a pacifier on the table. At first, I could tell he didn't realize what he was touching. I held my breath, and my heart started pounding in my chest as I watched him begin to take in his surroundings. Next, he eyed an empty baby bottle on the counter and a stack of diapers sitting on the chair.

"Got a babysitting job, huh?" he asked.

After a small pause, I decided the best thing to do was to rip that Band-Aid right off. I let out all the air I had been holding in my lungs and blurted everything out in one full sentence. "No, I got knocked up by Troy Hicks and gave birth to a baby girl a little over a month ago."

He laughed out loud. "That's funny." He looked at me and realized I was not smiling. Then he glanced back at the baby bottle. He surveyed the kitchen and living room, finally noticing all the different baby paraphernalia that lay around the house. I observed in real-time as the reality set in. I watched his face go through about five different emotions in a matter of seconds. I waited for him to freak out, but instead, four unexpected words came out of his mouth.

"Can I meet her?" It took me almost a full minute to register his response and finally answer.

"Of course. I just laid her down for a nap." We quietly walked down the hall to my room, I carefully opened the door, and we crept in. Rob stood there and stared at her in awe for a full five minutes before we slipped out again.

We sat back down at the table, and he said, "She's beautiful, Alina. What's her name?"

"I named her Faith after my mom."

"She would have loved that," he said with sincerity.

I knew he was wondering about Troy. To save him the pain of asking, I told him what happened. I took him through my journey from partying to pregnancy. I told him about being diagnosed with extreme morning sickness and how alone I felt. I shared with him how I had to attend a special needs class most of my senior year. I relayed how Troy had treated me and how his parents had moved him to another state so he could avoid his responsibilities. I even told him about the crazy ride to the hospital and how we almost didn't make it in time. He listened intently, nodding here and there.

"So, Troy's not involved?" he asked, once I finished.

"No, he's not. And honestly, I am glad for it. Don't get me wrong. I mean, I feel like one day, he will regret this decision and may want to be involved, but being a single mom isn't so bad." I smiled and noticed what I thought looked like relief on Rob's face. I couldn't be sure of it, but he almost seemed happy.

"This is the reason you stopped talking to me?" he pressed.

"Well, I mean, it's a pretty good reason, don't you think?" I chuckled, not sure what he was getting at.

"So, it's not because you want me out of your life? You just thought that I wouldn't want you because you got pregnant and had a baby?" I didn't realize what he meant until I saw the look in his eyes. My heart skipped a beat.

"I love you, Alina. I don't mean to put you on the spot; I know you have been through a lot but, I do love you. Ever since that day you came over to my house and beat the crap out of me, I knew it right then and there. It was never just about being friends for me. And having Faith doesn't change that."

There it was. I wondered how I had missed all the signs as his face turned a light shade of pink. It must have been tough for him to say that, not knowing how I would respond.

"I mean, do you have any feelings for me *at all*?" he asked.

I did love Rob and had for a long time. I had purposefully closed off that part of my heart, thinking that door had shut once and for all. In that moment, I finally opened it back up, allowing myself to feel for him again, and it quickly overflowed.

"Yes, Rob. I love you. I guess I always have." I choked back tears. He reached over and embraced me. I could not hold back the tears any longer. *I loved Rob Dunham, and he loved me.* He used his thumb to gently wipe away my tears.

"I'm here for a few months. Can we spend some time together? The three of us?"

"Of course, we can!" I exclaimed excitedly. I felt like doing a cartwheel. I didn't even know how this could possibly be happening. How could Rob accept the situation without even a single doubt? I could hear Faith starting to wake up from her nap and explained it was time to nurse.

"Should I leave?" he asked me.

"Absolutely not! Just give me about twenty minutes to feed her, then I'll bring her out." I jumped up and ran to my bedroom.

When I finished, I brought Faith out and handed her gently over to Rob. She stared at him, wide-eyed, listening to his deep voice tell her how beautiful she was. I couldn't stop smiling. He was a natural. Hours went by unnoticed by either of us. When Cameron walked through the door, he couldn't hide his surprise.

"Rob, how are you? Good to see you!" He shook Rob's hand and smiled at me, trying his best not to look shocked. "I see you have met our little rainbow." Cameron washed his hands in the kitchen sink then came over to take his turn holding Faith. Rob carefully passed her over. "Hello, sweet girl. I missed you today," Cameron said softly and rocked her back and forth. Faith smiled and cooed at the sound of Cameron's familiar voice.

That night, I wrote a prayer in my notebook of thanksgiving. God had surprised me once again. To think He loved me so much that He would bring restoration to my relationship with Rob; I was so amazed at the way things were working out. Everything I had been through, the good and the bad, had brought me to this very place.

That summer, Rob and I officially became a couple. Spending time with him and Faith over the following three months was the most precious time of my life. Rob bonded with Faith immediately and enjoyed bottle feeding her, burping her, and even changing her diapers. His parents were very supportive and offered to babysit occasionally so Rob and I could experience a few normal dates.

When it was time for Rob to return to college, I wasn't sure I could let him go. He reassured me over and over again that he would be back once a month, on holidays, and call me every day.

"It's only Tucson," he reassured me. I could tell it was very difficult for him to leave as well, but necessary for our future.

Throughout the year, Rob kept his promise. We spoke several times a day and wrote love letters back and forth. Herman had bought me a Polaroid camera after Faith was born, so I took photos of her and sent them to him weekly.

Gavin came home from treatment and was so excited to help me with his niece. He finally looked and sounded like his old self again. We never talked about what had happened. I figured he had done a lot of thinking and talking while in treatment, no need to rehash the past. He had missed months of school, so he decided to work on obtaining his GED.

One night, at dinner, Gavin announced that he wanted to join the police academy. Everyone was excited for him and discussed the details over Italian food at the Locke's house. Gavin reconnected with Cameron and spent time helping him and Herman work on cars for people who couldn't afford to go to a mechanic. On the weekends, the three of them would watch sports or attend games in downtown Phoenix.

I continued having dreams about Heaven and wrote every single one of them down. Sometimes I talked with Jesus and about a variety of topics; other times, I was alone, strolling through heavenly places taking in the mysterious creations and wondrous sights and sounds of the garden and the City of God. Many times, I tried to ask Jesus about my purpose.

He never answered me directly but, instead, would say things like, "You represent Me as a light in the world. A city set on a hill cannot be hidden away, nor do people light a lamp and put it under a basket. They put it on a stand, and the lamp gives light to the entire house. In the same way, let your light shine before others, so that they may see your good works and give glory to your Father, Who is in Heaven." My dreams always ended the same way: abruptly, with thunder and cracks in the floor of Heaven.

Rob and I got married the following summer. We said our vows under the old oak tree in our backyard, with only our closest friends and family in attendance. I can't explain why I wanted to marry him there. Maybe it was because it was my mom's favorite spot. That day it felt like she was present with us. It was a beautiful experience, one I would remember for the rest of my life.

CHAPTER 14
THE LETTERS

I had been saving money from my part-time jobs since I was a sophomore. With that money, plus a little help from Rob's parents, we were able to get a small apartment not far from my childhood home. Rob landed a job as an engineer, and I continued attending community college taking a few credits at a time. Doris and Herman bought us a computer for our wedding present so I could use it for school and Rob could use it for work. We had just enough money to get internet service.

I was fascinated with all things relating to Heaven. I loved spending hours at the local library or online, looking for anything having to do with the subject. I studied the book of Revelation in the Bible, determined to understand more about life after death and Heaven and Hell. I even searched for individuals who had had near-death experiences and claimed to have met Jesus or spent time in Heaven. I became fixated on finding my purpose and how it was related to my dreams. Sometimes the fascination turned into an obsession, and I would neglect my homework and housework.

One night, I stayed up until 2 a.m. reading a personal account of someone's encounters with Jesus in Heaven, after being fatally injured in a car accident and pronounced dead. They were finally resuscitated after ten minutes but gave a detailed report very similar to my dreams. This survivor spent their time traveling around the world, speaking at churches and venues about their experience with the afterlife. *Am I supposed to be doing that?* I wondered. *Maybe that's my purpose.*

"You're tired this morning," Rob commented, as I slowly made his breakfast, yawning every few minutes. Although he didn't say anything, I knew he disapproved of my obsession. Rob had never read my notebooks, and even though I had told him a little about my dreams, I knew he didn't understand the pressure I felt to figure things out. Even though he never said anything directly, the neglected errands and housework did not go unnoticed. Our daughter, Faith, was always cared for; but, I admit, there were times I could have been more attentive. I don't know why I had such a strong determination to find some type of connection between my dreams and my purpose, but I did.

One chilly, winter day, Rob was at work, and I sat on the front porch, going through the mail. Faith, bundled from head to toe, threw the ball for Buddy on a stretch of grass close to the front door. They both loved this game. Buddy would fetch the ball, bring it back, and drop it in her lap. She would giggle out of delight each time.

"Good girl, Faith. Good job, Buddy," I repeatedly said, as I thumbed through the most recent J.C. Penny catalog. I scooped up Faith and returned to the warmth of our apartment.

When I dropped the mail on the table, I was surprised to see an envelope addressed to me, written in pencil with a return address from the Arizona Department of Corrections. I picked it up, and I saw that someone named Ryan Sheridan had sent it to me. The letter had initially gone to my old address, but Cameron had scribbled "Forward to" and written in my new one.

What the heck? I knew mom had had a brother at one point, but she said he had passed away. She never said how or when he died and led us to believe we had no other relatives still alive.

I quickly opened the letter, and anxiously read it.

October 5, 1996

Dear Alina,

Hello. I know this might come as a surprise to you, but my name is Ryan Sheridan, and I believe I might be your first cousin.

I heard about you from an inmate here at the correction facility, where I currently live. Having lots of time on our hands, my cellmate and I got to know each other. He told me that a while back, he met a guy named Gavin Sheridan at a drug detox center. They became friends, and he learned a lot about your family. Unfortunately, my cellmate violated his probation and ended up in here shortly after leaving treatment.

Before my mom passed away, she told me that my dad had a younger sister named Faith. I put two and two together and set out to find you both.

My dad passed away when I was quite young, so I don't know much about him. I have spent most of my life with *little knowledge or connections to any extended family. I am an only child, so the thought that I might have relatives out there somewhere is exciting.*

I know that discovering you might have a cousin will be a shock to you, just as it was for me. I don't have high expectations that this letter will find you, but if it does, I hope that you will give me a chance. I, myself, have had a rough time since my mother passed away. The feelings of loss and grief led me to do some things that I entirely regret.

I have two more years left to go and am hoping that during that time, if you give me a chance, maybe we can get acquainted with each other. I am sure you have lots of questions. I hope this letter reaches you or your brother, Gavin; I would love to know that I have some family to reach out to when I'm released. This is an awful place to live, and despite my surroundings, I have worked hard to resist the prison mentality and dream of making a life for myself one day on the other side.

Sincerely,
Ryan Sheridan

My initial reactions were shock and disbelief. I reread the letter five times before setting it down. I could not wait for Rob to get home so I could tell him all about it. I called my brother right away.

"You are not going to believe what I just got in the mail, Gavin!" I said into the phone.

"Everything alright?" he asked, concerned. I realized I was speaking louder than necessary.

"Yes, sorry, I'm just surprised." I lowered my voice and took a couple of deep breaths to calm myself down.

"I think we have a cousin!" I announced.

"Wait; what? How do you know?" he asked skeptically. I explained the entire situation to him, then read the letter out loud.

Gavin paused for a moment, no doubt thinking back. "He must be talking about Chris Steadman. He was my roommate at the detox center, and neither of us could sleep much. We spent a lot of time talking late into the night. Man, that's too bad he's in prison. Nice guy, though. Are you going to write this Ryan dude back?" I hadn't thought that part through yet. I supposed I would.

"Probably" I replied. "I mean, it would be nice to learn a little more about our family, if what he says is true. Mom never wanted to talk about it." There was a part of me that wondered if this guy was trying to fool us. Faith pulled at my pants and said, "Mommy." She was ready for lunch and a nap.

"Well, I need to feed Faith. Do you want his information, too? I mean, it wouldn't hurt if we both wrote him. You could test out your detective skills." Gavin was halfway through the police academy with plans on becoming an investigator.

"Sure, I'll write to him," Gavin agreed. "Wouldn't that be crazy to discover we have a cousin after all this time? Did he say why he's in prison?"

"No, not really. Do you think I should ask? He said he has two years left until his release."

"Yeah, I think we should, but be careful, Nia, Gavin warned. "Don't give him too much information about our family until we are sure he's related. I wish Mom were here so we could ask her."

I could hear a little sadness in his voice. "I miss her too, Little Bear. We'll figure this out together, though. I love you."

"Love you too, Nia," he said.

Faith pulled at my pant leg again and let out a cry this time. "Sounds like my little niece needs you. Talk to you later, alligator."

"After 'while, crocodile." I hung up the phone and turned my attention back to my daughter. "I'm sorry, baby girl, come here. I will make you something to eat right now." I picked her up and walked into the kitchen. I couldn't stop thinking about the letter. After putting her down for a nap, I took out a pen and paper and wrote Ryan a letter.

October 10, 1996

Dear Ryan,

Thank you for writing to me. I was excited and, naturally, a little skeptical when I received your letter. I'm sorry for the loss of your mother. Our mother passed away several years ago, as well. My brother and I had a tough time recovering from her death.

Before I disclose too much about myself, I would like to know more about you and your family history. Excuse me for asking, but why are you in prison? Can you tell me more about your parents? Do you know anything about your paternal grandparents? My mom did not like talking about them for some reason.

We have no one left in our family to ask if what you are saying is true. However, for now, I am willing to give you the benefit of the doubt. Regardless, I believe God has brought you into our lives for a reason, so I have decided to correspond with you unless I'm led to do otherwise. My brother Gavin has also agreed to write you a letter. I'm sure he will have questions of his own.

Hope to hear from you soon.

Sincerely,
Alina Sheridan

I didn't know what else to say at this point, so I threw a stamp on it and popped the letter in the mail. When I walked back inside, I had an idea. I turned on the computer and waited for the buzzing and beeping to stop, signifying a connection to the internet was complete.

I typed in "Ryan Sheridan." After several searches on various sites, I found an article about a burglar in Mesa, Arizona, who had finally been arrested after a year-long string of break-ins. He had been found guilty on several counts of second-degree burglary. I waited as his mugshot slowly finished downloading. I desperately searched for recognizable features. Ryan had dark hair and freckles covering his face, unlike my brother and me, but there was something familiar about his chin, nose, and mouth.

I felt excited and anxious at the same time, so I went to my room and pulled out my prayer notebook. I asked God for wisdom, guidance, and protection in dealing with this situation. I closed my eyes and decided to take a short nap before Faith woke up from hers.

I had a dream I was walking through an orchard. Hundreds of trees, planted in straight lines, surrounded me on both sides. It looked like the ground was covered in snow. I bent down to grab a handful. To my surprise, it wasn't snow after all; it was delicate, soft, white flower petals. I had seen something like this before in a magazine; these were almond trees in full bloom. Every tree was completely covered in white flowers. It was a magical scene. The petals slowly dropping from the trees made it look like it was lightly snowing. I scooped up a big handful and threw them into the air. They floated down in slow motion, landing in my hair and on my shoulders.

I had never dreamt of the orchard before. As I was admiring this picturesque setting, I saw movement in-between the trees on my right. It was quick and disappeared before I could get a good look at what it was. I kept still, trying not to frighten away whatever was hiding from me. I slowly moved behind a tree and after a minute, peeked out from one side. There it was again, running fast as lightening to another hiding place behind a tree less than fifty feet away. Blossoms floated up in its wake.

I stayed very still, determined to uncover this mysterious being. It darted out again. and to my astonishment, I realized it was a little boy. He was quick as a whip and trying his best to stay hidden behind the tree trunks. He had pale skin and hair the color of a raven. He didn't see me; he was concentrating on something else. I wondered what this striking little boy was doing in an orchard all by himself. He couldn't have been more than four or five years old and he had a look like he was frightened.

I followed the direction of his gaze and saw movement again.

Something was following him. Out from behind a tree, chasing the little boy was a giant reptile. I recognized the evil serpent immediately. The snake paused, his tongue flickering in and out, tasting the air around him. I wanted to call out to the little boy, but I was afraid I would give his location away.

I watched as the snake slithered through the flower petals, no doubt following the boy's scent. Even though the child was quick, he was no match for the snake who was rapidly gaining on him. I knew what I needed to do and stepped out from behind the tree.

"Hey, you! Recognize me? Come and get me, I'm over here!" I waved my arms wildly.

The snake stopped abruptly and looked in my direction. The boy ran as fast as his short legs would carry him. The snake hesitated for a minute, looking my way then back toward the boy. I could tell he was contemplating his next move.

Suddenly, a lion's roar erupted in the distance. I had heard that roar many times before. It was so fierce and powerful that the ground shook, and the remaining petals still hanging from the almond trees all fell at once. It looked like a blizzard and gave the boy just enough cover to run unseen for a long distance. I was trying to decide what to do next when thunder quaked overhead. The orchard shook violently, stirring up the white petals that were on the ground and sending them back into the air, blinding me. I tried to steady myself but tumbled head-first into one of the many openings.

I woke up to Buddy, vigorously licking my face and the sound of Faith crying. I picked my little girl up and held her close.

"Good boy, Buddy." I patted his head. "You're the smartest pup on Earth." He wasn't a puppy anymore, though. "That was a crazy dream I had," I told them both. "I'm so glad it's over." I heard Rob come through the front door and went to greet him with a hug and a kiss.

"You are not going to believe what I got in the mail today!"

I told him about the letter over dinner. I pulled it out and let him read it.

"Wow, do you think he's telling the truth?" he asked.

"I don't know yet. I sent a letter asking him some questions. I searched for his information on the internet today and found his mugshot. He does resemble my family somewhat." Rob kissed my cheek and cleared the dishes.

"Promise me you will be careful," he said protectively.

"I will. I have to tell you about this crazy dream I had today, too." I told him all about the little boy with black hair and the dangerous snake pursuing him. Buddy, who was lying on the floor by my feet, let out a low but audible growl. I put my hand on his head, reassuring him everything was alright.

"I don't ever remember my dreams," Rob said, sounding a little disappointed. Did you write this one down in your secret notebook?" I smiled at his teasing. It wasn't necessarily secret. Even though I had told a few people about my dreams, I hadn't let anyone read my notebook besides Gavin. And that was many years ago; the night Mom was admitted to the hospital. One of these days, I would show it to Rob too.

A little over two weeks later, I received my second letter from Ryan.

CRACKS IN THE FLOOR OF HEAVEN

October 18, 1996

Dear Alina,

Hello, and thank you for writing me back. I completely understand your hesitation in believing we might be related. Let me answer a few of your questions.

I am twenty-five. My father passed away when I was two years old. He was shot in a gas station robbery and died a week later. He was your mothers' older brother by four years. My mother passed away from cancer when I was nineteen. I got involved with the wrong crowd and started burglarizing houses. After twelve months, I was arrested, convicted, and sentenced to seven years in prison.

My dad's name was Henry Sheridan, and my mom's name was Lucy. My mom's maiden name was Jones. I enclosed a photo of the three of us. It was taken five weeks before my dad was killed. Please keep it safe, and I beg you to return it in your next letter; it is the only photo I have of my parents.

I stopped reading for a moment and picked up the photo. A happy couple holding the hands of a little boy smiled for the camera. I held it up close and stared at the man in the picture whom Ryan claimed was my uncle. I couldn't believe my eyes. He looked so much like my mother that I gasped out loud. Buddy looked over at me and assessed the situation. Finding no danger; he laid his head back down to finish his nap.

Ryan's mother was beautiful, with long black hair, green eyes, and freckles that covered her face and exposed arms. Ryan had inherited his mother's freckles, eyes, and hair color; however, his nose, mouth, and chin looked like his father's. I continued reading his letter.

> My mother was strict, tidy, and organized. She liked to stay on a schedule, and I don't ever remember her being late to anything. She told me that my father was the exact opposite. He was spontaneous, a prankster, and had a great sense of humor. I wish I could have known him.
>
> The only thing my mom told me about my father's parents (our grandparents) is how they died. They were driving home from a weekend trip to the mountains. It was a week before Christmas and had snowed the night before. Grandfather was driving when he lost control on the icy roadway. Their car veered off the road and plummeted down a steep cliff. Both of them died instantly. My mom said that my dad never wanted to talk about it.

I took a moment to contemplate what I had read. No wonder my mom never wanted to talk about our grandparents. What a terrible thing it would be to lose both your parents a week before Christmas. I thought about her eccentric Santa Claus collection. It now made perfect sense to me. People grieve in different ways. I picked up the letter again and continued reading.

> I hope this helps a little bit. I don't know what other evidence I could provide, but I do believe we are related.
>
> I am glad that you have found God. I still have a lot of questions in that department. I can't help but wonder how a loving God could allow so much pain and suffering.
>
> I do have one favor to ask you, and I understand if the answer is no. I have a son. His name is Richard. He is five years old, and, I believe, living with his mother (my ex-girlfriend) in Tucson. My ex-girlfriend's name is Heather Stevens. She kept in contact with me for a while, but I haven't been able to get in touch with her for a couple of years now. Last I heard, she was addicted to drugs, and I believe my son may be in imminent danger.
>
> A mutual friend, who is here on the inside, gave me Heather's last known address. I've written to her dozens of times, but she will not respond to any of my letters. Richard is the only thing that has kept me going these last five years. I am asking you to check on him for me and make sure he is alright. I included

a photo of him, as well. Please send it back when you can. I am hoping to get custody of him when I get out of here. Please, Alina, if you can make sure he is safe, I would owe you my life, and possibly his.

Sincerely,

Ryan Sheridan

Ryan had written their last known address at the bottom of the page. I picked up the photo and stared at the picture of a little boy with dark hair and pale skin. I stood up so abruptly that I accidentally knocked over my chair. Buddy jumped up and whined a little.

"Oh my gosh!" I shouted. I stared in shock at the picture of the little boy with raven-colored hair. There was not a doubt in my mind. It was the same exact same boy I had seen in my dream two weeks ago.

CHAPTER 15
THE BOY

I knew what I had to do. It was as if God, Himself, had prepared me for this mission. When Rob got home, I handed him the letter and photos.

"It's the same boy I saw in my dream," I said, pacing back and forth. He shook his head in disbelief and looked up at me. Rob knew me well. He could tell that my mind was made up.

He picked up Faith, kissed her, and said, "I guess Mommy and Daddy are going on a road trip to Tucson."

I jumped up and down with excitement. "I'll call Doris and see if she can babysit."

Friday, after Rob got home from work, we packed our suitcases for a weekend-long trip. It was the first time I would be away from Faith for more than a few hours. I felt a little apprehensive at first; however, after praying about it, God filled me with His peace, and I knew we were doing the right thing.

We began the two-hour drive toward the city of Tucson, with Ryan's letters and photos safely tucked inside my purse. We sang along to country music on the way and stopped at a Mexican restaurant for dinner before pulling into a quaint motel.

I could barely sleep that night. I must have re-read both letters a dozen times on the drive there. I believed that Ryan was telling me the truth, and I was convinced that finding his little boy was a mission worth completing. I had no idea what I would discover, but I would trust God to lead the way.

The next morning, after breakfast, we obtained a map from the motel manager and directions to the address Ryan had provided. We found the address within fifteen minutes.

The apartment complex was not the worst I had ever seen; however, the paint was chipping off the stucco, and the wrought-iron gates surrounding the complex were rusted and threatening to fall over in some places.

We climbed the dilapidated stairs to the second story and knocked on the door of apartment number 202. Rob seemed calm and relaxed. I, on the other hand, was a nervous wreck. I tried to take a few deep breaths to calm down and slow my heart rate. After a minute or two, a rather large man answered the door. He must have been almost seven feet tall and had tattoos covering his neck and both arms. He had a bald head and a thick, red beard.

"What?" he asked, scowling down at us.

I couldn't manage to get words out, so Rob took over. "Hi, sorry to bother you. We are looking for a girl named Heather Stevens. She has a son named Richard." The goliath sized us up for several seconds before answering, distrust apparent on his face.

"She doesn't live here no more." He slammed the door on us. Disappointment settled in, and I had to fight back the tears. *All that way for nothing*, I thought. *A dead end. Now, what do we do?* I felt like knocking again, and demanding answers, but I dared not do it. I could tell he wasn't a man to be trifled with. When Rob and I turned to go, a Hispanic woman about five feet away spoke up. She had been chain-smoking on the balcony since we arrived.

She turned and addressed us in a thick accent. "You guys cops?"

Finding a little confidence, I answered, "No, we are looking for my cousin and his mom." I walked a little closer to her and smiled. "We were in the area and just wanted to say hi."

She eyed us suspiciously as she asked, "You looking for Heather?" She took a long drag off her cigarette and looked around like she didn't care one way or the other.

"Yes, and her son's name is Richard. He's about five years old with dark hair. My name is Alina, and this is my husband, Rob." I extended my hand as an offer to shake hers. She ignored it, turned her body away, and looked out over the street.

"Yeah, I know her. She moved a few weeks ago." Taking another drag off her cigarette, the woman looked away as if the conversation was over.

My heart sunk. *We'll never find them now*, I thought.

Suddenly, Rob asked, "Do you happen to know where she moved to?" The woman was quiet for a while, no doubt contemplating what she should disclose to us. We turned to go when she spoke again.

"She moved to the apartments at the end of West Alameda Street." She turned to look at us and glared right at me. "You better be telling me the truth, *gringa*." With that, she flicked her cigarette over the balcony, walked into her apartment, and shut the door.

After stopping for gas and looking at the map, we set out to find the next address. As we drove toward her street, we noticed the neighborhood got worse. Shady looking people were hanging out on each corner outside liquor stores. It was not a neighborhood I felt comfortable in despite it being the middle of the day. I couldn't imagine what it was like at night. Rob must have read my mind and locked the car doors. We found the run-down apartment complex at the very end of a cul-de-sac.

"Stay right by my side," Rob warned, eyeing people who were, in turn, checking us out. Dirty diapers, beer bottles, and trash littered the sidewalk and gutters. The apartment complex was in total disrepair, and loud music blared from various apartment windows. Cigarette smoke hung heavily in the air, and people were drinking out of paper bags. I was terrified, and I did precisely what Rob told me to. I tried not to make eye contact with anyone as we walked through the entrance.

Our main obstacle was finding the right apartment. Heather's neighbor hadn't given us specifics, so we were forced to knock on doors and ask around. After a while, we were directed to an apartment located on the third floor. Rob tapped lightly on the worn-out entryway and positioned me behind him in a protective stance. A woman my height, with light brown hair and blue eyes, opened the door. She would have been pretty, but years of living a hard life had aged her tremendously. She wore a halter top, cut-off jean shorts and her hair was up in a ponytail. Cartoons played loudly in the background.

"What do you want?" she asked, lighting a cigarette. "You guys cops?"

What is with the people around here? I wondered. *Are there a bunch of plain-clothed men and women law-enforcement agents combing the area in the middle of the day?* I moved out from behind Rob.

"Hi, my name is Alina, and this is my husband, Rob. We are in town for the day, and my cousin Ryan told me that you live in the area, so we thought we would stop by and say hello." She took a puff off her cigarette and looked me up and down. I held my breath as she blew the smoke toward my face.

"That lame ex-boyfriend of mine got himself in big trouble. He's in prison and left me to care for our son all by myself. I don't get any child support or have any help. Do you know how expensive it is to take care of a kid? Ryan's a loser, and I'm glad he's in prison." She walked out of the apartment and looked over the second-floor railing at the street below. "That your car down there?"

I nodded. Heather seemed to be contemplating something. "It' nice."

I couldn't help myself. As she was eyeing our vehicle, I turned around and peeked into her apartment. A little boy around five years old sat in front of a small black and white television. Cartoons flashed across the screen, but they were hard to see because of the poor picture quality.

She turned around, caught me looking inside, and said, "I suppose you can come in."

The apartment was utterly disgusting. Cigarette butts littered the floor, and on the couch were piles of clothes and fast-food wrappers. The smell of smoke was so over-powering that it was all I could do to keep from coughing. I spotted a cockroach scurrying across the kitchen floor. Trash overflowed from its container, and dirty dishes were scattered well beyond the sink. I was afraid to touch anything.

"Richard, turn off that television and meet your cousins," Heather demanded. He stood up and walked over to Rob and me with his head hung down. "Boy, what did I tell you about meeting new people? Don't make me smack you." He peeked up at us. I tried to hide my shock as I looked into the eyes of the boy from my dream.

"Hello," he said softly and looked back down. His skin was extremely fair, and freckles covered his cute little face and exposed arms. His eyes were a beautiful color of green, and his hair was black as night. He looked over at his mother, who was lighting up another cigarette. She nodded at him with approval. He walked over to the television, turned it back on, and sat down on the floor in front of it.

"He ain't too great around strangers," she said with a frown. "I can't get him to shut up most of the time, though. That's a nice car you got down there. You guys rich or something?" she asked, staring at my attire. We still had not sat down.

"No, we're not rich, but we make it work," Rob said. He smiled at me and put his arm around my shoulders. "We have a little girl. Her name is Faith. I work as an engineer in Phoenix, and Alina is attending community college." I smiled back at him, proud of our little family.

"I never attended college. Shoot, I didn't even finish high school. I had a job at the gas station but I couldn't find a babysitter. Now, I'm on disability." I don't know how, but I could tell she was lying. While I pondered her situation, a fight broke out in the apartment next door. We heard a crashing sound followed by a woman crying.

Heather rolled her eyes. "Stupid woman. She stays with her boyfriend even though he beats the crap out of her. He's going to kill her one of these days, I swear." I winced and looked over at Richard. He seemed unaware of anything but the cartoons in front of him. Sorrow for this young boy filled every part of me. I had no idea how I was going to tell Ryan about Richard's living situation.

"Hey, do you guys mind watching Richard for a minute while I run to the store for some cigarettes?" Heather asked.

"That's no problem," I said, trying my best to be friendly. If I wanted to see Richard again, I better hold it together.

Heather walked over to her son and stood in front of the television. "Richard, you better not give these people any problems, or else you're gonna get it, you hear me?" He nodded and looked down.

Heather smiled at us, "Alright then. Just leave him be. He loves his cartoons." She laughed obnoxiously. She said she'd be back soon and walked out the door.

Five hours passed by, and Heather had not returned. Richard kept silent, despite our best efforts to interact with him. I tried to make myself useful and clean the dirty kitchen. I washed the dishes, and Rob took out the trash. The cupboards were bare, and the refrigerator had a half-empty bottle of ketchup and soured milk.

"Rob, we need to feed him. There's absolutely nothing here to eat."

"Well, I'm not leaving you alone, so I guess we could write Heather a note and go get something to eat really quick," he said, concern in his voice. I noticed he kept looking at his watch. It was starting to get dark outside. Neither of us wanted to be in this neighborhood at night. I had an unsettled feeling in my stomach.

I pulled out a pen and piece of paper from my purse and jotted down a quick note for Heather.

I walked over to Richard. "Come on, Sweetie, let's go get some dinner." He obediently stood up, switched off the television, and grabbed his toy truck. It was the only toy I had seen in the entire apartment. He walked over by the door and put his shoes on. They had holes in the toes and looked to be too small for his feet.

Richard ate two cheeseburgers and a small order of french fries. The way he ate his food was shocking. He hovered protectively over his meal and barely chewed his food before swallowing. It was as if he hadn't eaten in days. That wouldn't have surprised me in the least, after what I had seen in the kitchen. We tried to hurry in case Heather returned during our absence. I didn't want her to freak out and call the police on us.

When we returned, Heather was still nowhere in sight. "Rob, what do we do now? We can't sleep here. Should we call the police?"

"She might come back tonight, so for now, let's take him to the motel with us." He scribbled down a note for Heather below the last one while I went on the hunt for pajamas. Dirty clothes covered every space in the single bedroom. I finally found a somewhat clean t-shirt and underwear.

I got on my knees in front of Richard and said, "We are going to have a sleep-over, little guy. Is that okay with you?" He shrugged his shoulders and rubbed his eyes. Poor kid must be exhausted. He let me pick him up and carry him to the car.

Back at the motel, I changed Richard's filthy clothes and washed his face and hands. We only had one bed, so Rob offered to sleep on the floor and grabbed a few extra pillows from the front desk. Richard fell asleep within minutes.

"I'm scared she is going to get back to her apartment tonight and call the police," I whispered.

"Well, if she does, we will tell them what happened. We left a note after all. What were we supposed to do, leave him alone all night?

"I'm also afraid she will come back, and we will have to leave Richard with her," I said, holding back tears.

"I know, Babe," Rob said, "but let's try to get some sleep."

I peeked over at the little boy. He was sound asleep with his arms above his head, his toy truck lying next to him. I listened to his breathing. *Dear God,* I prayed, *what do we do now? This little boy is in a terrible situation, and I know you brought us here for a reason. Please guide us and give us wisdom on how to handle the situation. Please rescue this sweet boy. He doesn't deserve to live like this. Amen.*

The next morning, we were up with the sun. I had barely slept. I kept anticipating a knock at the door with demands that we immediately return Richard to his mother. We got dressed quickly and headed straight back to the apartment. Richard still had not said a word. We knocked on the apartment door and stood outside for a couple of minutes before trying the doorknob. It was unlocked, so we went inside.

"Hello?" I called out. Maybe she was asleep after a late night of partying. I tip-toed over to the single bedroom and looked in. No one was there. I noticed that most of the clothes I had seen scattered on the floor and piled on the bed were gone. "What the heck?" I wondered, out loud, before raising my voice to call out, "Rob, can you come here, please?" He walked into the bedroom. "Do you see any women's clothes?"

He shook his head no. The few clothes that remained were Richard's. Only a couple of Heather's shirts were sticking out from under the bed. The closet was empty, as well. I looked at Rob as he registered what I was getting at. "She's gone," he whispered.

"Oh my gosh, what do we do?"

"Call the police," Rob said.

"What if they take him away?" I asked, trying my best not to panic.

"Richard would be better off almost anywhere but here," Rob said quietly.

I glanced around the corner at him. He was watching cartoons again. "What if we took him home with us?" I asked, already knowing in my heart that's what I wanted to do. I needed to protect him. "Temporarily, of course," I added.

Rob thought for a moment and looked deep into my eyes. He knew that my mind was made up. He reached out and took my hand. "Are you sure?"

"Yes," I confirmed.

"Alright. I am going to run down to the gas station and call the police. Lock the door and don't open it for anyone." He hurried off and I could tell he wasn't crazy about leaving us there alone.

Fifteen minutes later, Rob, accompanied by two police officers, entered the apartment. Richard looked up for a minute then turned his attention back to the cartoons. I was sure this wasn't the first time he had seen officers because it didn't even phase him. I couldn't help but wonder how many times the police had visited his apartment over the years. Probably a lot.

We spoke with them for over an hour and explained the situation and our intentions. After looking around the apartment, taking meticulous notes, and making some calls from their vehicle, they decided to go ahead and permit us to take Richard home with us until a social worker could follow-up on Monday. They would continue to be on the look-out for Heather in hopes of getting some answers as to why she would abandon her son. They also told us they were familiar with Heather and had responded many times to reports of domestic violence between her and past boyfriends. Several reports had been made to Child Protective Services over the years.

I looked over at Richard and couldn't imagine what his mother had put him through these past five years. My heart filled with so much love and compassion for him; it felt as though it would burst. It made me think of Faith and how I would do everything in my power to protect her.

We packed up Richard's belongings. He only had a few dirty clothes and that one toy truck he always kept with him. At least he wouldn't have to live in filth anymore. I thought of all the items I needed to purchase for him. We didn't have a lot of money, but I knew God would provide. Richard would have food to eat, clean clothes to wear, and, more than anything, love and safety.

I turned off the television and knelt down in front of him. "Richard, we are going to have another sleep-over, but this time it's going to be at our house in Phoenix. Will that be okay with you?" He nodded, and for the first time, asked a question.

"Is Momma coming?" A lump developed in my throat.

"No, Honey. She won't be coming with us. It's going to be me, Rob and our little girl. Her name is Faith. You will get to meet her tonight."

"Okay," he said and looked down at his toy truck.

"You can bring that with you," I said. I went to hug Richard, but he flinched, making me think maybe it wasn't the right time for physical contact. He had been through a lot, things we probably would never really know. I was determined to make sure the next part of his life was stable, happy, and secure.

The drive home was quiet. Rob and I were both deep in thought, wondering how it would all work out. God had shown me, time and time again, to trust in Him. I would need to do that now more than ever.

We got home around 8 p.m. and picked up Faith from Doris's house. She was already sleeping, so we did our best to get her home undisturbed. As she lay in her bed, I stared at her for a long time. I couldn't imagine anyone abandoning or abusing their child. Rob came in and stood behind me, massaging my shoulders. He understood me well.

"We are blessed," he said. I nodded in agreement. "I made him a bed on the couch for now. He's exhausted. I gave him one of Faith's teddy bears."

"Did he say anything?" I asked curiously.

"No, not a thing; he fell asleep pretty quickly." I went and checked in on him. He had one arm wrapped around the teddy bear, and the other one around his toy truck.

"Well, I am wide awake. I think I'll sit down and write Ryan a letter. He deserves to know what is going on." Rob kissed me goodnight and went to bed. I sat at the kitchen table and wrote down everything that had happened in as much detail as possible. I put it in the mailbox that night so that it would go out first thing in the morning.

By mid-week, Richard was still barely talking, but he had taken a real liking to Faith. He would throw the ball to her, and she would try to catch it. This game kept them entertained for over an hour. We didn't have cable, so there weren't any cartoons for him to watch; it was time for him to adjust to new types of entertainment.

Doris and Herman had gone shopping and bought Richard new shoes, pajamas, jeans, shirts, and a box of Legos. Cameron bought him some new trucks, a coloring book with crayons and a jacket. Gavin surprised him with a baseball and a little glove. My brother was bound and determined to teach Richard how to throw and catch a ball. I adored my family. No matter what, they were always there to help me whenever I needed it.

A social worker by the name of Pam came by the house late afternoon on Monday, just as the police had promised. She inspected our apartment, and I showed her all the items everyone had purchased for Richard. Rob's parents bought a twin-sized mattress with matching sheets, and we placed it on the floor in Faith's room. Everything checked out, and the social worker was happy to grant us temporary guardianship, pending a court date where a judge would approve or deny it. The police were still searching for Heather but had no leads on her whereabouts. There would still be a lot of things to figure out, but for now, Richard would be loved and well taken care of.

I received a letter from Ryan about eight days after I had sent mine. He expressed both sadness for the five years of pain and suffering Richard had gone through and thankfulness for the current developments. I could only imagine the guilt Ryan must have been feeling, and I wanted to be there for him.

Ryan provided Richard's birthdate and some other important information so we could take him to the doctor. I had no idea if he had received immunizations or had any medical issues. Ryan was little help in those matters because he had been in prison since before Richard was born. We were winging it, for sure.

The social worker applied for a copy of Richard's birth certificate so we could enroll him in kindergarten. Pam came by twice a month to check on him and ensure we had everything we needed. It was a lot of work but well worth it.

One night, I sat down and wrote a prayer of thanksgiving in my notebook. I knew that God had orchestrated the entire thing. Rob had supported me through the whole ordeal, and I was grateful for a husband who was generous, kind, loving, and thoughtful. Life couldn't have been any better. I decided to put my studies on hold for a while, so I could concentrate on being present for both Faith and Richard. It was also time to stop obsessing about finding my purpose. As far as I could tell, I had found it.

THE GIFT OF THE RAVEN

CHAPTER 16
CALL 9-1-1

The four of us had no problem getting into a natural routine. A couple of months after Richard came to live with us, he finally started to communicate more effectively. He quit hanging his head down, and his answers to questions eventually expanded past only "yes" or "no". Richard never asked about his mother, which I thought said a lot about their relationship and what he had gone through in the first five years of his life.

We slowly started introducing Richard to the idea that he had a father who loved him very much. Ryan wrote letters to his son and enclosed them with his letters to me. Each night before bed, we would read them to Richard and say a little prayer before tucking him in. One night, after our normal routine, I crawled into bed, extra tired from the day's activities and fell right asleep.

I dreamt I was floating thousands of feet up in the sky. Fear and adrenaline pumped through my veins as I instinctively froze, afraid any second I would plummet to the Earth below. I squeezed my eyes shut and tried to wake myself up.

Ever since I was little, I had an extreme fear of heights and apparently this carried over into my dreams. One time, Mom took us to the Grand Canyon, and I wouldn't go anywhere near the ledge. I stayed at least fifty feet or more away from it. Mom and Gavin tried to coax me into going closer, pointing out the safety fence, but I refused.

"You're missing the best views," Mom would say.

"It looks just as beautiful from back here," I would argue.

Suddenly, I heard a familiar voice. I opened my eyes and saw Jesus floating next to me. I was so relieved to see Him.

"Help me, Jesus! I am afraid I'm going to fall!" I yelled in a panic.

"Do you trust Me?" He asked.

"Help me, Jesus," I continued to scream, terror rushing through me like a freight train.

"Do you trust Me?" He asked again. Did I trust Him? Now's not the time for this!

"Please help me, Lord," I started to cry as the phobia continued to attack me.

"Alina, do you trust Me?" He pressed.

"Yes, I trust you!" I would have said anything. I would have done anything. I just wanted down from there. The terror was overwhelming.

"If you trust Me, then follow Me." Jesus stretched His arms out like Superman and shot toward the ground like a bullet. He landed on the top of a tall mountain ledge and waved for me to do the same.

I was immobilized. *Trust Jesus, trust Jesus,* I repeated to myself. I put my arms out in front of me as He had done. When I did that, I sped up. It scared me to death, so I quickly tucked them behind my back, which immediately slowed me down. Jesus kept waving me toward Him. I slowly brought my arms forward again and learned how to move at a more controlled pace. *I wasn't going to fall after all.* For the first time, the fear subsided, and peace took its place.

I surveyed the ground below me. I caught sight of the Garden, stretching out as far as the eye could see. Majestic mountain peaks gave way to lush green valleys. I saw hundreds of different types of animals, making their way to and from multiple feeding grounds and watering holes. An incalculable number of lakes and streams sparkled, and on the horizon, the City of God radiated light. The praise and worship songs of the saints drifted high up into the Heavens. It was a glorious sound.

I looked down at Jesus, and He waved at me again. Slowly but surely, I made my way to Him, eventually, landing gently by His side. He smiled at me.

"See how that worked out?" He asked.

"I thought I was going to die!" I said, relieved to be standing on solid ground.

"To trust in Me when things are going well takes a small amount of trust, but to trust in Me in times of trouble requires it to grow and expand."

At that moment, I noticed how close I was to the edge. It looked like we were on the highest mountain peak in Heaven. I closed my eyes as my heart began beating fast, and fear filled my mind once again.

"Fear is one of the enemy's most popular weapons against you. When you are afraid, you must put your trust in Me." It sounded so simple but was very challenging to implement. I opened my eyes and looked at Jesus. He grabbed ahold of my hands. "Keep your eyes on me, and you will never falter." I looked deep into his rainbow-colored eyes. Peace replaced fear in an instant as I realized I was safe with Jesus.

"Be strong and courageous. Do not be frightened, and do not be dismayed, for the Lord your God is with you wherever you go." I wanted to ask Him what He meant, but before I had the chance, thunder boomed, and the mountain shook. The ridge where we were standing began to rip apart, but I was not afraid. I kept my eyes fixated on the face of Jesus as I fell down through the center of the mountain.

My alarm was going off when I woke-up. It was time to get ready for church. I could hear Rob joking with the kids at the breakfast table. My head hurt as usual; I downed a couple of Tylenol and got in the shower. We were running late, so I threw on some make-up, put my hair up, and headed out the door with my family.

The pastor had an interesting message that morning. It was all about trusting in God. I knew it was no coincidence that the sermon matched my dream from the night before. It had happened many times and didn't surprise me any longer. I knew God was always up to something. Our pastor read Romans 15:13.

"'May the God of hope fill you with all joy and peace, as you trust in Him, so that you may overflow with hope by the power of the Holy Spirit.' Psalm 84:12 says, 'O Lord of hosts, blessed is the one who trusts in You.' It's not easy trusting in God when we are going through really challenging times. The definition of trust is: A firm belief in the reliability, truth, ability, or strength of someone or something." As I listened to him speak, I confirmed that I wanted to be a person who could entirely trust and depend on the Lord.

On the drive home from church, Rob and I always enjoyed talking about what we had learned from that day's sermon.

"You are not going to believe this, but I had a dream last night about Heaven, and this time, I was flying way high up in the sky."

"How cool! Was it fun?" he asked.

"It was crazy scary at first, and I was freaking out." We both laughed. "It ended up being a lesson about trusting Jesus."

"How did it turn out?"

"By the end, I was getting the hang of it," I said.

"Maybe He's trying to tell you something."

"I don't know what that would be. I mean, I already trust Him."

Rob pulled into the driveway and helped Richard out as I unbuckled Faith from her car seat. Gavin's new black mustang was in the driveway.

"Oh, look, your brother's here." My brother had a key to our apartment. He borrowed our computer and internet as needed since he didn't have them at home. He met us outside and took Faith from my arms, tickling her until she was laughing uncontrollably.

"You missed church," I said.

"I know, I had too much homework." Gavin gave Richard a high five as we filed into our tiny apartment. He had only two months left until his graduation from the police academy and had grown into a handsome and compassionate man. Mom would have been so proud of him; I knew I was.

"How's Cameron?" I asked. I put Faith in her highchair with some peas and carrots while I started lunch for the rest of us.

"He's fine. I kind of wish he would meet someone again. Doris and Herman come over frequently to play Dominos with him. I feel sorry for the guy, you know? I don't have a lot of time to hang out with him now." Faith finished her lunch, and I put her down to play with Richard as we ate ours.

Richard had eaten his sandwich and was building something out of Legos on the floor near Faith, when Gavin said, "Oh my gosh, you would not believe what I found out today. There's this guy in the Academy who used to be a guard at the Columbia Correctional Institution in Ohio, where Jeffrey Dahmer was incarcerated."

Rob interrupted him, "Didn't he get beaten to death by another inmate about two years ago?"

"Yes, but here's the crazy part, he became a Christian in prison and helped lead other inmates to Jesus. Then it got me wondering, so I searched the internet this morning, and other infamous serial killers became Christians in prison as well." He had our full attention. "So, it seems that Tex Watson, one of the Manson family members, Westley Allen Dodd, Michael Bruce Ross, and David Berkowitz, all converted and helped spread the gospel while incarcerated."

"Wasn't David Berkowitz known as the Son of Sam or something?" I asked.

"Yes," Gavin answered, with a mouth full of spaghetti. Buddy rested his head on Gavin's knee just in a case a piece of food dropped; he would be sure to catch it.

"If you have spent your entire life murdering people and accept Jesus before you die, do you still get to go to Heaven?" Rob asked. It was a fair question. All three of us considered it carefully.

"Let's ask the expert," Gavin teased and winked at me.

"Why not?" I answered. "There's no stipulation I can think of that would keep you out of Heaven. If you accept Christ, doesn't that mean that you are just as forgiven as the rest of us?"

"I have a hard time believing that," said Rob.

"Well, I don't know, but maybe you could ask Jesus in one of your dreams." Gavin joked again.

"Well, maybe, I will." I teased and stuck my tongue out.

Suddenly, Buddy turned around, ran over to Faith and started barking loudly. I looked over to see what was going on. Faith's face was beet red.

"Hey, there's something wrong with Faith," I yelled. Everyone jumped up and ran over to her. She was choking on something, and her face was starting to turn blue.

"Oh, dear God! She's choking, do something!" I screamed. Rob was opening her mouth and trying to see what she had in there. I saw Richard back away and stand in the corner.

"I can't get it! Gavin, call 911!" Rob yelled. Gavin jumped up and ran to the phone as Rob smacked Faith on the back, attempting to dislodge whatever was in there.

"The ambulance in on their way," Gavin said.

"Oh my gosh! Oh my gosh! Get it out, Rob!" I screamed in full panic mode. Just then, I recalled my dream from last night. A soft, calm voice from inside spoke to me and asked, *Do you trust Me?*

"Dear God, please help my baby! Please help her, Lord!" I cried out loud. My entire body was shaking. It looked like Faith was starting to pass out. I had no idea how long she had been choking. Richard began to cry, and Gavin scooped him up.

"It's alright, Richard. It's okay," I heard Gavin say. I could hear sirens in the distance.

Do you trust Me? Jesus asked again. Faith was now blue, her eyes were closed, and she wasn't moving. *Not again, God. I can't lose another person close to me. Not my daughter.* A deep, dark feeling of fear and trepidation took hold of me, like a chill on a cold winter day; it settled inside my entire body, mind, and soul.

Do you trust Me, He pressed. Did I trust Him? Truth be told, I did not. My mind replayed the Bible verses from church that morning, but I pushed them away.

Gavin swung the door open as the EMTs rushed in and took over. They were able to dislodge a Lego out of Faith's throat in a matter of seconds and started performing CPR. Rob grabbed ahold of me and held tight as I watched them work on my daughter, bawling uncontrollably. I could not take my eyes off her. After a minute or two, the color started returning to her face, and a tiny trickle of hope flickered inside me. They continued CPR, loaded her onto a gurney, and rolled her towards the ambulance.

One of the EMTs asked if I would like to ride with her. All I could do was nod yes. Rob kissed my forehead and told me he'd follow behind in the car. Gavin would stay home with Richard. I climbed into the back of the ambulance and watched as they continued to work on her. She was breathing, but still unconscious. They had placed an oxygen mask over her tiny face and were hooking her up to an IV. I was crying so hard; I couldn't even ask questions. I reached out and held her tiny left foot in my hand.

Dear God, I prayed, *please do not take my baby girl. You gave her as a gift to me. I'm sorry that I do not always trust You. You took my mother and my best friend. Please, please do not take Faith as well.*

We pulled up to the hospital and piled out of the crowded ambulance. Rob must have driven like a madman because he was by my side, holding my hand in no time. The paramedics rolled the gurney through double sliding doors and told us to please stay in the waiting room and that a doctor would be with us soon. That was torturous; I wanted to be with her.

I buried my head into Rob's chest. He held me close, whispering assuring words in my ear. I tried to stop shaking but couldn't. We stood close to the doors for what seemed like an eternity. When they finally opened, a doctor with grey, thinning hair called out to us.

"Mr. and Mrs. Dunham?" he asked as he scanned the waiting room.

"Yes, doctor, that's us," Rob notified him.

"Hello. My name is Dr. Brown; I've been attending to your daughter," he began. I took a deep breath and willed him to tell me good news.

"Faith is breathing on her own at this time but remains unconscious. This is not abnormal under the circumstances; however, we are running tests to ensure that her brain is functioning normally. We are also doing some lab work and an X-ray to confirm we extracted the entire object from her throat." I let my breath out. I felt some relief, but the fact that Faith was unconscious scared me to death. I wanted to ask more questions but couldn't speak.

"As soon as we finish these tests, you can be with your daughter. I want you to know; we are doing everything we can for her and should have more information soon."

"Thank you so much, doctor," Rob said and shook his hand.

"Thank you," I managed to get out. The doctor put his hand on my arm, trying to reassure me, and then walked back through the doors separating the emergency room from the waiting room. Rob led me over to a chair and sat me down next to him. My surroundings were a blur, but I was acutely aware of the fear and anxiety that had positioned itself within me.

"She's going to be alright, Babe. She's breathing on her own. That's the most important thing right now." I know Rob was trying to reassure himself, as well.

About an hour later, a nurse came through the emergency room doors and called out our names. We stood up and hurried over to her. "Hello, come with me, please."

We walked through the automatic doors, and down a corridor past several closed curtains. The nurse pulled the fourth curtain aside and showed us into the emergency bay where Faith had been admitted. She was lying in a mobile hospital bed and hooked up to a variety of different machines. The nurse showed us which ones were recording her oxygen levels and her heart rate.

"The doctor will be with you shortly to go over the test results and lab work." She walked out and closed the curtain. Faith looked so small and helpless lying there; I started crying again.

"Oh my Gosh, Rob. Is she going to be alright?" I leaned over, kissed her forehead, and gently took ahold of her hand. I whispered to her, "Mommy and Daddy are here. I love you, Baby. You're going to be okay," my voice broke off. The curtain opened again as Dr. Brown, and the nurse walked in.

"All of her test results came back normal. It's not uncommon for someone to stay unconscious for a while after an incident like this, especially a small child. She's been through a lot. Her body and mind are most likely in recovery mode." Rob squeezed my hand. "Your quick response saved her life. You are welcome to stay here with her. We are going to keep her here until she regains consciousness, which I expect will be less than twenty-four hours. I'll be back in a while to check on her. Please try and get some rest."

The nurse read the data from the machines and wrote her findings on a sheet of paper. She took Faith's vitals and recorded them as well. She asked us if we needed anything and made sure we knew where the call button was, smiled and left us alone.

I tried to calm down, but until she was awake and at home with us again, I remained on high alert. I kept my eyes on her for hours, jumping every time an alarm or unusual beep went off on one of the machines. Nurses would wander in and out every few hours, checking her IV bag and vitals. The only time Rob left my side was when he went out to call Gavin.

It was around three in the morning when Faith finally started stirring. Rob had fallen asleep, but at the sound of the commotion, woke immediately. I called for a nurse as Faith opened her eyes, reached for her oxygen tubes, and started yanking at them. My poor baby was frightened and disoriented, but she was *awake*.

The nurse hurried in. I kept my hand on Faith's arm and the top of her head, trying my best to reassure her. She reached for me and started to cry. I bent down so she could wrap her little arms around my neck as the doctor on call came in to check her pupils and reflexes. *Thank you, Jesus,* my heart cried out. The nurse administered something into her IV line. Almost immediately, Faith closed her eyes, and it looked like she was unconscious again.

The nurse could see the panic on our faces and said, "It's alright, I gave her medication to help calm her down, so she can sleep through the night." The doctor explained how they wanted to keep her under observation until tomorrow.

I sat back down next to Faith's bed as Rob paced the room. Instinctively I knew it was going to be a long night. Rob finally wore himself out and sat down next to me. He held my hand and coaxed me to lay my head on his shoulder. My determination to stay awake lost its battle to fatigue, and I fell into a dreamless sleep.

CHAPTER 17
THE SNAKE

Snakes. I hated them. My mom had told me a story once when I was little about a frog and a snake. A venomous snake approached a fast-moving riverbank, wondering how he was going to get across. He watched as a frog hopped great distances between rocks, crossing the river to his side with ease. The snake slowly approached the frog and asked if he could crawl on the frog's back and hitch a ride to the other side.

The frog protested and said to the snake, "I'm not giving you a lift. You are my enemy. As soon as we get to the other side, you'll bite me, and I will certainly die."

"Don't be silly," the snake replied. "Surely, if you help me, I will not bite you."

The frog thought long and hard about it. "Alright then, if you promise not to harm me, I will help you."

"I promise," the snake assured the frog.

So, the snake climbed onto his back, and the frog hopped to the other side of the river. Just as they landed on the opposite bank, the snake drove his venomous fangs into the frog's back.

In shock, the frog asked, "Why did you bite me when you promised that you wouldn't? I helped you, and now I shall indeed die."

The snake replied, "Because you see, dear frog, I am a snake, it's in my nature to bite you." And with that, the snake slid off the dying frog's back and slithered away.

Life is like a snake, sometimes. It convinces you that everything is going to be okay. You have a good life, a good future. It makes assurances and promises. Sometimes the frog escapes the snake unharmed, but most of the time, it doesn't.

Faith was discharged from the hospital the day after her incident, and within an hour, was running around the house as if nothing had happened. I was not as fortunate. A dark cloud of depression developed over me, and no matter how hard I tried, I could not shake it. I wondered how I could go from feeling normal to feeling so deeply depressed.

It began with anxiety, and that anxiety turned into fear. I thought about everything that had gone wrong and everything that could go wrong. The loss of control was overwhelming and it paralyzed me. For weeks, I struggled to get out of bed. I stopped showering and refused to go to church or talk with friends. Nothing tasted good so I barely ate. My clothes hung loosely around my already small frame. Rob was working full-time, playing the part of father and mother. At first, he was very patient with me. I'm sure he thought maybe if given a little time, I would recover, and everything would go back to the way it was before the event.

Then, his patience turned into frustration. His frustration turned into anger and resentment. The angrier he got, the more I withdrew. Doris, Herman, and Gavin all did their best to help when Rob was at work. I could feel their patience with me dwindling as well. Everyone suggested I see a counselor, but I refused. All I wanted to do was sleep.

It didn't make any sense to anyone why this was happening, and quite frankly, it didn't make sense to me, either. Faith was healthy and Richard was thriving. So, why was I so depressed? Why couldn't I shake this unbearable feeling of despair and fear? My family needed me. Shame and guilt were an ever-present reminder of how I was failing them. The tension between Rob and I worsened as time went on.

Terrible thoughts entered into my mind. *"You are a failure. Everyone would be better off without you. Give up."* I hated to admit it, but I didn't feel like I could handle life anymore. *What horrible things were in store for me in the future?* I started getting paranoid that bad things would continue to happen to the people I loved. I would insist that Rob call me as soon as he got to work safe every morning. Doris caught a cold and I was convinced she was going to develop pneumonia and die. I knew I was being irrational, but I couldn't help it.

One night, as we lay in bed, I began to weep softly. Rob had witnessed this occurrence on many occasions over the last two months. In the beginning, he had done his best to comfort me, but that night, his heart hardened, and I felt like he was giving up on me. I couldn't blame him; I was giving up on myself.

"Alina, what is the problem?" he said as he rolled toward me with a heavy sigh. "I feel like you aren't even trying. I don't know how to help you. I've suggested counseling and medication. You won't even make the smallest effort. Do you really want Faith and Richard to grow up seeing you like this?"

I didn't have any answers for him. Rob gave me several minutes to reply, but when I didn't, he rolled back over on his side and faced away from me.

I climbed out of bed and went into the living room. I got down on my hands and knees and prayed for the first time in months. It was only four words: *Please, God, help me.* I collapsed to the floor and cried myself to sleep.

I dreamt I was standing at the edge of a fast-flowing river. A cool breeze stirred up dandelion seeds in the grass nearby and sent them drifting up into the air and a symphony of cicadas made it sound like someone was playing the maracas and a family of possums scurried up a tree to my right. I watched in awe as a deer and tiger drank together in harmony several feet away.

I noticed that the feelings of fear and depression were gone entirely. The weight of sadness and anxiety that I had experienced for months dissipated, and peace, joy, and hope replaced it. I sighed with relief.

I felt His presence before seeing Him. I scanned the horizon, finally catching a glimpse of Him sitting under a large Ponderosa Pine tree. He motioned for me to come near. My soul rejoiced at the sight of Him, but when I tried to take a step, I couldn't.

I looked down and was stunned to see a heavy chain wrapped

tightly around my ankles and wrists. I was desperate to get to Jesus, but my movements were limited. I shuffled my feet the best I could, but the uneven ground made it impossible to make any progress without falling on my face. I thought about getting down on my hands and knees so I could crawl to Him; however, the chains around my wrists were too tight. I closed my eyes, trying to work out the problem in my head.

When I opened them, I saw a rabbit hopping across the grassy garden floor. The bunny stopped and looked up at me for a moment, then continued on its way. That gave me an idea. I carefully balanced my weight evenly and jumped with both feet. I made a little headway, so I tried it again. The progress was slow and tedious. I fell over half a dozen times, but when I looked up at Jesus, He just smiled, and encouraged me to keep going. After what seemed like an eternity, I finally reached Him.

"You did it, Daughter!" Jesus exclaimed and helped me sit down next to Him.

"Jesus, why do I have chains around my ankles and wrists? I can hardly move," I said, out of breath and exhausted from the exertion.

"These are the chains of sin and disobedience." He answered with sadness. He gently took hold of one of the links.

"I don't understand, Lord. What have I done that was disobedient?" I asked, confused. "I have tried to live a good life. I know I have been depressed lately, but I couldn't seem to shake it."

"I want to tell you a story about a snake," He responded.

"Yes, I have heard this story. The snake and the frog," I replied.

"No, this is the *true* story of Adam and Eve, my first human creations. Close your eyes," He said and gently placed His hand over my face. "Now open them."

When I did so, I was surprised to see a naked man and woman walking around, tending to the Garden. An illuminating and transfiguring light enswathed them both. In the middle of the Garden stood a tree I had never seen before. It was a very interesting looking tree. Its leaves were pink, and it had the most delectable fruit I had ever seen hanging from its branches. The scent filled my nostrils and licked my lips.

Jesus began narrating, "What you see here in the middle of the Garden is the Tree of Knowledge of Good and Evil. I told Adam and Eve, You may eat of all that I have created in the Garden except you shall not eat of the Tree of Knowledge of Good and Evil lest you die." I thought back to the book of Genesis and was confused because Adam and Eve did not die after eating the fruit. They went on to have children and live for hundreds of years.

Jesus answered my unspoken question by saying, "I was not only referring to physical death in this instance but spiritual death, as well. Sin and disobedience cause spiritual death and separation from God. Failure to heed and obey the Word of God is the cause of every single sin, and it all started here in the Garden with Adam and Eve." Just then, I witnessed a snake drop down from one of the branches of the forbidden tree. It hung at eye level with Eve. The snake began speaking to her as Adam stood close by, listening.

The snake said to Eve, "Didn't God say you may eat of every tree in the Garden?"

Jesus continued explaining, "The serpent was subtler than any beast of the field, which the Lord had made. He had the quickness of sight, swiftness in motion, intelligence and adaptiveness. Before the fall, beasts of the field were fully able to communicate with Adam and Eve. The snake itself was not evil. Satan had full knowledge of this reptile's abilities and chose it specifically when he entered into the snake to deceive man." I was captivated by this narration and watched the book of Genesis play out before me.

Then Eve spoke to the snake, "We may eat of the fruit of the trees of the Garden, but God said we shall not eat of this tree lest we surely die."

"You shall not surely *die*," retorted the lying snake. "For the day you shall eat of it, your eyes will be opened, and you shall be like God."

Jesus continued by saying, "This serpent's statement was the first proclamation of an outright denial of the Word of God." I wondered why God would even allow such a temptation if He knew all things, and why didn't He know Eve and Adam would fail this test?

"Tests are essential to spiritual development," Jesus stated as He answered my unspoken question again. "And free will is the bedrock on which mankind was created."

Jesus looked at me and said, "Pride, disobedience, and lack of trust lead to spiritual wreckage. It was not the fruit itself that caused the fall of Adam, Eve, and the rest of humanity, but the failure to obey and trust the Word of God."

Eve paused for a moment then plucked one of the delicious-looking

tree. She lifted it to her nose and closed her eyes, taking

vatering smell. I wanted to yell at her, "Don't do it!" Eve

opened her mouth and took a bite of the fruit, then handed it to Adam, who also partook of it. After Adam shared in eating the fruit from the Tree of Knowledge of Good and Evil, the snake dropped to the ground and slithered off. The light of purity that emanated from Adam and Eve went out, and they looked at each other in fear. Adam dropped the fruit to the ground, and they took off running.

"Fear was the first reaction of the fallen man. They ran to hide, but you can never conceal yourself from Me," Jesus said.

I started sobbing. I couldn't help it. The full effect of what I witnessed was utterly overwhelming. Adam and Eve had ruined it for us all. Jesus reached out and pulled up the garment that exposed the scars on his wrist.

"Do not cry, Child. I had a plan for this all along. Satan used a woman to attempt to bring down humanity, but I would use a woman to redeem you. Her name was Mary, and these scars are that redemption. The answer to the dilemma of the human race is Me, Jesus Christ, through my crucifixion."

I felt a sudden sadness as I realized what I had done. "Not only did I fail to trust You, Jesus, but I also blamed You for the pain in my life. I see that now." Just then, the chains that bound my ankles and wrists fell to the ground in a heap, and I was free.

The sound of thunder exploded overhead, and the ground fiercely shook. The floor of Heaven fractured, cracked open, and devoured me in a single gulp.

I sat straight up, still on the floor in the living room where I had fallen asleep and grabbed my head between my hands. It was dark out, and everyone was still sleeping. I looked at the clock; It was only four in the morning.

I waited for the familiar cloud of depression to show its ugly face, but much like the chains, I was free of it. I tiptoed into my bedroom and grabbed my notebooks. I recorded the details of my dream and wrote down a prayer of thanksgiving for God's delivery from the shackles of despair.

When I finished, I quietly opened the door to the kids' room and peeked in. They were fast asleep. Gratefulness and hope replaced the spaces where sadness and hopelessness had lived for far too long. I walked into the kitchen to start some coffee and looked around. I know Rob had tried to keep up on things, but the apartment was a mess. I started cleaning the kitchen from top to bottom. I even rearranged the drawers and wiped out the cabinets. The kitchen was spotless in no time.

Rob would be up soon, so I made him a gourmet breakfast. I had a lot of making up to do. Embarrassment and shame tried to work its way into my heart. I couldn't help but wonder if Rob would forgive me. Doubt joined in and tempted to derail me once more. I closed my eyes and concentrated on what I had learned last night in my dream. *Follow the word of God and trust His promises.* Several verses entered my mind about God's good plan for my life. Then I heard His voice whisper, *"Do you trust Me?"*

"Yes, I trust You!" I responded, and I knew in my heart that it was true. Joy and peace broke through, pushing out the lingering remnants of doubt and fear. It was so powerful that I shivered, and my knees almost gave out.

An hour later, I heard footsteps coming down the hallway. I said a quick prayer for restoration in my marriage and held my breath.

Rob stopped in his tracks when he saw me at the table. He eyed the big breakfast sitting in front of me and scanned the clean kitchen.

"I'm so sorry, Rob," I began. "I was a mess. I couldn't. . ."

"You're better!" he interrupted.

I smiled at him, "Yes."

"Oh, thank, God!" He said and rushed over to me. "I knew you could do it." He pulled me into his arms.

"Jesus did it," I whispered.

"I was so scared, Alina. I didn't know how to help you. I thought I had lost you." Rob's voice broke, and I heard him cry for the very first time. The last bit of doubt melted away as we held each other close.

God had gone to great lengths to pursue me. He had seen me through the toughest of times. He loved me so much that He visited me in my dreams. I would never doubt Him again.

CHAPTER 18
AN EARLY ARRIVAL

For a year and a half, my cousin and I communicated via letter and phone several times a month. Along with those letters, I would send pictures of Richard and the family. Ryan was only allowed one fifteen-minute call a week. We laughed and cried together, sharing stories of our childhood along with current events. Richard was always encouraged to talk to his dad on the phone but, being so young and shy, he would only hold the phone up to his ear and listen intently, never saying a word.

One day, Richard asked some very grown-up questions, "Aunt Nia, who is my dad?"

"His name is Ryan. He is the one who calls and writes you letters, remember?" I asked. "And you will get to meet him very soon."

"Will he live here with us?" Richard cocked his head to the side in a curious manner.

"Yes, for a while, he will live with us so the two of you can get to know each other."

"Where is he? How come he doesn't live with us now?" he asked, pushing his toy car around on the floor. I looked over at Rob, motioning for some help with answering.

"Richard, he has been far away," Rob said. "He is trying to get to us, but it takes time." He looked over at me and shrugged his shoulders.

"Momma said he's in jail cause he's bad."

Uh oh, I thought before trying to explain. "Well, Richard, Momma was telling you part of the truth. Yes, your dad is in jail because he did some bad things, not because he's a bad person."

"Am I going to jail?" he asked while playing with his new Spiderman action figure.

"What? No! Why do you think that?" I asked.

"Momma said I'm a bad boy. She said I'm going to grow up and be like daddy." He hesitated for a moment then added, "And Faith got sick cause she ate my Lego." My heart sunk. What a terrible thing for his mom to say to him. And the incident with Faith had happened over a year ago by this point. Had Richard been blaming himself all this time?

I knelt next to him and lifted his head so he would look me in the eyes. "Richard, first, you are a very good boy. Your momma should not have said that to you. Second, Faith was younger then and was going through a phase where she put everything in her mouth. That was not your fault, and little boys and girls don't go to jail. We love you, Richard. Buddy loves you; Faith loves you, and your daddy loves you. You are not a bad boy." I really emphasized that last point. Oh the things people say to their children. I would never understand it.

"Ok," he said. "Can I have some chocolate milk?"

"Yes," I said. "Of course, you can!" I leaned over and wrapped him in a big hug. He started wiggling to get free, so I tickled him until he was laughing hysterically. He had been through so much and still had a rough road ahead of him. It wouldn't be easy adjusting to a new life with his father, and one day, he would have to face the fact that his mother abandoned him.

Two months later, there was a knock at the door. Richard was at school, and Faith had been put down for a nap. When I answered, I was surprised to see Ryan standing there.

He looked a little older than his mugshot and was wearing clothes two sizes too big for him. He was holding a single shopping bag containing his personal items and must have read the shocked look on my face.

"I'm so sorry to surprise you like this, Alina. I tried calling a few days ago when they notified me that I would be released a couple months early due to overcrowding. I rode a bus here." He looked down, flushing with embarrassment. "I didn't know where else to go."

I snapped out of it and welcomed him properly. "Oh my gosh! I'm so sorry, I was just surprised! I can't believe it's really you! Please don't apologize; come in, come in!" We embraced, and I led him into the house. "Richard is still at school."

"I'm so excited!" Ryan said, almost shouting. "I know it may be uncomfortable at first, but still, I can't wait to see him." It was uncanny to see how much he resembled our family. Ryan and Gavin had similar chins, and there was something familiar about the shape of his eyes. It had been hard to tell from his mugshot, but seeing him in person, I was sure he was my cousin. I led him to the kitchen table and poured him a glass of water.

"Are you hungry? I have chicken breasts in the oven, and I'm making a side salad for lunch. Does that sound good?"

"You cannot believe how good that sounds. The food in prison is terrible. I lost a lot of weight, especially these last few years." He was so skinny; I could see his collarbones protruding.

"Well, we will have to put some weight on you then." We chit-chatted as I fixed lunch. Ryan was straightforward and an easy conversationalist. By the time we got done cleaning up the kitchen, Faith was waking from her nap.

"She's a little shy around strangers," I warned him. "She adores Richard though." I smiled at the thought of them and how quickly they had bonded with each other almost two years ago when he came to live with us.

Faith surprised me. She took to Ryan almost immediately. He played with her on the floor as we continued to get to know each other without the limitations of letters and fifteen-minute phone calls. When it was time to pick up Richard from school, I suggested Ryan stay behind so they could have their first meeting at the house, and he agreed.

On the drive home, I explained to Richard that he was about to meet someone very special.

"Are you talking about my daddy?" he asked curiously. *What a smart boy*, I thought and beamed with pride. *Ryan will be so proud of him.*

"Yes, Honey, I'm talking about your daddy."

He was silent for a few minutes then asked, "Is he going to take me away, so I don't see you anymore?" I knew it was only a matter of time before he asked this question. Richard was becoming more and more attached to us. I wasn't sure what Ryan's plans were.

"We love you, Richard, and we will always be a part of your life." This was the best answer I could give him right now. My response seemed to suffice because he didn't ask any additional questions.

Ryan greeted us at the door. I could tell he was excited and nervous. At first, Richard hid behind my legs, matching his dad's nerves.

"Hi there, little man," Ryan said and bent down so he could be at eye level with him. "Wow, you are so tall and handsome." Richard refused to move from behind me and had latched on to my legs like a parasite. Understanding the situation, Ryan stood up and slowly backed away, giving us some room so we could enter the house.

I put Faith on the floor, and she surprised me again. She reached her arms up for Ryan and said, "Hold me."

Ryan obliged and bent down to pick her up. This behavior surprised Richard as well. He moved out from behind me, and slowly inched toward his favorite spot on the floor where his toy cars lay. Ryan was very patient with the process. He didn't pressure Richard, but instead, played with Faith, inviting Richard to join them every so often. Richard curiously watched his dad interact with Faith. Every now and again, Richard would smile or giggle at something Faith said or did.

After a couple of hours, Ryan stood up and informed me that he had to meet with his parole officer by five.

"Do you need a ride?" I asked.

"No, thank you. I have the bus schedule and plan to use that as often as possible."

"Our sofa folds out into a couch and is very comfortable. I'll warm your dinner up for you when you get back." I could tell he felt awkward, and I instinctively knew why. "Ryan, you are welcome to stay here until you get back on your feet." We had already discussed it in our letters, but I knew he felt like a burden. "Seriously, Ryan, it's no big deal," I reassured him.

"I'm so embarrassed," he said and held his head down. In that instant, he reminded me of his son. There he was, with nothing to offer and totally dependent on someone else. I couldn't imagine how humbling that must feel.

"Somehow, at some point, I will repay you, Cousin." He looked up at me, and his eyes glistened with tears.

"I know, Ryan. I'm glad you're here." He left the house for his meeting, and I started dinner. Rob would be home from work soon, but I felt like I needed to tell him about Ryan's early arrival. I dialed his work number.

"You are not going to believe who showed up today." I tried to keep my voice down so Richard couldn't hear me.

"Who?" Rob asked.

"Ryan."

"Really? I thought he wasn't getting out for another couple of months."

"Me too, but he was released early. I wanted to give you a head's up before you got home," I said.

"Well, . . . what do you think?" Rob asked me.

"He looks a lot like Gavin. He's sweet and very grateful. Faith warmed up to him immediately."

"Wow, that's surprising! How did Richard respond?"

He's keeping his distance right now. It can't be easy for the little guy."

"For either of them," Rob added. "Thanks for letting me know. I'll see you soon. Love you."

"Love you."

The following week, Richard finally started interacting with his dad. Ryan played games with him on the floor and threw the baseball to him at the park. Before long, he was tucking Richard in at the end of the day; however, I was always summoned in to say a good-night prayer. Ryan would bow his head and listen to me as I thanked the Lord for His protection and blessings. I wasn't sure if Ryan had a relationship with Jesus or not, but I was about to find out soon enough.

Sunday morning rolled around, and it was time for church. Everyone was rushing, getting ready. Ryan was pacing throughout the house, acting very skittish for some reason.

"Hey, are you feeling alright?" I asked him while putting on my shoes.

"Yes, I'm fine but..." He paused for a second, then continued. "I have only been to church once. Are you sure God isn't going to strike me down with a bolt of lightning? I don't want the church to catch on fire and burn down." He said it with such a serious look on his face that I couldn't help myself; I started laughing hysterically. Then Rob began to laugh, which made me laugh harder. Faith giggled like she was in on the joke, and then Richard started laughing at Faith. Ryan looked at Faith and Richard; then, he started cracking up. We laughed so hard at the thought of the church burning down because of Ryan that tears rolled down our cheeks, and my stomach started cramping. I hadn't laughed that hard in a long time.

"Well, at least we will all die together as a family," Rob managed to get out in between fits. Ryan's nerves calmed, and we all loaded into the car.

We met up with Cameron, Gavin, Doris, and Herman at church and filled up an entire pew. I looked down the row at our family and shook my head in disbelief. I remembered when I was twelve years old and wanted nothing more than to be surrounded by a large family. I wished Mom could have been here to see this. She was probably smiling at us from Heaven, doing a little dance and commenting in a French accent.

The pastor read from Matthew 18:12: "What do you think? If a man has a hundred sheep and one of them has gone astray, does he not leave the ninety-nine and go into the mountains to seek that which has gone astray? And if he finds it, verily I say unto you, he rejoices more over that one sheep than over the ninety-nine that never went astray. Even so, it is not the will of my Father which is in Heaven that one of these little ones should perish." I had never heard of the story of the lost sheep. I thought about God's pursuit of me through my dreams and our first encounter at camp when I was twelve.

The pastor continued explaining the verse. "Your Salvation came at a great price; therefore, all who accept that Salvation become the property of God the Father. This verse describes the extensive efforts the Lord will go to for the lost."

At the end of the service, Pastor announced that the church was going to start an outreach program.

"Every Saturday afternoon, we will be feeding and ministering to the homeless." He encouraged church members to volunteer at least one Saturday a month. This particular ministry really spoke to me. Since meeting Cameron, I'd always had a special place in my heart for the homeless. I printed my name and phone number on the volunteer sheet in the foyer and was signed up to help the following Saturday.

Cameron hugged me and said, "I knew you would be the first one to volunteer. They are blessed to have you, Alina."

"Thanks, Cameron." I gave him a quick hug and headed out to the car with my family. Ryan was very quiet on the ride home. I had a feeling he was digesting what the pastor had said at church. Hopefully, I could find the right time to answer any questions he might have. I smiled as I thought of how patient Amy had been with me all those years ago.

"I'm so excited to help volunteer," I said, breaking the silence. "Ryan, do you mind helping Rob with the kids for a few hours next Saturday?"

"Of course not. I'd love to help. I'm also going to start looking for a job first thing Monday morning."

"Department of Child Protective Services will be at the house Tuesday to check on things and start the reunification process," I reminded him.

"I'll do whatever they need me to do," he reassured us. He looked over at Richard and said, "Daddy's going to get a job." He put his hand up for Richard to high-five him. Faith, sitting next to him, was the first to slap his hand. Her daddy taught her that. Richard, not wanting to be left out, leaned over and high-fived Ryan, too.

That evening, after everyone had gone to sleep, Ryan and I stayed up late talking. Sure enough, when the house was quiet, he asked several questions.

"Do you think God really chases us?" he asked. "I mean, what if we have done terrible things? It's hard to believe that God loves me. I'm a nobody."

"I can see how difficult it may be for you to believe that God loves you." I wanted so badly to say the right things to Ryan. However, I had never witnessed to anyone before. What could I say that would convince Ryan that Jesus wants a relationship with him? How could I assure him that if we ask Jesus to forgive us for our sins, He does?

Then, a voice, gentle as a breeze, spoke to me. "Hold on one second," I said. I tiptoed into my bedroom and quietly gathered all my notebooks.

I sat down next to him. "Ryan, I have only shown these notebooks to one person in my life and have only told a few people about their existence. These three notebooks here are prayers that I have written down since I was a teenager. And these three are the recordings of God's great pursuit of me. Since I was twelve, I have been dreaming of Heaven and have had almost a hundred encounters with Jesus. I've seen fantastic beauty and felt a love so strong, that is not of this Earth. It's challenging even to find the words to describe it accurately," I explained. "Every time, just as my dreams are coming to an end, there's loud booming thunder, an earthquake, the ground cracks open and I fall through it. I always wake-up with a splitting headache.

"Why do you get a headache every time?" he asked, as he opened one of the notebooks.

"I've been trying to figure that out for a long time. I think it's because Jesus is so holy and righteous, and Heaven is so magnificent and incredible; our Earthly bodies can't physically handle it. I also think that is why my dreams are so short in duration.

We spent hours going through the notebooks. Ryan was mesmerized by the detailed descriptions. As expected, he had dozens of questions. Some I could answer, and some I could not. Ryan found it fascinating how my prayers and dreams matched up perfectly. I used the same analogy that Amy had used. I told him that we are dirty in the sight of God and that we needed to get cleaned up. I explained that when Jesus died on the cross, our sins—past, present, and future— were forgiven. All we had to do was believe in Him and ask Him to be our Lord and Savior.

"I've always wondered why God allows so much pain and suffering. But now, reading these notebooks, I can see connections that were never apparent before. These are amazing; I feel so honored that you would share them with me. Do you think God has a purpose for me?"

"Of course, He does, Ryan!" I exclaimed.

"Have you found your purpose yet?" he asked.

"At first, I thought it had something to do with you and Richard, but now I believe God may have something else in mind. That's why I signed up at church to help with their outreach program."

I told him the story of Cameron and how he came to be in our lives. "Since then, I've always wanted to help the less fortunate. No matter what, I'm not giving up. One of these days, I will figure out what God's purpose is for my life. There must be something important I am meant to do." I smiled at him.

In the early morning hours, with tears of joy running down our faces, I led Ryan to Christ. It was one of the most extraordinary moments of my life.

CHAPTER 19
A GOOD PLAN

Saturday arrived, and it was time to volunteer at church. I had to admit, I was a little nervous. I started off helping in the kitchen by mashing a giant pot of potatoes. I helped set up tables and chairs and transported giant containers of meatloaf, mashed potatoes, green salad, and brownies to the main serving table.

Most of the women volunteering were quite a bit older than me, except for one. She was at least six feet tall with blonde hair and gorgeous blue eyes. When she entered the room, everyone stopped what they were doing and looked. Her name was Victoria, and the elegance of her name matched her demeanor perfectly. She started a conversation with me in the kitchen, and I discovered her inner beauty was just as attractive. She was single, had just finished getting her master's degree from Pepperdine University, and had recently returned to Arizona to take care of her ailing parents.

When it was time to serve the food, I found Victoria to be genuine and kind-hearted to every single person. She was outgoing and always seemed to know what to say to break the ice. It was a little more challenging for me. It's not that I didn't want to communicate with those I was serving, but I had never learned how to converse easily with others, especially people I didn't know. Making small talk with strangers had never been my forte. I carefully observed and listened to her, desperately wanting to learn this critical skill. I did my very best, smiling at each person as I served them a scoop of mashed potatoes. Toward the end, I was even able to add, "How are you today?" or "God bless you."

Victoria and I had the job of wiping and stacking the tables and chairs. We carried them to a small storage area in the back of the church. It was hard work, but we had a great time getting to know each other. She was a deep thinker like me and had a wonderful sense of humor. She seemed to enjoy my company, as well. I invited her over for dinner that night, and she accepted. I explained the living situation with my cousin and nephew.

"You are a saint!" Victoria declared.

"Thank you! You are too! Coming home to take care of your parents right after graduating from college can't be easy, either," I responded.

"Then, we'll be sister saints!" She tossed her head back and laughed, her blonde hair swaying side to side. It almost touched her waist. "Saint Victoria and Saint Alina!" I knew right then and there that Victoria and I were going to be best friends.

Every Saturday for over a year, we volunteered at church, feeding the homeless, showing them compassion and love. My ability to interact with them improved tremendously. I had Victoria to thank for that. I learned their names and got to know their personalities. Then, after a long day of volunteering, Victoria would join us for dinner. Sometimes we included Cameron, Doris, Herman, and my brother. It was a tight fit with so many people crammed into our tiny apartment, but we always had fun telling stories and playing Dominoes. Ryan was the reigning champ and always the one to beat. We laughed and gave each other a hard time. Doris would always bring over a popular dessert, and Cameron would bring one of his favorite dishes.

"I guess all those hours of playing Dominos in prison paid off," Ryan would joke.

For a while, we assumed that Victoria and Gavin would end up dating each other, but for whatever reason, that never happened. It had been a year since Ryan's release, and his bond with Richard had grown very strong. He was an incredible father to his son, and Richard copied everything his dad did. Ryan got a job at the hardware store where Cameron had become the manager. The family court judge also ordered Ryan to take parenting and self-improvement classes. Ryan was attending the last one and well on his way to gaining full custody of his son. Everyone was incredibly busy but happy and thriving.

Career-wise, I was still trying to figure out what I wanted to do with my life. Because Faith was in school part-time, volunteering Saturdays at the church was great but not enough to fulfill me.

Victoria's father had passed away six months ago, and her mother joined him two months later. It was a tough time for her, losing both parents so close together. I did my best to help her get through it. She was at a crossroads in her life, as well. Victoria's degree was in business and finance, but she had a heart for helping others.

One Saturday night after dinner, Victoria and I were enjoying some quiet time on the patio and started talking about helping the homeless on a larger scale.

"I feel like there is so much more we could be doing to help those in need," I said.

"I agree. I've been thinking about it a lot lately now that my parents are gone," she said with a sigh.

"What if we started our own outreach program?" I suggested. "We could help line-up job interviews and find people willing to donate appropriate work attire. We could also help connect them with other non-profit organizations in town. You have a business degree and could research grants and funding," I suggested.

"And you know all the local resources," she added.

We talked for hours, brainstorming ways to help the less fortunate in our area.

"Let's do it!" she exclaimed and jumped up.

"I'm in!" I jumped up, too, sharing her enthusiasm. We hugged each other, excited about our new adventure. I could barely sleep that night. When I told Rob about it the next day, he was a little hesitant.

"I understand what you want to do, Honey, and I admire it. You have such a giving heart, but don't you think it's a little dangerous?" He saw the disappointment on my face, leaned over and kissed my cheek. "I'm just worried about your safety is all."

"What if I promise that Victoria and I will always stay together? We won't ever go out or meet with anyone alone."

Rob considered it. He knew by the determined look on my face that I had my mind set on it.

"You promise?" he asked.

"I promise."

"Alright, then."

I thanked him with a kiss.

Faith and Richard were working on a five-hundred-piece puzzle. Faith asked me to help her; I obliged and sat down at the table to spend some quality time with them. Faith and Richard were growing up too fast.

Ryan came into the kitchen and said, "Hey, what's all the excitement about?" I told him about our new idea. He shared in my enthusiasm but also echoed Rob's concerns.

"I've got some good news myself," Ryan said, smiling from ear to ear. "I found an affordable apartment and have saved enough for a deposit. The court approved it, so I'll be getting out of your hair at the end of the month." He was ecstatic, but truth be told, I felt a little sad. I had gotten used to having him and Richard around. However, they were ready to start their life together, and I was happy for them.

"I'm so excited for you, Ryan, but I'm going to miss our late-night pow-wows." At least once a week, Ryan, Gavin, and I would stay up late, make popcorn, and talk about topics we found interesting or engaging. It had become a family tradition.

"There's no reason why we can't still do that. I appreciate you both so much. I could not have done any of this without you two," Ryan added. "My life is forever changed because of your generosity and kindness. I promise, Alina, if there is ever a way I can pay you back, I will."

"We are family. Family is there for each other, no matter what," I reassured him.

Rob agreed. "It has been a pleasure, Ryan." Rob and Ryan had become best friends. They often golfed together and watched sports on television.

Gavin had also developed a close relationship with Ryan. After becoming a police officer, he frequently saw the ugliest side of society. Getting to know Ryan had given Gavin hope that people can make changes in their lives. Having a little confidence in humanity was exactly what he needed. Ryan was able to give Gavin insight into what factors can cause people to go off-track, as well as what motivates people to get the help they need.

For several months, Victoria and I worked on our business model for our outreach. While I developed relationships with community resource agencies and other non-profit organizations, Victoria put her business degree to work and applied for 501C3 status to turn Eternal Life Missions into an official non-profit organization.

We met with the director of El Modena Emergency and Transitional Shelter. They were willing to allow people who weren't staying at their facilities to use the shower if needed. They also agreed to give priority housing in their transitional shelter to anyone who found steady employment. They would then work closely with that person, in hopes of moving them into affordable, permanent housing.

Herman and Doris agreed to assist with transportation to interviews and would purchase bus passes for those who found employment. We still needed to figure out a few more logistics, but things were progressing quickly.

One day as we were finishing up a meeting with our local bank, I fell very ill. I was so sick that within a few days, Rob made me see our family doctor. He confirmed I had contracted a virus that was making its rounds. For days, I suffered from a high fever, chills, and nausea. I was weak and had a constant, painful headache. Night four of my illness, I had a dream that would change the entire focus of Eternal Life Missions.

I dreamt I was in a large room surrounded by four white walls. I did not recognize the location; I had never been to this place before. There was an altar in front of me. It was made of gold and had a statue of two angels, one on each end. Their wings pointed forward, and their heads bowed in reverence. It was approximately four feet high and six feet long. There were words engraved on the base of the altar, but they were in a language I did not recognize. It was one of the most beautiful things I had ever seen. In the center of the alter, a fire was burning brightly enough to light the entire room. The flames burned continually and were as high as my shoulders. Other than the alter, the room was empty except for two doors; one on the left and one on the right. Suddenly, Jesus appeared before me.

"Where am I?" I asked Him.

"Daughter, that is of no concern at this time. The question you should be asking is, where are you going?" He answered with a firmness that made me a little nervous. "It is written man shall not live on bread alone but by every word that proceeds out of the mouth of God."

"I don't understand, Lord," I said, anxiety slowly creeping in. I was confused. *Have I disappointed the Lord?* I wondered. *Why did He sound so serious?* I felt like I was in the principal's office, about to get in big trouble.

He continued, "Your plans for helping the homeless are honorable and Scriptural. Truly I say to you, whatever you did for one of the least of these, you did for Me. However, you are missing the most important piece of the puzzle. People are in need of the living Word of God. For the Word of God is alive and active. It's sharper than any double-edged sword. It penetrates even to dividing soul and spirit, joints and marrow; it judges the thoughts and the attitudes of the heart."

I wanted to ask questions, but Jesus continued. "I have given you a special gift. You have visited My City and Gardens many times. We have spent countless hours together, but I am a fair and just God. My judgment is eternal and final. Those whose names are not found written in the book of life will be thrown into the lake of fire and eternally separated from Me. It is time for you to witness what happens to those who refuse to believe in Me, and do not seek forgiveness for their sins."

With that, He pointed at me, and I watched Him use His finger to draw a circle in the air around my entire body. I noticed a translucent material, transparent as glass but hard as stone, encompass me. I reached out and felt a solid barrier. I found myself trapped inside a giant glass bubble. It began floating a couple of feet off the floor. Jesus walked toward the door on my left, and my translucent home floated towards it. The door had no handle, only a giant lock with a keyhole. Jesus pulled out a key and unlocked the door.

"Come and see." It was pitch black on the other side, and I immediately felt frightened. "Do not be afraid, Daughter, you are protected by My mighty hand." The bubble moved me into the darkness; the door immediately shut behind me, and I heard the lock click loudly.

"No, no, no, no!" I yelled. I didn't want to go further into the darkness. The fear I felt hearing the door click behind me was indescribable. It didn't matter if my eyes were opened or closed, the darkness was not only outside of me but inside of me, as well. I became acutely aware of the temperature change when I saw my breath. It was bone-deep cold. I shivered uncontrollably, and my toes and finger went numb.

Still, it was nothing compared to what I experienced next. Every good thing, every bit of love, joy, goodness, kindness, gratitude, hope, and peace evaporated immediately upon entering this dark realm. Everything I knew about life; relationships, love, decency, graciousness, fascination, excitement, compassion, and humanity was gone. So was any and everything that had to do with God. I searched deep in my soul for the still, small voice, but there was nothing. Exclusion from the Lord wrecked my soul and filled it with despair and rejection. I felt as though I had been banished to the farthest planet in the galaxy, so far from the sun's light that the remoteness caused shivers to run through my spine and penetrated my very being. The isolation from everything and everyone good made me sick to my stomach and I wanted nothing more than to wake from this nightmare.

I did not want to be here. I turned my head and looked for the door, but it was pitch black, and I couldn't see anything. I had never been afraid of the dark before, but this was entirely different. I stuck my arms out and pushed on the glass-like surface with all my strength. I pounded on it and yelled again for help, but it floated forward, driven by someone other than me. That's when I heard them; a countless number of voices around me. Some were softly crying while others were screaming with terror. Awful things came out of their mouths. Many were cursing God and making accusations against Him. Others expressed defiance, hatred, and blame. I could hear a mix of anger, pain, desperation, and suffering in their tones. I also heard whipping sounds, followed by shrieks and moaning. Unseen tormentors howled and laughed after each flogging. The bloodcurdling sounds were frightening, and it was then that I realized, I was in Hell.

At that moment, the smell hit me. It was a stinking, putrid, sulfuric stench. I tried to breathe out of my mouth, but then I could taste it. I gagged, and stomach acid crept up my throat, threatening to come all the way out. An overwhelming smell of decomposing flesh filled my enclosure and clung to my hair and clothes. The foul odor burned my nose and throat. A dying world surrounded me and penetrated every sense, seeping deeply into my flesh.

The bubble stopped its forward motion and slowly began to rise up into the air. I reached my hands out to steady myself, as I was now shaking uncontrollably. The complete darkness gave way to a very subtle light in the far-off distance. As I rose higher, I saw a fire so vast; it was immeasurable. As we got closer, the heat was so intense that every cell in my body became instantly dehydrated. My mouth dried out, and my eyes and throat burned from the smoke. My thirst for water was overpowering, and I could think of nothing else. Within seconds I was drenched in sweat, and the bubble's surface became too hot to touch.

The endless lake of fire was blinding, and its flames were taller than skyscrapers. An unholy light cast foreboding shadows and illuminated things better left unseen. Cages made of thick bars floated above the highest flames. The bubble transported me closer to one of many prisons that hovered over the lake of fire. Flames licked the bottom of each cell without ceasing. Inside the cage was a man cowering in the corner with his hands protectively wrapped around his head. He was covered in maggots that crawled in and out of open, seeping wounds. He was filthy, skin and bones, and I could smell his burning flesh.

Then out of the shadow, in the corner of the cage, emerged a horrendous beast. It stood at an astounding height and walked toward the crouching man. The demon was holding a whip with metal hooks attached to each strand. As it raised the whip high in the air, readying to strike, it turned around and locked eyes with me. When I saw its hideous face, all I heard was screaming. It took me several seconds to realize the screams were coming from me.

In an instant, a door opened, and I exited Hell abruptly. I had to close my eyes and slowly adjust to the light. The smell of death and sounds and sights of horror dissipated, and I instantly noticed a transformation within me. Goodness, love, faith, and joy washed over me and took back their residence within my heart.

I was back in the room with the golden altar. The bubble vanished, and I collapsed into the arms of the Lord. Tears ran down both of our faces, and we cried together. As Jesus held me, my heartbeat steadied, and the fear finally dissolved.

He waited for my breathing to calm and my tears to cease before He said, "Do you now see, Daughter?"

And I did see. I saw what was going to happen to all the people who refused to accept the gift of forgiveness, readily available to every person through confession and faith. In Hell, there was no rest, no love, and no peace. It was a complete separation from God; therefore, a complete separation from anything and everything good. Hell did exist, and there were horrific things awaiting those who do not believe in Jesus, confess their sins, and accept His saving grace.

Jesus said, "There are only two kinds of people in the world, in the end. Those that say, 'Jesus, I am Yours; Your will be done,' and those who reject my forgiveness and refuse to admit their sinful nature. They shall be turned away from Me for I will know them not."

"But I don't want anyone to go to Hell," I said emphatically.

"Hell was created for Satan and his demons. It was never My will that anyone should perish for eternity. The right to choose through free will was my gift to humanity. So, I yield to the stubborn mans' steadfast, willful rejection of Me. I give them up to their sinful desires and accept their decision to exclude Me from their lives. Hell exists because there is no excuse for sin; it is punishable by death." I felt like crying again.

Jesus continued, "Take heart, Child! I already paid the price in full."

I stood back and looked at Jesus. At the instant, my love for Him grew exponentially as I realized just what He died to save us from. He didn't want anyone to go to Hell. He suffered the tortures of death and took sin upon Himself to save man from being alienated from Him for eternity.

"I have a lot to do, then," I said with conviction.

"And I will be with you," He said.

The sound of thunder echoed within the four walls, and the ground shook and cracked open in front of me. I winked at Jesus, crossed my arms over my chest, and jumped in.

I woke up covered in sweat, but my fever was gone. Everyone was still sound asleep, so I quietly retrieved my notebook from the nightstand drawer. It took me almost an hour to record my dream. I shivered from time to time, recalling the details. Even though it was the worst dream of my life, I thanked Jesus for allowing me to experience it.

Victoria visited later that day and brought me some chicken noodle soup. I told her about my dream and said, "We need to share the love of God to the homeless. We need to minister to them and lead as many to Christ as possible. It's so much more important than anything else we can do for them."

Victoria was in total agreement. She even offered to make calls to several local churches and ask them to donate Bibles. We decided to practice sharing God's word on Saturdays while feeding those in need at church. At first, I found myself stumbling around, trying to find the right words, but I improved with practice. I started reading the Bible more frequently so I could answer questions that arose, and I practiced praying out loud in case someone responded "Yes" to the question, "Can I pray with you?"

For the next four months, Victoria and I worked hard at obtaining donations from local businesses and churches. We also spent that time becoming spiritually mature and aligning ourselves with the word of God. Finally, we were ready to launch our program.

It was a cloudy Saturday when Rob woke me from a late afternoon nap.

"Hey, Babe, something is wrong with Buddy."

I jumped up. "What do you mean?"

"He isn't eating, and he can't get up from his bed." It had been getting harder for Buddy to move around. He was to turn fourteen soon. I would be turning twenty-six, and we always celebrated our birthdays together. I went over and sat down next to him.

"What's wrong, Buddy Boy?" He licked his lips and whined a little. I had a bad feeling in the pit of my stomach.

"Rob, we have to get him to the vet," I said, holding back tears.

"Okay, Babe. I'll get the car started and call your brother to see if he can watch Faith."

Gavin arrived within minutes and sat down next to Buddy and me.

"Poor Buddy. We love you. You are a good boy." A tear ran down my brother's face and I knew he was saying goodbye to our dog. Even though I recognized this day was coming, it was impossible to face.

My mother had surprised me with Buddy for my twelfth birthday, but really, he had belonged to all of us. Dozens of memories flashed through my mind. There was the time that Buddy ran off a stranger that had been creeping around outside our house. And the time he protected Gavin from a vicious dog that had gotten out of his backyard. Buddy had been the one to alert us when Faith was chocking and had been a great comfort to me when Mom and Amy passed away. He was there for me during both my trials and my triumphs and had been a friend to me in times when I had no one else. He was the most loyal companion a girl could have ever wanted, and I wasn't ready to lose him.

Gavin and Rob gently loaded Buddy into the back of our car. Gavin said one last goodbye, hugged me, and watched us drive away, tears streaming down his face. At that moment, he looked like a little boy again. I cried the whole way to the animal hospital.

It was terrible news. I had expected as much. The veterinarian said that several of his organs were failing and that it was just a matter of time. The options were to take him home, so he could pass away on his own, or have the doctor put him out of his misery now. I hated both options. As Rob and I started discussing which one was best, Buddy took his last breath. He had decided for us. I held his head in my arms and sobbed until there was nothing left of me. I felt like my heart was breaking in two. It took weeks for me to recover from losing him. Thankfully, I had Eternal Life Missions to keep me busy. And, it did.

CHAPTER 20
PURPOOSE

For four years, Victoria and I worked countless hours helping the homeless in the Phoenix area. Almost every church contributed in some crucial way. They donated Bibles, food, clothing, money, and many other things. We used these and other resources to help people get off the streets and back on track.

Most of all, we shared the gospel with them. I'm not going to lie, it was hard work, and our message of Jesus' saving grace was rejected more than it was accepted. It was the harsh reality of the true stubbornness of man's heart and the sobering reality of a fallen world. We live amongst drowning people, and when offered a life-saving raft, they reject it.

That's not to say that there weren't many successes. During our four years of outreach, we led exactly one hundred and three people to Christ. That's one hundred and three people who will find themselves forever locked into God's grace, mercy, and forgiveness. We had also helped almost two hundred and twenty people find jobs and, eventually, permanent housing

On my thirtieth birthday, Victoria took me out for lunch to celebrate. She would be attending the party Rob was throwing for me that night but wanted to treat me to a special meal at my favorite Italian restaurant. She even surprised me with a chocolate cupcake with buttercream frosting and a single candle positioned in the center.

"I have a weird question. I hope it's not too personal," she said, half-way through lunch. "Why didn't you and Rob have more children together?"

"That's not a weird question," I reassured her. "We've talked about it, that's for sure. The timing just hasn't been right. When we first got married, we couldn't afford it. Then, we were going to try when Faith was around two years old, but Richard came to live with us, and after that, Ryan. They were with us for over a year, and we had such a tiny apartment at the time, there wasn't enough room."

Rob and I had finally been able to purchase a lovely house a few years ago. Even though I loved my new house, I had adored that little apartment. Beautiful memories had been made there.

I continued, "Then, you and I started Eternal Life Missions. There hasn't been time, you know?"

"You're both young. There's still time." She was right. Maybe it was time to have that conversation again. Money and space were not an issue any longer. Time was a different matter. I would need to make some adjustments, that's for sure, but it was doable.

"You're right. Although it's hard to imagine diapers, baby bottles, and all-nighters again." I shook my head and smiled at the thought of it. "That reminds me, how is David doing?" David and Victoria had an on-again, off-again relationship for a couple of years now.

"David and I decided to call it quits for good this time. I can't handle his controlling nature, and he can't handle my shopping." She laughed and showed me her new designer purse.

"I'm sorry, that's too bad. I thought David was making some changes."

"I thought he was, too. I'm ready to get married and start a family, but when I finally got honest with myself, I realized David was not the kind of person I wanted to settle down with."

"Well, God has the perfect person out there for you. I'm sure of it," I reassured her again. She smiled and agreed.

I mulled the baby conversation around in my brain for the rest of that day. Having just turned thirty, I figured I had better bring it up quickly if I was going to do it at all. Lying in bed that night, I broached the subject with Rob.

"So, I was thinking; maybe it's time for you and me to have a baby." Rob almost jumped out of bed in excitement.

"Are you serious?"

"Yes, while we're still young. What do you think? " I asked.

He threw his arms around me and kissed me passionately. "I think it's a wonderful idea. Are you sure you're ready? You've been so busy with your non-profit organization. "

"I think I'm ready. I mean, I believe I could handle both. I could reduce my hours at work and rearrange some things."

"That would be amazing, " he said and kissed me again. "Give me a few more months to scale things back with my job. Then we can give it a go." He nuzzled my neck. I smiled at the thought of having a baby with this incredible man. Faith would make a terrific big sister. We talked late into the night about it and fell asleep in each other's arms.

A young man by the name of Michael frequented the outreach program at our church on Saturdays. Over the years, I had developed a solid connection with him. He was only twenty-one years old and a regular drug user. He often slept under benches or bridges, begging for money during the day on busy street corners. My heart broke for him. For some reason, he reminded me of my brother, and what could have happened had Gavin not turned his life around.

Michael and I were on a first-name basis, and he would often start our conversations off with a joke. They were usually corny, but it was his way of connecting with me. I would always tell him a joke of my own in return.

"Hey, Alina, why do we tell actors to break a leg?" he asked, one Saturday afternoon as I served him a giant scoop of baked beans.

"Why do we? " I asked.

"Because every play has a cast," he responded with a big smile on his face. He was missing one of his front teeth.

I laughed, "Good one! Michael, did you hear about the actor who fell through the floorboard?"

"Nope," he answered, waiting expectantly for the punch line and grinning from ear to ear.

"He was just going through a stage."

He threw his head back and laughed loudly. "Hey, I'm going to use that one!" he said as he continued down the food line. I had tried to share God with Michael many times, but he was disinterested and would get angry if you pushed the topic.

"Church is for people who need to feel good about themselves," he would often say.

He was especially jovial today, which usually meant he was high. When he was sober, he became temperamental, edgy, and unpredictable. I had heard rumors about violence; however, Michael had been nothing but kind to me. Unfortunately, it was much safer to be around him when he was under the influence. I had been around him once when he was coming down and, truth be told, he scared me a little. Victoria and I had made multiple attempts to get him the help he so desperately needed, but to no avail.

The following Friday, Victoria and I spent the day ministering to the homeless at a park about ten miles away from my house. There were two rules Victoria and I followed. One, we never went out alone, and two, we never worked after dark. Most of the homeless knew us and were usually friendly and thankful for our help, but we were always cautious. Drugs and desperation can cause people to make impulsive decisions.

The sun was setting, and it was time to leave. Victoria and I hugged, said our goodbyes, and got into our vehicles. As soon as my car door was shut and locked, Victoria backed out of her parking spot. I put on my seatbelt and inserted the key into the ignition. When I turned the key, nothing happened. I tried it again, nothing. I tried a third time. The car was dead. I glanced in the rearview mirror as Victoria started pulling out of the parking lot. I quickly unbuckled my seatbelt, opened the car door, and jumped out, waving my arms wildly. Victoria didn't see me, however, and drove off.

Located about four blocks away was a corner store, and I

remembered seeing a phone booth in the parking lot. I would have to walk there and call Rob. I was a little nervous because I wasn't in a good neighborhood. Tall chain-linked fences enclosed abandoned warehouses and empty, dirt lots, outside the park. I grabbed my purse, locked the car, and started walking at a good pace. I was sure I could make it there in fewer than ten minutes if I hurried. The light of the day was almost completely gone but luckily a few working streetlamps did their best to illuminate the shadows.

I was about half-way there when I heard footsteps a short distance behind me; the hairs on the back of my neck stood straight up. I walked a little faster, but as I picked up the pace, so did the person behind me. I could see the lights from the corner store in the distance. *Just a little bit further*, I willed myself.

Suddenly, I heard the person behind me close the distance in a matter of seconds, and felt my purse being yanked forcefully. I tried to let it loose in exchange for my safety, but somehow it got tangled around my arm. As the shadowy figure pulled again, the force swung me around sharply, and I fell toward him. It was at that moment, two things happened; I felt a sharp pain, and I faced the identity of my attacker. I looked down, surprised to see the black handle of a large knife sticking out of my chest. I couldn't grasp what was happening. *Am I hurt?* I collapsed into the arms of Michael and witnessed the horror on his face as he recognized me.

"Oh my god! Oh my god!" he repeated. I could see his pupils under the streetlamp. He was sober and, no doubt, trying to steal for his next fix. "I didn't know it was you, Alina! I didn't know! I'm sorry! Someone,

please help us!" he yelled, looking around wildly.

I noticed changes happening to my body, and fear rose up inside of me. I gasped for air and shivered as my extremities turned to ice. I knew I was going into shock, but I couldn't understand why.

I would like to say that in my last moments, I thought of my family, but I did not. I thought only of Michael. This young man that I had gotten to know was lost, broken, and on his way to a horrific eternity unless something drastic happened to save his soul. I reached up with the little energy I had left and gently touched his face. Tears ran down his cheeks as he begged me to stay alive, apologizing in between sobs.

I took in a gulp of air and whispered, "Michael, I forgive you." These were the only words I managed to get out before I took my last earthly breath.

In an instant, I found myself in a bright room with four white walls. I recognized the two doors, one on my left and one on my right. The stunning golden altar with its beautiful angels burned intensely before me. Peace like a river flowed through me, even though I knew my life on Earth was over.

Every memory, great and small, flashed through my mind going all the way back to my time in Heaven before my earthly birth. I remembered Jesus saying, "I have an important purpose specifically designed for you. Are you ready to be born?"

Just then, Jesus, in all His glory, appeared before me. My love for Him expanded and enlarged. I had never seen His full glory before, not during my time before Earth or in my dreams of Heaven. His countenance was brighter than the sun. Purity and love poured out of

Him, unabated, and you could see it visually. It flowed out to me, occupying my being until it overflowed and filled the entire room. I fell to my knees and bowed before Him, knowing instantly I was not worthy of His presence.

"Rise, Alina Gabrielle Sheridan," He commanded. It was the first time Jesus had ever called me by my name. I obeyed Him. "Alina, your name has been written in the Book of Life. Well done, my good and faithful servant. It is time to test your good works against the flaming fire. Jesus reached into my inner self and pulled out what looked like a living sphere of my life. The sphere contained every thought, every word I had spoken, and every deed I had done. Jesus then placed it over the altar. It floated within the flames, and I watched as many things burned up. After several minutes, the flames grew smaller, and the Lord reached into the fire and brought out what was left of my life.

"These good thoughts, words, and deeds have been tested by fire and survived the Altar of Truth. Now you will receive your rewards according to what you have done for the Kingdom of God. "

"Jesus, I am not worthy of rewards." Again, I fell on my face before the Lord.

"My blood that was shed on the cross has covered your sins. Receive your rewards and eternal payments."

"But, Lord, I failed you," I said. "You sent me to be born for a purpose, but I barely even got started before you called me back home." I was thinking of the four years I spent helping the homeless.

"Your definition of purpose is much different from mine," Jesus responded. "It was about My purpose all along, and it was not limited to the time you spent ministering to the homeless. It was not in any single accomplishment or success. My purpose shone through in every act of kindness, forgiveness, mercy, and love you showed. Do you not remember how you forgave others for hurting you?" I nodded yes. "Do you not remember how you became a loving granddaughter to an older couple who had lost their only son to drugs?" I nodded, thinking of Doris and Herman. "Do you not remember how you rescued a broken, lost child and reunited him with his father?" I nodded again, tears streaming down my face. "Do you not remember how you used your pregnancy to minister to other teens who were suffering both emotionally and physically?" I was starting to understand. "Do you not remember how you spent weeks raising money to help a man you met on a street corner and accepted him into your life as a father figure? And do you not remember how, with your last breath, you forgave a drug-user who took your very life?"

"Yes, Jesus," I answered sobbing. Jesus had seen everything. Nothing had gone unnoticed under His almighty gaze.

"These deeds and millions more were recorded in this Book. Everything you did out of love, kindness, and mercy had a purpose. Every prayer you prayed was meticulously written down, and angels were charged to work on your behalf. Even your name, that which you have despised your entire life, had purpose. Alina means 'light.' You were a light in a very dark place for many. Gabrielle means 'gift from God.' You were My gift to the world. And your last name, Sheridan, means both 'bright' and 'seeker.' You have an especially bright soul, and you have sought after Me with determination and tenacity your entire life on Earth. Even the nickname Nia, given to you by your brother, means *Purpose*."

It all became crystal clear in that moment. It was never about me. It was all about what Jesus did on the cross and letting that shine through for all to see. And sometimes that was through the simple, daily acts of goodness, kindness, love, and forgiveness. His purpose worked through me during the times of pain and in the times of triumphs and was never limited to one single accomplishment or deed.

"I understand now, Jesus, but may I ask you a question?"

"You always have such great questions, Alina." He smiled at me, and I recalled this familiar phrase from the very beginning of it all.

"Will my family be alright without me?" I knew it was a trivial question under the circumstances, but I had to ask.

"Come, I will show you the remaining gifts I have given to you and the people you love."

Jesus touched my forehead, and I immediately had a vision of the future in my mind's eye. I saw Rob and Victoria, a happy couple holding hands at the park. Faith was playing with a young boy who looked just like Rob. God had remembered my family and had brought me a best friend who would become a beautiful mate to Rob and a loving mother to Faith. I saw Victoria and Rob welcome another baby, and I saw Faith grow into a beautiful woman of God.

I saw Gavin at his wedding, marrying an attractive redhead. I saw him promoted to lead detective and watched as they grew as a family. I thought that was the end of the vision, but Jesus had another surprise for me. I watched as Ryan gathered all my notebooks out of my nightstand. Years later, Ryan would marry a Literary Agent who eventually published the hundreds of dreams I had about Heaven. It was titled, Cracks in the Floor of Heaven by Alina Gabrielle Sheridan Dunham.

Then, I saw Michael, the young man who had taken my life. The man I joked with on Saturdays and tried to minister to and pray for. He was in prison but had become a Christian and was sharing the gospel with other inmates. I saw him lead many prisoners to Christ during his incarceration. When he was released from prison after two decades, I witnessed him dedicating the remainder of his life to the mission field.

I cried as I watched how my life's good works continued even after my death. Jesus removed his hand from my forehead and wiped my cheeks.

"Those will be the last tears you ever shed," He said and led me over to the door on the right. He pulled out a golden key, unlocked the door and opened it wide. Bright light poured in, and I could hear the familiar sounds of the Garden and see the sparkling City of God, off in the distance. Mom, Amy, and generations of relatives I had never met lined up, ready to greet me. And wouldn't you know it, Buddy, the dog, and Buddy, the lion, were there too, waging their tails and welcoming me home.

The End.

IN CONCLUSION

Know this, there is life after death, and you will spend eternity in either Heaven or Hell. If you don't know Jesus as your Savior, I want to give you an opportunity to do so. God made it as simple as possible for us to have forgiveness of sin and share in his eternal reward. Believe me when I tell you, God is chasing you. There is a beautiful song that I encourage you to listen to about this very thing. It's called *Reckless Love* by Cory Asbury.

In Matthew 18:12-14, it says; *What do you think? If a man owns a hundred sheep, and one of them wanders away, will he not leave the ninety-nine on the hills and go to look for the one that wandered off? And if he finds it, truly I say to you, he rejoices over it more than over the ninety-nine that never went astray. So, it is not the will of my Father who is in Heaven that one of these little ones should perish.*

2 Peter 3:9; *The Lord is not slow in keeping his promise, as some understand slowness. Instead, he is patient with you, not wanting anyone to perish, but everyone to come to repentance.*

And John 3:16; *For God so loved the world that He gave his one and only Son, that whoever believes in him shall not perish but have eternal life.*

Finally, in Romans 10:9 it says; *If you declare with your mouth, Jesus is Lord, and believe in your heart that God raised Him from the dead, you will be saved.*

Pray this prayer, believe it, and you will be saved.

Lord Jesus, for too long I have kept you out of my life. I know that I am a sinner and that I cannot save myself. No longer will I close the door when I hear You knocking. By faith, I gratefully receive Your gift of salvation. I am ready to accept You as my Lord and Savior. Thank you, Lord Jesus, for coming to Earth. I believe you are the Son of God, who died on the cross for my sins and rose from the dead on the third day. Thank you for bearing my sins and giving me the gift of eternal life. I believe your words are true. Come into my heart, Lord Jesus and be my Savior. Amen.

If you prayed this prayer in sincere faith, you are saved. Find a local church. Read the Bible daily. Buckle your seatbelt, God is going to do amazing things in your life. Please send us an email; we would love to pray for you. Next, share this book with others. Share it with someone that is suffering or in pain. Share it with someone who may or may not know the Lord Jesus as their Savior. Share it with a friend or a stranger. You never know whose life you can change by a simple act of faith and love.

michelederouin58@gmail.com.

REFERENCES/CREDITS

- Heaven by Randy Alcorn 2004

- Crossfire Deluxe Edition-The Expositor's Study Bible, Holy Bible Concordance King James Version Published by Jimmy Swaggart Ministries 2005

- 23 Minutes in Hell by Bill Wiese 2006

- The Sinner's Prayer by Ray Pritchard www.crosswalk.com

- Story of the Snake and the Frog, Llenrad.com/story-of-the-snake-and-the-frog/

- www.desiringgod.org

- Heaven, Hell and the Judgement Series by Tom Sefik through Kailua Community Church

- www.theodysseyonline.com

- www.openbible.info

ABOUT THE AUTHOR

Michele grew up in Bakersfield, California before earning a degree in Child Psychology and embarking on a twenty-year career in social services. In 2001, she moved to the mountains of Arizona where she learned to hunt, fish, and rock climb. It was during that time that God first began to speak to her about writing a book. In 2017, she moved to the island of Oahu, Hawaii, where she retired from social work and began the process of writing her first novel.

Michele has two grown children and one grandchild. She spends her days writing, swimming, and helping others. In addition to the outdoors, Michele enjoys painting with watercolors and digital mediums. She has sold over 200 pieces of art, one of which came second in being chosen to furnish rooms at a popular hotel in Hawaii.

Michele's strong faith in God has helped her overcome many obstacles. She has endured her fair share of heartache which, inspired much of her book, *Cracks in the Floor of Heaven*. She has also been blessed with many gifts from God, who has taught her how to have joy despite pain and hope in the midst of hardship. Michele is an optimist, has a heart for helping others, and plans to write many more books that she hopes will bring light into the darkness and healing into the lives of hurting people.